JUSTIN

KRIS MICHAELS

KMRW LLC

*U*ndetected, invisible, a mere shadow melding into the warm December night's inky darkness, Justin King ghosted toward the side entrance of the Perth mansion. Every facet of his attire was custom fitted—both to the man and to his purpose. His customary thousand-dollar, handmade, Italian leather dress shoes had been replaced with equally expensive, specially crafted ankle-high boots, highly flexible with soft suede soles that left no distinguishable footprints. The ten thousand dollar bespoke Seville Row business suit of a successful restaurateur was replaced by a uniform of black, body-hugging tactical material, a skull cap of black wool and black leather gloves that molded themselves to his fingers so snugly they did all but leave fingerprints. He drifted to the left behind a large acacia bush. The move kept him out of the camera's angle as he merged further into the shadows. The make and model of security camera installed outside the home picked up only indistinct movement where he was standing. He used the environment and moved when the wind shuffled through the branches to further disguise his approach.

Three feet farther up the wall, next to the water meter and electrical panel, sat controls to an alarm system. Whoever had installed the 'state of the art' equipment didn't have a fucking clue how to protect their clients or the information they tried desperately to conceal. Justin skirted a small shrub and lifted his gloved fingers to the alarm panel door—only to stop short. The door to the panel box was open a fraction of an inch, almost undetectable. The adrenaline-fueled charge that hummed through him intensified and swelled.

He crouched and flattened against the exterior of the massive home and visually scanned the area before he fished his thermal imaging scanner from the pocket of his black tactical vest and palmed it. Similar to a cell phone set to vibrate, the apparatus would pulsate if it detected another body within the scanner's two-hundred-yard range. His forefinger slowly pushed the device—the size of a deck of cards —two, 360 degree, rotations before he dropped the device back into its carrying pocket.

Satisfied he was alone, he pushed off the wall and rose silently. The pad of his index finger pressed the thin metal door of the alarm panel box open a further fraction of an inch. He glanced around one more time before he focused on the interior of the alarm panel. *Sweet.* He sent a furtive glance around him again before he shut the alarm panel as far as the disarmed and dissected panel would allow. The work was professional, but personally, he would have used a lithium polymer battery. At a mere 500 microns, the thin casement was bendable, and with a less than three percent self-discharge, the battery life supporting the digital looping device currently deceiving the human alarm monitor, assuming there was one, would last for up to a week. There would be no need to reassemble the system if an emergency arose. Not that most operators in his line of work went to the trouble of masking their entry. He did. It was a mark of a true professional, and it was one fucking hell of a thrill ride. Get in, get out, and nobody knows you were there or how you did it. Fuck, the rush was intense. It was better than base jumping or skiing down a double black diamond slope after launching out of a helicopter.

Justin dropped into a crouch and worked his way toward the side entrance. According to the intel he'd received, there was a redundant camera system backing up this alarm system. The rigged loop on the alarm panel would work on all but the entry point cameras and the camera fixed on his objective: the safe. Taking out the entry point camera wasn't necessary and could alert the guards. Justin pushed a tiny pen-light from its compartment on his vest. He used the glow-in-the-dark sites he'd painted on the device to line it up perfectly with the light sensor on the top of the fixture and sent a laser-point of light to the photo-sensitive lens at the top of the porch light. The light immediately darkened. Justin lifted and entered an already open door. He replaced his equipment in its proper pocket while moving into the home quietly and efficiently. He had planned on forty seconds to pick the locks on the back door and enter, but thanks to whoever was already here, it took him four.

The blueprints to the house didn't do justice to the opulence that surrounded him. A younger version of himself would have taken the scenic route to his objective. The ever-present need for danger and excitement hadn't diminished, but he'd learned to control it...somewhat. The older version of himself would settle for a trinket of nominal value that he could carry away from the mission. His trophy room held pens, coffee cups, figurines and countless other tiny treasures. *Stupid?* Maybe, but then again, the thrill was worth the risk. The pounding of his heart while engineering the acquisition and extraction of his handler's required information and beating high tech systems manufactured to keep people like him out...well, it was a life-affirming rush and one he would never get tired of feeling. Knowing that someone else at least as competent as himself in the art of covert entry was already here? Fuck, that was a heady sensation, and his blood, supercharged by that bit of information, thrummed through his veins. He fucking loved the thrill. He made his way from the back of the home to the front stairway. He took a moment to scan the design of the room. The target had excellent taste, but he could admire furniture another time. A glance at his watch dropped him to a crouch beside a Fendi couch. Justin glanced at the luminescent hands of his ten thousand-dollar Breitling watch and waited. Right on schedule, the slight tap of a soft heel sounded. Justin drew quiet breaths, pushed back into the darkened corner next to the couch and watched.

It was the top of the hour, and security guards were unwaveringly predictable. Ninety-nine percent of the time, if a guard was going to make the rounds, it would be at the top, bottom or quarter of the hour. This guard ambled through the front of the house and headed toward the back of the first floor. Justin pushed to his feet and watched the man through the spindles of a grand stairway. He waited until he couldn't hear the soft tap of footsteps and sprinted around the couch and up the stairs then dropped beside an antique table at the second-floor landing. He angled his head and swept the visible area using his peripheral vision to ensure he observed the entire area without making unnecessary movements. Nothing disturbed the quiet. Silent strides took him to the suite his target used as an office where he paused and listened. Although silence met his senses, he erred on the side of caution. He pulled out a flexible snake with a micro camera mounted on the tip, opened the door slightly and angled the device through the crack. The two inch by two inch, low-light display revealed an empty outer office. Justin retracted the camera and stowed it away before he slid into the room. He smiled as he neared the next door. As he approached, a soft click caught his attention. He knew that sound. That was the unmistakable sound of a mechanical lock. The safe he was supposed to infiltrate tonight had two locks. The key code his handler had sent rested in his pocket. Unless the person behind the door had the code...The solid thump of the safe's wheel dislodging the four-way moving bolts sent a buzz unlike any other through him. So that eliminated any question; the person inside had the key code. Whoever was working this retrieval was elite...and the adrenaline kick of observing them - unseen and unaware of his presence - was too much to resist. *Fuck it.* Justin opened the door a fraction of an inch and stood so he could see over the ornate wooden desk that blocked his view. His smile grew. It couldn't get any better than this. A *woman* reached in and pulled out the external hard drive Justin had been sent to clone. *Intriguing.* He shut the door as she turned around. If it were him, he'd survey the area before he focused back on the task at hand. He counted a slow ten and cracked the door again. Her features concealed by darkness, the woman leaned over and worked a large, clunky, cloning device. Whomever she worked for needed to upgrade their tech, but then again, not everyone could work for

Guardian. Justin wished he could reveal his presence to the woman. Hell, it would be nice just to talk to another expert about the intricacies of their shared profession. Justin smiled and soundlessly closed the door. Meeting her could never happen, but damn, wouldn't that be a rush? He headed out, pausing only long enough to grab a small glass paperweight off the edge of the desk. Memento pocketed, he retraced his steps, quickly and silently, leaving as he had entered.

He'd have to make a phone call. Someone else had the information Guardian wanted him to obtain. But Justin knew his role, and he knew his restrictions. Jason, his brother, and CEO of Guardian International had only one standing order that he demanded Justin obey. Never disclose himself to anyone, for any reason. In accordance with Jason's directive, he didn't make contact with the other specialist. Besides, what would be the point? He assumed people of his caliber probably tended to avoid making friends in the business. It could end badly...or at least he believed it would. As there were only three people who knew what he did for Guardian, *his* identity would never be exposed. Justin waited at the back door until he heard the guard start his time regimented walk and slipped out of the house. He hoped there was only one sentinel on duty. If not? Well, his little friend upstairs would need to hunker down and wait for the excitement to abate before she left. Hell, on one mission, he'd spent almost twenty-four hours in a janitor's closet hidden behind six ten-gallon buckets of floor wax. The risks came with the territory. Justin moved through the outskirts of the property. He jumped up, grabbed the top of the eight-foot stone wall and pulled himself to the top. He'd hidden his equipment bag under a bush on the other side. Justin dropped down, grabbed the backpack, and unzipped the main compartment before he pulled out a pair of running shoes. His black pants and long sleeve shirt were carefully rolled up and pushed back into the compact back-pack. Sweat saturated the athletic shorts and black shirt he wore under his work clothes. The light breeze weaving through the bushes cooled his over-heated skin and sent goose-flesh down his arms. From a small pocket, he pulled out a pair of wireless headphones and plugged them into his ears before slipping his arms through the straps of his gear bag and nesting it between his shoulder blades. With a glance up and down the street before he left the bushes next to the wall, he turned in the general direction of his rental vehicle and started jogging. It

may be winter in New York, but the warm summer
night in Perth couldn't have been a more perfect
reason to take a run and enjoy the city—even if it
was two o'clock in the morning.

Justin admired the small estates along the road
where he jogged. A 'For Sale' sign caught his attention, and he studied the well-lit drive leading up to
an old style mansion. The striking example of
American Colonial architecture punctuated the
knoll where it sat and captured his attention. Book-
ended by the neighboring Queen Anne homes, the
manor stood out as even the landscape lighting
varied from the neighborhood norm and cast beautiful rays through the massive limbs of the established trees that accentuated the sprawling yard.
He'd studied the map and knew how to get back to
where he'd parked the car, but he ended up jogging
around that block three times. There was something about the old home that called to him. He
glanced at the address and decided to have Danielle
Grant, his Chief of Acquisitions, come check it out
with him. Justin pulled out his phone and activated
the voice notes. He rattled off the address and spit
out the questions that popped into his mind as he
circled the home. The manor had potential... bed
and breakfast, higher-end clientele. Was there a

market for such a thing? Did the manse have enough rooms? Was it updated? If it wasn't, what would it take to bring it up to speed? The location was close enough to Elizabeth Quay to be attractive to those who wanted the privacy that a hotel could not give.

Justin slowed his pace as he approached the late model Mercedes he'd rented. Walking to calm his breathing after the jaunty five-mile run, he smiled at the thrill of watching the specialist work. She was damn good. Her equipment? Not so much. That could mean she was a freelancer, or it could mean the company that sent her wasn't as concerned about their people as Guardian. Justin threw his gear bag into the back seat of the car and leaned against the vehicle, stretching his calves and hamstrings. He had a busy day ahead. Working without sleep wasn't new, and he could deal with the long hours. Working with leg cramps? That was a different story, and it wasn't going to happen. He took his time and stretched out, making sure to cool down before he grabbed a liter of bottled water out of the front seat. A marked police vehicle rolled at a brisk 5 mph through the parking lot adjacent to a small park where he'd left his car. Justin turned and reclined against his door as he took a long drink of water.

The driver window slid down. "What are you doing out here so late?"

Justin lowered the water bottle and smiled at the officer. "Well, it may be late for you, but my jet lag is telling me it's the middle of the afternoon. I'm sorry if I'm in the wrong area, but when we arrived yesterday, this looked like a safe place to jog."

"Ah, an American?"

"Yes, sir."

"Well, we don't have many people out and about at three in the morning. Just checking to make sure you're not up to any evil."

Justin laughed, "No sir, just trying to exhaust myself. I'm going to finish my water, drive back to the hotel, and try to get some sleep before my meeting in…" Justin glanced at his watch and grimaced. "Damn, five hours."

"What's your name?"

"Justin King. Would you like to see my passport?"

"Please." The officer got out of his vehicle and watched as Justin leaned in, opened the glove box of the rental vehicle and pulled out his wallet and passport. He handed the dark leather holder over to the officer. The man looked at the cover of the passport and flipped it open. "Here on business or pleasure, Mr. King?"

"Business mostly, but I hope to enjoy a day of fun if I can squeeze it in."

"That so?"

"Yes sir, I'd love to abseil down Gordon Dam."

"That's one hell of a drop."

"The largest man-made, commercial, vertical descent on record." Justin couldn't wait to wrap up his work, take a short flight to Tasmania and rappel down that four-hundred-twenty-feet concrete surface. It would be a major rush. At least that was his plan until tonight's mission crumbled.

"Where are you staying, sir?" The police officer's question brought him out of his musings.

"COMO, The Treasury, on Cathedral Avenue."

"Well now, those are nice digs. What business did you say you are in, Mr. King?"

I didn't. "I recently purchased a building overlooking the Quay, and I'm here to hire some local contractors to help me convert the structure." He had started to tire of the third degree but kept his cool, his professional veneer wrapped tightly around his internal musings.

The police officer took one more glance at his passport and handed it back to him. "Enjoy your stay, but at this time of night, stick to running on the treadmill in the hotel's spa, right?"

"I'll take that into consideration. Thank you, sir." Justin took another long drink of water, capped the bottle and stretched his lower back. The taillights of the cruiser signaled a left turn. Watching them disappear around the corner Justin bent at his hips and touched his palms to the ground. He was getting too old not to stretch out after exercising. He chuckled at his normal exercise regime. If his brothers ever got wind of what he did to keep in shape for his night time job? Hell, he'd never live it down.

He glanced at his watch and calculated the time difference between Perth and Washington D.C. before he got into the car and pulled his cell phone out of the glove compartment where he'd stowed it when he'd finished his run. He'd wait until he got back to his hotel room before he made the call. It was lunch hour in D.C., and he'd be damned if he'd be the reason his brother missed a meal. According to a conversation he'd recently shared with his mother, Jason tried to go home for lunch with his wife at least three times a week. His brother worked like a fiend, but he was devoted to his wife and son.

Justin flipped his phone in his hands. Gabriel might be free, but he doubted it. For a retired man, Gabriel kept his fingers in just about everything going on at Guardian. No, this phone call could wait until he got back to the hotel, or even later.

Making sure to fasten his seatbelt, Justin started the car and pulled out, heading toward Elizabeth Quay. His mind returned to the mission he was supposed to have conducted tonight. Guardian would know soon enough if the specialist who copied the hard drive was friend or foe. Justin had a few more days in Perth before he had to get back to the insanity of his world. If Guardian wanted him to take another shot at it, he could send one of the entourage currently traveling with him to convey his desires to the construction, design and engineering teams. More than likely, his representative would be Danielle. Dani had made herself indispensable. Among other things, she was his right hand in all acquisition matters. Her sharp mind and intuition were only a couple of her assets he coveted. The woman was his cornerstone in his day-to-day business, and he trusted her—a statement he didn't make lightly. He trusted only a handful of people.

Justin drove the nearly deserted streets and relaxed. Until Guardian told him otherwise, he was personally overseeing the restaurant design in the newly acquired building overlooking Elizabeth Quay. The location was prime for development. The construction company that had started the venture had encountered a financial backing issue. His acquisitions team had been looking for a suitable property in Australia, in either Sydney or Perth, for months. When Danielle's team discovered the opportunity, Justin swooped in, bailed the company out, and his business machine started planning his fifteenth restaurant. He wanted to showcase Australian wines and cuisine while adding a distinct European flair. The chef he wanted was currently working in London, but he was a native Australian. Justin conceded to himself that he might be heading to London next if the phone calls and video conferencing couldn't entice Chef Melvin Williams to agree to his very generous terms.

Justin glanced at the rear-view mirror, his gaze flicking over his appearance. The smile on his face wasn't a surprise. He'd enjoyed tonight. For him, everything revolved around the next thrill. He and his therapist continued to work on that. He laughed out loud. Hell, he was an addict to the feeling of the pound of adrenaline when the anticipation of intense danger spiked, or when he'd mastered something like speeding around a high banked track in a car, going insane speeds…whatever it took to get his blood screaming through his veins, he wanted it.

Fuck, he *needed* it. The thrill of near destruction obsessed him. His therapist had called it a "specter of insanity" after he'd described bungee jumping off the Bloukrans Bridge in South Africa. Two-hundred-sixteen-meters of free falling adrenaline rushing through his body. The first fall was amazing, but the moments that fascinated Justin were the ones when the bungee recoiled, pulling him back up and then suspended him, weightless, unfettered, before he dropped again. That perfect sensation of risking everything, and knowing you'd won, was better than any drug on the planet.

He pulled into the valet station at the hotel and hopped out of his car, tossing the keys to the young woman who ran out from the glass enclosure. She was the same one who'd retrieved his car hours earlier.

"Good morning, Mr. King. Will you need it again this morning?"

"No, I have a car service for later. You can put it away for the day." He handed her a tip large enough to make her do a double take. Justin winked and smiled. He made it inside and up to his room in minimal time, with good reason—nobody else was awake. The hotel keycard flicked across the sensor and unlocked the door to his suite. He pulled off his t-shirt and toed off his shoes before he grabbed his computer and flopped down on the sofa. He powered up the computer and logged into his work email letting the inbox populate.

He grabbed his phone and hit the favorites, calling his brother's number.

"Good Afternoon, Mr. King. Please stand by while we locate your brother." The female voice at the switchboard never changed.

He didn't bother to respond; the woman was gone before he assigned meaning to her words. The efficiency of Guardian baffled him. It had to be the military background of the employees. Lord knew his own organization was extremely effective, but the precision Guardian had obtained was eerie. Justin had never been in the military and had no desire to duplicate his brothers' career choices.

He and Jared were the only two of the five brothers who chose other paths. Of course, only Jason knew about his 'other' job, so he got a load of crap from his big, bad, Alpha snake-eater type brothers. *If they only knew.* He sighed. It was yet another reason he tended to avoid any family get-togethers. He'd made a pointed effort to avoid being around his family for so long declining invitations was the norm now.

"Justin, how are things?" Jason's gravelly voice pulled him out of his musings.

"Not so good. I'm afraid I'm under the weather." The code phrase he'd never uttered before brought silence from Jason's end of the connection.

"Really? Do you need a doctor?"

In other words, were you made? "Nah, I think I caught something from someone else. Which is strange because I can guarantee you I don't think anyone else wants to catch this crud." Justin cleared his throat. He didn't like the taste of telling his brother someone had beat him to the target.

"Someone else got sick first?"

"Yeah, some woman." Justin picked at the hem of his athletic shorts.

"Ha. Sucks to be you. Do you have meetings all day?"

"Yeah, no rest for the wicked."

"You're not wicked, just slightly weird, but we love you anyway. You should get some rest. I'm sure you'll be fine. A bug like this isn't easy to figure out, but give it some time. I'm sure between the two of us we can figure out a remedy."

"Yeah, I'm sure. I'll be down here for a couple more days, and then depending on several factors,

I'll either be flying to London or heading back to New York."

There was a long pause on the line before Jason asked... because he always asked, "How are you, besides the cold?" Justin couldn't miss the concern. It was always there.

"Fine." It was his standard answer. He was successful and damn good at the night job. What else was there? Justin pushed away his brother's concern, hell, his family's concern. He pushed away everyone, well almost. It was a gift or a curse.

"It's been a long time since we've seen you." Of all his siblings he was closest to Jason and maybe Jade, but one never knew with that one. She was...unique.

"You know how it goes. Life is busy."

"Bullshit. You know I worry about you. I know about addictions. Mine were chemical, yours are, hell, they're batshit crazy, but you've pushed us all away. You take risks that I'd never let any of my people take. If we didn't need your skill set, I'd fire you."

"You can't fire me. Gabriel hired me, and my agreement is with him." They'd had this conversation before. Same song different verse.

"Do you have anyone? A friend, someone constant in your life?"

Justin stared off into space at his brother's question. Yes, he had Danielle. She was his constant, but he couldn't walk down that path because if he did, he'd end up driving her away, too. It was inevitable. He was a self-labeled thrill seeker more interested in the next adrenaline spike than a relationship. He couldn't give the women he dated what they wanted because, simply stated, he didn't want the same thing. A wife and two point five kids would suffocate him.

"Justin?"

"What? Oh, right. I'm good. No need to worry about me." He knew his words sounded as fake as they were. The problem was, he didn't really care. He kept his family out of his life and out of his business except for the most necessary of occasions. It had been different, to a degree, before his dad's murder, but that seemed like a lifetime ago. He didn't fit in with his brothers growing up. His interests were vastly different than theirs. Hell, it seemed like the person he was then and the one he was now were totally different entities. The only similarities were the scars they carried.

"You know I'll always worry about you. I hope you feel better. Give me a call before you go to your meetings and let me know how you're doing."

"Can do. Take care." Justin glanced at his tablet and accessed his appointment calendar to set the alarm to activate and remind him to call Jason. Knowing himself, he didn't doubt he'd fall headfirst into work and forget to call his brother. He'd forgotten to do so many times.

"Don't forget to set a reminder. Talk with you soon." Jason's last-second dig about setting a reminder was nothing new.

Justin threw the disconnected device to the end of the couch. He glanced at over one hundred new emails since he'd last logged off. His executive assistant, Max, would go through the inbox when he woke up this morning and handle most of them, flagging only those that he needed to read. Max kept him from drowning in an ocean of emails. Justin scrolled through the notifications stopping when he noticed Danielle's name. She'd sent him an email last night about an hour before he left for the target's location. He popped it open and nodded at the content. The facts and figures, spreadsheets and breakdowns, were exactly what he needed to redirect his attention from last night's assignment. But first...he slid the laptop onto the sofa table and headed for a shower. Justin changed direction a second before he hit the bathroom door. Coffee...he needed coffee and gallons of it. He pulled out the room service menu and ordered coffee to be sent up ASAP and two breakfasts to be delivered at seven. He and Danielle had a standing breakfast meeting. The amount of work that could be done over the morning meal never ceased to amaze him. It didn't hurt that he genuinely enjoyed Danielle's company. Probably more than he should. Whatever, it was just business with them. He'd kept it that way. *Unfortunately.* Justin shook the thoughts out of his head and scratched his chest. He wrinkled his nose at his own stench. Yep, time to head to the bathroom for a quick shower.

CHAPTER 2

anielle Grant hung her head under the pulsing spray. The pressure of the jetted water loosened the tightness from her muscles, but nothing could clear the mountains of information careening around in her mind. She'd never been so ill-prepared for one of her morning meetings. The JK Holdings' executives, basically she and Justin King, were making the final decisions on vendors, allocations of space, and most importantly the remodel of the three-story restaurant that would be the crowning jewel atop a thirty-story bastion of all things luxurious. Even the lower level office space was going to cost an arm and a leg to rent, but those with money were flocking to the meetings tomorrow to sign leases on the highly sought after real estate.

The hot water pounded down on her back. The steam and white noise was a needed buffer that allowed her to strip the day into the sequences of meetings that she would need to tackle. She was with Justin King for the majority of the day, not that *Justin* was a hardship. Danielle allowed herself a small smile as she braced her hands against the shower wall. The man was gorgeous, and most likely oblivious to the fact that she existed, outside her role as his acquisition manager. Over the years she'd watched him date a host of beautiful women—models, businesswomen, lawyers, and the latest, an investigative reporter. All were beautiful, undeniably successful women, and all were history. Not that Danielle was keeping track...okay, so she watched and maybe even secretly cheered each time Justin told her that he was no longer seeing the flavor of the month. Was she harboring a crush on her boss? Oh, heck yeah. Could she do anything about it? Nope. That wasn't going to happen. Through their unique breakfast meetings and random impromptu lunch and dinner meetings, she probably knew Justin better than anyone in the company, much to his assistant's chagrin. Justin kept his personal and professional life distinct and separate. She had nothing to offer him to make him jump that line. So, he dated and she...well, she amused herself with "what-ifs". What was the use trying to have any real relationships when she ended up comparing the men she went out with to Justin? She'd had a couple strings of quasi-serious dates, but she attributed those to the fact she was the daughter of an influential and wealthy man. It had become uncomfortably clear that her dates were men who wanted what a connection to her could bring them rather than what she, Danielle, was willing to offer... which admittedly wasn't much. She rolled her shoulders under the water and reached for her shampoo.

When she'd first been asked to work for JK Holdings, she'd agreed immediately. It was a small up-and-coming company with a dynamic, magnetic CEO. Justin King had the Midas touch, and even though her father had almost forbidden her to work for such a small start-up, the new diploma on her wall from Brown gave her the credentials and the confidence to make the leap. So, leap she did. Four years later, JK Holdings had businesses around the world, and the corporation's growth rate had quadrupled.

Danielle rinsed her hair and grabbed her conditioner. She loved what she was doing. In her capacity, she had carte blanche to travel to any country and scout new venues for the expansion of JK Holdings' empire, and the company was most definitely an empire. What a ride. Justin King had started with fine dining restaurants, then acquired office buildings. He had the foresight to franchise three of his more profitable restaurants, but nobody expected the explosively successful franchises currently rolling out in seven countries and twenty-seven of the fifty states. He then expanded his real estate holdings into thriving and developing areas in the healthiest, most vibrant cities around the world. Currently, Danielle managed over six hundred million dollars in real estate assets. She had no idea how much Justin King's net worth was or what divine power had blessed his meteoric rise as the emperor of the haute cuisine movement, but there was no disputing the fact that anything Justin King touched turned to pure, unadulterated profit.

Jet lag from the flight to Australia clung to her tenaciously. Danielle groaned and coughed. She also seemed to have brought a bug with her from the States. To say her night had been unpleasant, well, that was an understatement. The chills that ran through her now weren't from the air conditioning being set too low. With the multitude of tasks that she needed to accomplish, there was no way she could crawl into that soft, warm bed and sleep all day…no matter how much her body demanded she do just that. Danielle turned off the water and stiffened her spine. She'd suck it up so she could get the day's meetings and mandatory accomplishments out of the way. Tomorrow she could be sick. Not today.

Fifteen minutes later, with her make-up on and her freshly washed and dried hair pulled back into a tight dark brown ponytail, Danielle felt almost human. She glanced at her skin's pallor in the mirror and grabbed her contour brush…but no, any more and she'd look like a circus clown. She'd just rock the lack of color like it was a fashion statement. Danielle snorted…then coughed…*oh, just freaking great.* She padded into the bedroom and stepped into a light green, wrap-around dress. Normally, she would wear the thin cashmere dress to accent her green eyes and dark brown hair, but today she wore it because it was the warmest thing she'd brought with her. She wrapped a white angora scarf around her neck in a loose cowl and hoped the contrast of the white against her skin would give her some semblance of color. She grabbed her briefcase and stuffed the reports, contracts, and documentation she would need into the side pockets. The external hard drive lay beside her purse where she'd dumped it last night. The documents she'd downloaded onto them couldn't be left in the hotel room, so she scooped them up and put them in the small side compartment within her computer bag before zipping the entire mess closed.

Danielle searched her purse for the keycard to her room, and when she couldn't find it, she started a pat down of the clothes she wore last night. The damn thing had to be here. She'd gotten in the door, hadn't she? Five minutes later she found it...in the side pocket of her purse. God, today *was not* going to be a good day.

She replaced the card, zipped the compartment closed and grabbed her briefcase as she headed out the door. Two rooms down, she knocked on Justin's door. The smile on his face when he opened the door never failed to take her breath away. This morning his crisp white linen shirt wasn't buttoned, and his hair was uncombed. The image could stop traffic; it definitely stopped her heart. Her eyes dropped to the light dusting of black hair on his very nicely defined chest. It was the most casual she'd seen her boss in a very long time.

He stepped back from the door and extended a

hand toward the sitting area. "Hi. Sorry. I got distracted reading the reports you sent over, and I'm running a little behind. Breakfast is set up. I'll be right in. Pour me a cup of coffee, would you?"

"Sure." She dropped her purse and computer satchel onto the couch and headed to a small bistro table already set up. She poured herself a cup of coffee, added a packet of sugar and a healthy drop of cream. The hot fluid felt wonderful against her sore throat. Damn it, she wasn't about to admit she was sick. Especially not day one on a trip. The front end was when Justin relied on her, even though the majority of the things on the agenda today weren't technically her job. It could be said that none of it was her job, but somewhere along the line Justin had started depending on her, and she was needed—even though the six-feet-five-inches of sexy perfection in the next room didn't even know she was alive. Well, that wasn't true. He counted on her for her business acumen. The problem was she wanted to be so much more.

She set her cup down and poured Justin's coffee, adding honey and cream. She was hopeless. She knew how he took his coffee, knew that he switched to water at ten every morning and drank at least eight bottles of spring water every day. She knew he was a fresh food fanatic and rarely had more than one drink of alcohol at any social event. She was with him while he studied and passed his master sommelier tests in Colorado. The feat was one very few could master. In fact, the organization allowed you to fail one of the portions and retest during the next testing cycle. It was expected that a person would fail. Justin didn't have to retest. He passed each of the three phases the first time and never looked back.

She also watched as he studied languages during long flights and could testify that he worked like a madman. Danielle made sure he knew what was on his calendar, went with him to the meetings he wanted her to attend and still managed to run the acquisitions branch of his business—all while hiding a side of herself most people wouldn't understand. Happily, there was no need to let people in on what she did in her private time. It wasn't like Justin would care, as long as she was there when he needed her. So, she usually scheduled her...events...when he took time off. At random times during the year, Justin's calendar blanked, and he dropped out of contact. There was nothing to indicate where he went or what he did, so Danielle usually scheduled her more exotic activities around those dates. This trip was the exception to the rule.

Justin walked into the sitting area fastening his cufflink. She set his coffee by his plate and lowered into her seat. She watched him move across the room. He didn't walk so much as prowl. She cocked her head and allowed herself a moment to take in his pure masculinity. Her boss was breathtakingly sexy and completely unaware she desired him. She sighed to herself. That was for the best. She'd just end up dumped like the long list of women before her. Working for him after that? No, she couldn't see it, so she kept her wants and desires to herself.

"What is the first order of business?" His words snapped her out of her moment of self-pity.

She cleared her throat, which hurt, and got up to grab her tablet because she had to have backup today. She should have familiarized herself with his schedule and the meetings, but there were things that couldn't be put off if her after hour activities were going to be successful, and she'd been very successful last night. When he arched his eyebrow at her, she blinked...*oh, right...schedule*. "I believe we have a nine o'clock with the construction company contracted to reno the restaurant. At ten thirty we will be reviewing proposals for the design. There are three. At one, you have lunch with Klaus Schmidt, Franklin Hayes and Terrence Lloyd at Le Château."

"You will accompany me to lunch."

Danielle blinked at the interruption and lifted her eyes from the day's itinerary. "Why?" She had no reason to attend. Justin was hosting the luncheon to shmooze the affluent businessmen in the area. Besides, she had a few errands to run that couldn't wait.

"We'll leave from the restaurant. While I was running last night, I saw a piece of property I'd like to take a look at." Justin didn't raise his eyes from the tablet he was scrolling through.

"I have a few things I need to work; being at that meeting would be difficult." She cleared her scratchy throat and closed her eyes while pinching the bridge of her nose. Her head ached under her fingertips. She waited for his answer. When he didn't respond, she opened one eye and peeked up at him.

"How long have you been ill?" He leaned back in his chair and hit her with a taciturn stare.

Dani blinked in surprise at his question. She thought she'd concealed her mild illness well. She flicked her wrist and shook her head. "It's just a bug. I started feeling it last night. I'm good to go through the meetings this morning, but I'd rather pass on the luncheon. I want to get some things done that I couldn't do last night. I can meet you at the restaurant. Give me the address. I'll contact a local realtor and set up a viewing. Commercial or residential?"

Justin put his tablet down and lifted his coffee cup. "Never mind about the property. Go back to your room, Danielle. I don't need you with me today. I'll have Miranda fill in for you."

Her mind skidded to a screaming stop, and she paused with her coffee cup halfway to her mouth. Miranda Tschetter *would not* fill in for her. The woman had been on the hunt for Danielle's position with Justin for two years. Miranda was sickeningly sweet and a back-stabbing character assassin. Danielle had watched the manipulative witch slice and dice her way to the executive floor of JK Holdings. She shrugged. "I'm fine, Justin. I promise not to breathe in your airspace if you're worried I'll contaminate you."

Justin threw back his head and laughed. The action relaxed his features making him appear younger and carefree. His dimples queued up and dazzled at the spontaneous outburst. It was a good look on the serious work-a-holic. "I haven't been sick in years. I was more concerned about you."

"Not going to sideline me, boss. I'm going to get a

good look at the growth and dynamics of the city. If it is as strong as the numbers suggest, another building in this area would be an investment worth researching. That is why I'm doing my thing while you wine and dine the locals. I'll meet you at the restaurant. Now, what was the address?" She took another sip of her coffee as Justin's executive assistant opened the door to the suite. The man pocketed his key card as he entered.

"Max, good timing. I need you to set up a Skype chat for me tonight. I need to close the deal with Chef Melvin Williams in London. If he is my guy, I want him in on the renovation and design of the kitchen here at the Perth location. Jorge and his team will oversee the front of the house after I choose a design. Which reminds me, make sure Jorge gets the information on the design firm we select today as soon as the ink is dry on the paper. He is going to be working behind the power curve on this establishment if we want to meet our grand opening date. I also need the quarterly reports for the franchises. Break them out by franchise and by country, please. The spreadsheets sent by accounting are too large. Make sure they get the memo to send them to me in that format. I spent entirely too much time trying to sort them and make sense of them this morning."

Max used his stylus and scribbled across his tablet. Danielle glanced at the man who'd been Justin's assistant for as long as she'd worked for JK Holdings. The thirty-something man was attractive and professional to the point of being cold. He didn't acknowledge she was in the room, but that was expected. She and Max had a love-slash-hate thing going on. He hated her, and she loved that her presence bothered the screwed-down-too-tight man. Ever since she'd started having breakfast meetings with Justin, Max had taken offense at her presence. So what if Justin had given her access to his calendar, and she briefed him on the day's schedule before Max could? Justin had told her Max was territorial. Danielle didn't doubt it. From the way Max's look lingered on Justin after he'd turned his attention elsewhere, she'd lay odds the man wanted more than control of Justin's schedule. She got it. She understood what it was like to desire the man. However, she enjoyed pissing off Max. Honestly, in the beginning, she couldn't have cared less about Justin's uptight assistant, but now, doing things to spin Max just a little tighter had turned into a fun game. Besides, she coveted her morning meetings with

Justin and because of those one-on-one hours, Justin had become...more. He was a constant in her life, and for someone like her, a constant was important.

Danielle tuned out as, for the next ten minutes, Justin went about the morning task of running his empire. When it was empty, she filled his coffee cup and added honey and cream, not that he noticed. He loaded Max with tasks and duties and sent him to his own suite to coordinate the efforts of the day.

Justin turned his attention back to her. "Are you sure you're well enough to work? You didn't even give Max the stink-eye this morning." Justin lifted the chilled glass dome off the fruit plates and served her a selection of her favorites along with a small bowl of yogurt. He added a bran muffin to his plate and a larger portion of fruit and yogurt.

"I don't know why he is so threatened by me. I've never been anything but supportive." Danielle tried to suppress the smile that turned the corners of her mouth up.

"Right." Justin laughed and shook his head. "Max is a control freak. It's why I hired him, and why he is so good at his job. The fact that you've stood up in his canoe and tipped it sideways will always bother him."

"I *could* stop briefing you on your schedule."

Danielle quipped before she dipped a small spoonful of yogurt. With her scratchy, sore throat, the thought of eating the fruit, no matter how ripe and luscious it looked, didn't appeal.

"I wouldn't allow it. What pretense would we have to continue having breakfast every morning?"

Her head whipped up at his comment, but he was reading his tablet while eating his yogurt. She lowered her eyes to her yogurt dish and pulled the spoon through the smooth offering. He couldn't mean it the way it sounded. Because it sounded like... It sounded like Justin enjoyed having breakfast with her as more than an employee? Could that be right? No, she was reading into his words and imagining things. *Wasn't she?*

She licked her dry lips and lifted her eyes from the yogurt to the man across from her. "I guess we would have to stop and return to the normal routine of discussing your acquisitions via email, boardroom meetings and video conferencing." She waited for him to respond.

He lifted his gaze to her. A puzzled look flashed across his face. "Excuse me? What did you say?"

"I simply stated that if I didn't give you a rundown on your schedule, there is very little we do at these breakfast meetings that couldn't be done via email or video conferencing." Danielle reached for the coffee pot, not because she wanted more, but because it gave her something to do while she waited for a reply.

Justin remained quiet while she added sugar and cream to her cup and stirred the mixture. She looked up at him as she leaned back in her chair.

"I enjoy these morning get-togethers. It isn't a stretch of the imagination to believe we get work done, because we do. I'm afraid I'm not willing to give up my time with you, so you'll have to endure giving me a personal briefing on my day for a while longer." Justin stood and glanced at his watch. "I ordered a limo. It should be outside. I hate to ask, but if you'll excuse me, I need to make a quick call back to the States, a family matter."

Danielle rose and pivoted on her heel to retrieve her purse and briefcase. "Of course, I'll wait in the car." She took four strides across the small sitting room before she stopped and rotated back toward him. "For some reason, I sense my comment upset you. Let me assure you I enjoy our morning inter-ludes as much as you do." She gave into the desire to reveal exactly *how* much she enjoyed them by running her eyes down his sexy physique and back up to encounter his bemused smile. "I'll be waiting."

Danielle turned and let herself out of the suite. Outside the elevator, her heart bounced like a timpani drum until the elevator door opened and she walked inside. The polished brass doors reflected her wide-eyed shock at her own brazenness. "Chalk that up to being sick. Either that or I've lost my mind." Her words bounced around her in the tastefully decorated elevator car. She'd basically told Justin King that she liked him. Like a schoolgirl. As if. Her innocence was lost long before it should have been. *Why in the world did she open her mouth?* Her shoulders shook as she tried to stop a yawn. *Because she was sick. That was her justification, and she was sticking to it.*

JUSTIN STARED AT THE DOOR. He'd crossed a threshold he never assumed he'd cross. Danielle had been a constant in his life for almost four years. She was a shrewd businesswoman. Her intelligence was second to none, and her work ethic mirrored his. They'd fallen into the comfortable habit of having breakfast together. It was the part of each morning Justin coveted just for himself. Danielle's off-handed remarks this morning had sliced through the professional veneer he'd placed on their time together. How would they disguise the time they shared if they stopped the pretense of business? Justin wasn't willing to risk losing his mornings with her. The time they spent together centered him, and he missed it when either one of them was traveling on separate business trips. Ice infused his spine, leaving him suddenly cold and uncomfortable at the thought of not having that time with her. The realization of how much he enjoyed his mornings with her should have sent up warning flags and alarms. It didn't. Which was remarkable.

The alarm on his tablet sounded again. Justin silenced it with an offhanded swipe at the screen. He went into the bedroom and retrieved his phone to call Jason. He was directed to Jason's office with smooth efficiency.

"How are you feeling? Better after a few hours' sleep?" The gravel in Jason's voice rumbled over the connection.

"Who slept?" Justin walked into the sitting room and found his shoes. He sat down on the couch and tucked the phone to his ear, so he could tie the laces of his thousand-dollar Italian leather shoes. "Shame, but I think I found a solution to your medical problem. One of the doctors we do business with has the remedy. Well, they have been told the remedy has been obtained, but the medication hasn't been received."

Justin stopped tying his shoe. Interesting that another agency had gone after the same product as Justin. In the years he'd been working for Guardian he'd never had competition on a mission. He knew there were others used by the different agencies Guardian worked with, but actually being in the same location at the same time as another operative was...intriguing.

"Strange. We need to talk when I get back. It has been awhile." Justin wanted Jason to know he had concerns. If he knew his brother, and he did, Jason had already sorted out the why's of the snafu.

"That sounds good. Are you coming back to the States then?"

"I'll know more tomorrow morning. I'll throw you a text when I find out."

"Sounds good. I'd wish you luck in your meetings, but dude, you know with the Midas touch thing you got going on...you don't need it."

"That's right. Preparation and skill outweigh luck, every time." Justin laughed as his brother groaned and hung up. He might push them away, but he still cared for his family.

CHAPTER 3

The bell on the pharmacy door clanged loudly as Danielle opened it. She glanced at the signs suspended from the ceiling and zeroed in on the home health section. An attractive older man dressed in a summer business suit came in behind her. She smiled, apologized and stepped aside to allow him through the doorway. He gave her a curt, brief nod before marching to the side of the store. Her briefcase strapped over her shoulder, and her purse hooked into the crook of her arm, she made a straight line for the familiar and not so familiar boxes that hung from the metal pegs. She didn't waste time reading the boxes of the brands she didn't know. Instead, she swiped up two boxes of a world-wide brand, one for nighttime and one for daytime.

She sent a silent prayer heavenward that the, "fights congestion, headache and stuffy nose, so you can sleep medication" would do a magic trick on her.

Four minutes later, she walked out the door and headed back toward the hotel. She'd had the limo drop her outside the pharmacy two blocks away. The heat of the summertime sunshine in December felt amazing, even if breathing wasn't as pleasant. Danielle glanced back when the door chimed. The same man followed her out. Danielle nodded at him and plunged her hand into the bag, pulling out the daytime medication. She unwrapped the cellophane from the box and pulled out a sheet of blister sealed pills. Popping out two, she made a last second decision to enter a small coffee shop. The line wasn't long, and thankfully within minutes, she had an iced coffee. She tossed the medication into her mouth and sipped her coffee chaser as she glanced at her Rolex with a sigh. She was late. Damn it. Grabbing an empty table, she pulled her phone out of the pouch and made her call.

"You're late." The grumbled dissatisfaction was expected.

" I know. Sorry, but I do have a day job." Danielle dropped her head into her hand and stared at the tabletop allowing the noises of the coffee shop to fall into the background.

"I don't need attitude, Danielle."

"Right. I know. Sorry." She took a sip of her coffee and glanced around the small cafe before she spoke. "I got the information and documents you wanted, although I really don't understand why you needed it."

"Since when do you question my intentions?" A hint of laughter tinted his voice.

"Umm...since forever?" She couldn't remember a time she hadn't.

"True. Suffice to say I need the information to secure my position and fortify it against any attempts to subvert my goals."

"Oh...cryptic. Nice, Dad. Did you watch a spy movie last night? I'm in a coffee shop right now, I can log onto the Wi-Fi and send it, unless you'd rather me encrypt it."

"If it is intercepted, nobody will understand it without context. Please forward it now. I have a meeting in thirty minutes. I will need to look at it before that conversation." His voice sounded more tired than usual, although that was a measure of extremes.

"You're working too hard again." She said the words without thinking.

"I work to keep myself from going insane."

"I'm sorry." And she was. Their history had been rough.

"As am I, but we each do what we must. Your...activities, shall we say, are worse than mine."

Danielle leaned back in her chair and stared sightlessly out of the storefront's large window. "We've agreed not to talk about that anymore. It just ends in arguments."

"That it does. Promise me that you'll take care of yourself."

Danielle smiled at the request. "I will if you will."

"No promises."

"As always."

"Send me the information, please."

"I'm taking my computer out now. Give me time to boot it up, and then I'll send it." The line went dead. She didn't expect anything less. They'd made a pact years ago to never say goodbye or actively mention their feelings for each other. They knew, and that was enough.

Danielle shoved her medication into her purse and pulled out her laptop. She booted up her computer and accessed the Wi-Fi using the password on the placard centered on her small table. She fished around for the thumb drives she'd thrown into her purse this morning and zipped the information into a compressed file before she signed into her internet account and sent the documents. She'd never use her JK Holdings account to send these. Justin King employed one hell of an IT team, and she couldn't afford to have him question her activities. Besides, they didn't affect JK Holdings, so no harm...no foul.

CHAPTER 4

*J*ustin walked into the summer sun and let his eyes adjust to the brightness. His limo waited at the curb. He darted in between the moving human throng on the busy sidewalk and entered the car through the door that was being held open by the driver. A blast of cool air met him as he lowered himself onto the leather seat.

"How was lunch?"

Danielle sat across from him. Her long, slender legs crossed at the ankle. Justin didn't allow himself the pleasure of a sweeping glance up that tempting expanse of skin, although it was exactly what he wanted to do.

"It went well. We established useful business contacts for our endeavors here. The local businessmen anticipate expanding the horizons of Perth and see JK Holdings as a vehicle to accomplish it. I wish to make money and enhance the city, and I see their positive interest as a boon. Win-win for all parties." Justin unbuttoned his jacket and leaned back in the seat.

"Okay, a more important question." A wide smile spread across her face. "How was the food?"

Justin laughed and shook his head. "It had flashes of excellence, but the overall level was lacking. The front of the house had numerous issues that could be resolved with proper management. I could make it a gem. There are possibilities."

"Of course, you could. The question is do you want me to see if Le Château is for sale?" Danielle pulled her tablet out of her briefcase.

"You could put out feelers. We've got our hands full with the new endeavors here, but once the projects have advanced and are manageable, I'd give consideration to acquiring this property if the owners were interested in selling. The location is perfect for business district clientele."

Danielle made a few notes on her tablet. She stopped typing, grabbed a folder off the seat beside her, and held it out to him. "I've had a conversation with the realtor representing the property you're interested in purchasing. The home is designated as 'historically significant', is in a restricted residential area, and it isn't zoned for a business. I contacted our Australian legal team and asked them about the zoning laws here. To boil down the four-page response in that folder, there hasn't been a precedent to allow for a waiver so it would be a legal tussle for us to present an argument that would suffice to amend the zoning. That's a lot to go through to set up a bed and breakfast, but we've done it before and given time, we would most likely prevail." Danielle swiped at her tablet before she blinked up at him.

Justin's hand itched to push back a lock of hair that had slipped from her ponytail. He fisted his hand to keep from making that stupid move and looked out the window instead. Fuck, what was wrong with him today? It had to be the lack of sleep. He'd never had impulse control issues around her. Well, none that he couldn't handle. He'd been interested in Danielle for years, but he'd never acted on it. Today, however, not acting was proving difficult.

"Justin?"

Her question returned him to the moment. "Excuse me? What did you say?"

"We could also purchase the property as a residential investment."

"No, cancel whatever you have set up with the realtor. I don't need another home, especially since I already have an apartment planned for the building we are renovating. The business idea was a late-night, jetlag-fueled inspiration. Thank you for tracking down the information."

He watched her tap out an email. She tugged her bottom lip between her teeth as she always did when she was concentrating.

"Are you okay?" Danielle's eyes traveled over him and damn him if he didn't like the sensation.

"I'm fine. I'm just tired. I couldn't sleep last night."

"That makes two of us. We should have ordered room service and had a movie marathon." Danielle threw the comment out as she worked on her tablet, not really paying attention to him.

Justin closed his eyes and let his head fall back against the seat. He allowed himself to imagine her feminine curves tucked against him on the couch. "Hmmm...I think I would have enjoyed that."

"Me, too. Maybe next time."

Danielle's soft voice did nothing to dissuade his mental mock-up of a night alone with her. The only thing that stopped his musings was the limo pulling over and stopping. Justin blinked open his eyes. Damn, sex and sleep were on his mind, not business.

He leaned forward and rubbed his face. "What are we doing now?" He glanced out the window.

"Meeting with legal. Just a quick glance over the agenda shows they have a briefing on Australian labor law, the status of the work permits for our company and the people we are bringing in from your other businesses, and numerous other bits and pieces. The usual song and dance before we can start working. There were no issues red flagged, so that's good. They have three hours blocked, and then you have a meeting with your bankers. Same conference area. It shouldn't last long as they are just a conduit for the incoming funds, but, I'm sure this is their push to be more than a repository."

Justin dropped his head and rolled it, right to left, relieving the tension in his shoulders. *He needed to get a grip.* Her low, sexy voice running down the afternoon's agenda went straight to his balls, and that was unacceptable. He bit the inside of his cheek and winced. Enough. Time to focus on business, not his unrequited desires. "Right, let's see what kind of preference the banks can give us before we close that door."

Justin didn't wait for the driver to open the door but stepped out into the summer heat and extended his hand back to Danielle. Her hand was ice cold in his. He gripped her hand, covering it with his free hand. "You're cold?"

She gave a small laugh. "Freezing, but the tablets I took about an hour ago have kicked in, and I'm feeling almost human."

Justin stood on the sidewalk and looked down into her green eyes. She was tall, five-feet-nine-inches. Her beautiful green eyes and dark chestnut brown hair set her up as a magnet for every male eye. She wasn't classically beautiful. The spray of freckles that spanned her nose and the slight gap between her front teeth marred what could have been perfection, but it was those things, small things, that she didn't try to hide that drew him to her. She was different than the model-perfect type he usually dated. Year round she had a tan, but not the sprayed-on type. He could tell her skin had actually been kissed by the sun. Her nails were neatly trimmed, no fake coverings or fancy polishes. While she wore makeup, it wasn't enough to hide or mask the natural woman beneath it. In his world, she was exceptional and unique.

Justin dropped her hand as if it scalded him. *Fuck, he needed to get through the day and get some sleep, before he did or said something he couldn't take back.*

He moved to allow her to adjust her purse and

briefcase before he put his hand on the small of her back and escorted her across the sidewalk into the building. It was a simple act he'd done many times before, but today he noticed how her waist fit against the palm of his hand, how the muscles in her back flexed against his fingers. He pressed his palm against her soft cashmere dress and felt firmness under his hand, not soft contours but a toned, muscled body. He removed his hand as he reached for the door. His fingers skimmed along her back and lower, over her gorgeous ass. The wayward touch was completely unintentional as her sudden stop at the door created the contact of his fingers. Her eyes darted to his with a questioning look. He carefully blanked his expression and opened the door. Danielle Grant was... *an employee...and his friend.* Fuck. He needed to drop the infatuated teenage angst. If he acted on his desires, he had far too much to lose when the relationship failed, and there was no doubt in his mind the relationship would end. She deserved better, and he wasn't foolish enough to alienate one of the few people he counted as a friend.

"As you can see the projections lead us to believe that if JK Holdings utilizes our line of credit..." *Blah, blah, blah...*

Danielle tried desperately not to roll her eyes. She'd heard this song and dance too many times to count. The things they needed to know had been covered two minutes into the presentation, but Justin was a consummate businessman, and he'd have the bankers eating out of his hand even when he told them he wouldn't be using their banks as anything but a local repository. She pulled out her tablet, held it in her lap and worked through her numerous emails. She glanced up at random points during the briefing, but nobody was paying her any attention. She opened her business email and dealt with the most recent issues and tabled the matters she needed to work through, acknowledging receipt of information and confirming commitments and meetings for the following week. That finished, she sat back and tried desperately not to fall asleep. The monotone drone of the speaker did little to keep her eyes open.

She swiped the face of her phone and hit her personal email account. The first email she saw made her glance around the room and move the phone so she was certain no one could see it. She hit the email and read the message:

Your request is confirmed. Be available 0800hrs, Saturday. We cannot wait.

"Are there any questions, sir?"

Danielle glanced up and hit the phone's side to blank her screen then shot a look around the table. *Please, no. No questions.*

"Thank you, Mr. Woolworth. I believe I have all the information I need. I'll examine your numbers and determine if the potential profit would be within the margins we deem as acceptable." Justin stood, sending all the bankers around the table scurrying. Dropping her tablet into her briefcase, she picked up her purse and followed Justin, who stopped at each person to shake their hand and speak a few words, as he made his way out of the room.

She clutched her phone in her hand as if her grip could safeguard the email on it. The slice of fear and internal trepidation brought on by the email eradicated any scrap of fatigue. She followed Justin's wide back as he worked his way through the meeting participants. *Saturday.* The rest of this business trip had to go as planned or she was royally screwed.

CHAPTER 5

*D*anielle had been quiet, inordinately so, during the ride back to the hotel. Justin had attempted to draw her into conversation, but her distracted, vague answers stilted his attempt. He pretended to read his email as he thought back through the afternoon. What happened? His mind jolted to the incident at the door. Could the accidental brush of his hand over her ass be the reason? He closed his eyes and dropped his head back onto the seat. Fuck, he'd been so distracted by his attraction to her that he hadn't considered if the feeling was mutual. Had he misread her interest and misinterpreted her comments? Hell, he didn't know. It was probably fate biting him in the ass. He'd basically placed Danielle onto a three-tiered pedestal as employee, friend and possible lover. She'd long since been more than an employee to him. She'd been firmly entrenched on the friend tier...until this trip. For some reason, his mind had catapulted her onto the third tier, and fuck him if it didn't sting that she didn't return his attraction. It was best to acknowledge her distance and reel back his feelings. He needed some space and time to deal with the fact that he'd overstepped. She probably did too.

The car pulled into the drive at the hotel and stopped. He exited and allowed the driver to offer Danielle a hand out of the vehicle. She didn't notice or seem to care. Justin followed her through the lobby and hailed the elevator. The ride up was as silent as the trip across town.

Danielle stopped at her door. "I'll see you in the morning?" She flashed her keycard against the reader.

Justin stopped in front of his door. "No, not tomorrow."

Her head whipped up. Her eyes went wide and then narrowed. "Why?"

He shrugged. "Max and I need some time to work some issues that don't involve acquisitions. I'll need you to represent me at the closing with the title company tomorrow afternoon. The rest of the meet-

ings I can handle with Max or Miranda. Good night."
Justin pushed his door open and walked into his
suite. The door closed behind him, and he drew a
deep breath. He'd apologize for his errant touch
when they got back to New York.

The phone in his suit pocket vibrated at the same
time someone pounded on his door. Justin spun and
opened the door without checking to see who was
knocking.

"That is complete and utter bullshit. What did I
do to get that attitude?" Danielle's face was flush
with anger—the last thing he'd expected.

"You didn't do anything." Justin stepped back as
she planted a hand on his chest and pushed him to
the side as she strode past.

She clicked angrily past him on her heels and
spun around glaring at him. "I'm not stupid, *Mr.*
King. I've heard that tone from you. Usually when
you're brushing off one of your many conquests. You
do not get to treat me like one of your floozies!"

"Floozies?" Justin repeated the ridiculous word.
The women he'd dated were career-minded profes-
sionals.

"Yes, *floozies*. I'm your friend. What in the hell was
that?" She flung her arm out and pointed toward her
suite. "Max drives you crazy with his hovering at

meetings, and Miranda Tschetter will replace me *over my dead body*." Justin blinked as she growled out the end of the sentence. He opened his mouth to speak, but Danielle spun away from him and threw her hands up in the air. "What did I do? Did I miss something in the meeting? I wasn't paying attention to the bankers, but I never do. Did I embarrass you somehow?" She spun around again and put her hands on her hips. She drew up tall and lifted her chin before she spoke, "Don't clam up on me and pretend I'm not your friend. Tell me what I did, and I promise it won't happen again."

Justin ran his hands through his hair. Still standing in the small hallway leading into the suite, he dropped his hands and looked at her. *Time to bite the bullet, King.* "I'm sorry." He put his hands in his pockets and rocked forward onto his toes as he searched the Carrara marble floor for the words he needed.

"You better be. I deserve to be treated better. Now, why the dismissal?" Danielle kicked out of her heels and walked over to the couch, sitting down and tucking her legs under her.

Damn it, she wasn't making it easier. "I could tell you were upset."

"What? When?"

"In the car."

A surprised look flashed over her face before she shook her head, narrowed her eyes, and pointed at him. "You know I have had, like, two hours of sleep in the last forty-eight. I'm running on fumes, and so are you. There is something else. Something else that prompted you to act like that."

He walked into the suite and unbuttoned his suit jacket, as his phone vibrated in his pocket again. He ignored it as he sat down across from her. "I thought maybe I offended you and I was trying to give you some space." He glanced out the window. He didn't want to see the confirmation of his trespass in her expression.

"Justin, look at me." He drew a breath and swung his gaze back to her. The confusion clearly written on her face startled him. "What do you think you did that offended me?"

He looked down at his hands and steepled his fingers. "I accidentally..." hell, how did he say it..."copped a feel of your ass this afternoon as we went into the meetings." He lifted his eyes when she snorted.

She leaned back on the couch and shook her head. "You are always a perfect gentleman, Justin. I never thought for a second that touch was anything more than what it was, an accidental brush of your hand. Remember. I. Know. You. Besides, I am *so* not your type."

An explosive chuff of air burst from his lungs before he could stop it. God, she was exactly his type, and he'd just figured that out. How in the hell did he tell her?

She frowned. "Right? I know you aren't interested in me. We're good. I need to order some food and go to sleep."

Justin blinked at her response. There was something off, a brittleness to her voice, as if she was talking politely to a stranger. She grabbed her heels and stood, heading toward the door. He shouldn't correct her, but he needed her to know how wrong her assumptions about him were. "You're wrong, you know."

She stopped and turned around. "About what, exactly?" Exhaustion dripped from her question. She looked defeated and small. Black circles under her eyes marred her light complexion.

"I am interested in you. I care about you." He'd probably said those words in some form or fashion to all of the women he'd dated, but after saying them to Danielle, he realized he'd never given weight to them before.

She relaxed, her tense shoulders fell, and she smiled softly at him before she nodded. "I know. You're my friend. I care about you, too." She turned around and spoke as she went down the short hall. "I want eggs tomorrow morning."

Justin smiled at her parting shot. His confession hadn't been the liberating event he'd hoped, but knowing they were good and Danielle considered him a friend gave him hope.

The phone in his pocket vibrated again. He snatched it out and answered it without looking at the caller. "What?"

"Well, that is a hell of a greeting." The voice of his brother Jacob snapped him to attention.

"Hey, what's up?" Justin shook his arm out of his suit jacket, transferred the phone to his other hand and dropped the coat onto the sofa.

"Jason wanted me to get ahold of you after your workday ended and since I'm here, I was magnanimous and agreed—that and he'd fire me if I didn't." Justin laughed at his brother. Jacob was the clown among them. He laughed often and enjoyed life. "He had to go to a student-teacher thing at Reece's school, so he asked that I contact you." Justin glanced at his watch. It was obviously a late night or very early morning for Jacob. "He wanted you to know that what you discussed earlier is a moot point. Someone else has the information and he doesn't need you to do anything else for him." Justin grabbed his tie and loosened it with one hand. "Can I ask what in the hell he was talking about?"

"You could ask, but if Jason wanted you to know, he would have told you." Justin smiled as he yanked his baby brother's chain. As far as he knew, Jason hadn't let any of the brothers in on what he did for Guardian—not that Jason's silence had stopped Jacob from suspecting. Obviously.

"Listen, that shit wasn't funny growing up, and it isn't funny now. I'm surrounded by asshole brothers." Jacob mumbled the last part into the phone.

"Poor widdle Jacob." Justin taunted.

"Fuck you, meathead."

"Oh, so eloquent, little man. Please tell me you don't work in communications for Guardian." Justin flopped onto the couch and put his feet up on the coffee table. Fuck, he was tired.

"I send messages, but usually not with words." Jacob gave an evil chuckle.

"I don't even want to know."

"Good. You know that old saying, 'If I told you, I'd have to kill you?' It applies here."

"Well then, by all means, keep it to yourself. I enjoy breathing."

"Noted. Hey, when are you coming back? We need to get together. You won't recognize the boys. They are growing like weeds. Tori wants to start doing a family reunion once a year. She says it is the only way the boys will see all of their aunts and uncles at the same time, but with Jewell's wedding, we may pass on this year and start planning it for next year."

"That sounds good. I just need to know a date as soon as possible, so I can schedule my meetings and travel around the event." The thought of a family reunion made his stomach flop. He was good with short periods of intense questioning, like at weddings, but a weekend of interrogation? Not so much.

"You can't blow this off. We never see you. I want the boys to know their uncle, and don't you dare tell anyone this, but I miss your ugly ass, too."

"It hasn't been that long." That was a lie. It had been...

"Years, Justin. Two fucking years and that is two fucking years too long."

"Yeah." What else could he say?

"You still calling Mom?"

"Weekly. She'd hunt me down if I didn't."

"Well, at least that's something. Do me a favor, come home. Let us see you."

"I'll try. My schedule is insane, but I promise, I'll try." He wasn't sure if he was lying or not. Maybe he would drive down to D.C. and surprise them. That way he could leave on his schedule, not theirs.

"You travel more than anyone I know." Jacob laughed and added, "Which begs the question who, or what, are you running away from?"

Justin flinched because his therapist had asked almost the exact same question about a month ago. He responded to Jacob with the same words he gave Doctor Morrissett, "What makes you think I'm running *away* from something, and not running *toward* something?" His doctor had raised an eyebrow and stated Justin shouldn't ever run towards death or serious bodily injuries. Jacob just laughed. His brother had no idea who or what Justin had become.

CHAPTER 6

*D*anielle pulled the suede wrapped elastic from her hair and literally let her hair down. The conversation from a few moments ago played on a loop in her brain. She couldn't shake her disappointment. There was nothing between them but friendship, and she knew it, but she'd always nurtured the hope there could be something more...until today. Justin hadn't denied she wasn't his type. No, rather than hurt her, he offered a consolation prize. He said he *cared* for her.

The little part of her mother she couldn't eradicate pushed into her thoughts. It had been years since her mother had slid over the edge of sanity and been committed. The last months they were together had scarred Danielle in ways she probably would never recover from, but meeting her father had helped. They'd formed a relationship based on trust—something she hadn't had before mental illness took her mother. Regardless, at times like these, she could still hear her mother's voice, "You are worthless, Danielle, just a stupid, worthless, girl. You'll never be of any use to anyone." She pulled her hands through her hair before she dropped face first into the down duvet that covered the king-sized hotel bed. She grabbed a pillow, shoved her face into it and screamed in frustration and disillusionment.

Flopping onto her back, she stared up at the ceiling. Well, she was better off knowing. Right? Maybe. She batted that thought around like a badminton birdie. She careened from one side to the other until she just couldn't run it through her mind again. Realistically, she'd just have to suck it up and deal with the fact that Justin King would never be anything more than a friend. On the bright side, she didn't need that complication in her life. She already served two masters. She wouldn't taint the brand Justin was building with the hallmark of her other...well, employer, for lack of a better term. A shiver of apprehension ran through her at that thought. No, not employer. That didn't come close to describing her relationship to the owner of Phoenix Armament.

Her phone vibrated in her purse and her tablet pinged a few seconds later. That meant a direct message...which meant work, probably the New York office. JK Holdings' personnel were just beginning their day. Danielle rolled to her side and grabbed the handle of her purse and pulled it toward her. She read the message and rolled her eyes. Sleep was no longer in the equation.

THREE HOURS LATER, with all the fires put out and tasks assigned to the department heads, she padded out, freshly washed and wrapped in a pair of ancient shorts and an extra-large cotton t-shirt. She pulled the hotel-supplied robe and slippers from the closet and wrapped up in the voluminous, plush terry cloth. She would have killed for this earlier when she was freezing, but whatever bug she had last night and most of the day was leaving, because, with the exception of being overly tired, she felt almost human. She picked up the room service menu and turned on the television. Crawling up into the middle of the bed she opened the menu. Oh, wow...the hotel had some decent offerings. Hmmm, Justin would have already tried the Mediterranean menu. It was packed with fresh offerings. Danielle chuckled to herself. Her boss was a bit of a fresh food snob. She stopped and corrected that train of thought immediately. He was actually a culinary elitist and had every right to that claim. The man made his name providing only the best of haute cuisine to the most discerning palate.

Danielle reached for her phone nestled in the charger and glanced at the time. If Justin wasn't awake, no harm, no foul and she'd pick for herself. If he was, she'd see what he recommended.

>Have you tried room service? The Med offerings?

She watched as the three little bubbles started immediately after her text delivered. So... he wasn't asleep.

>*Looking at the menu now. Max just left. Have you eaten?*

>No.

>*Come over. Eat with me.*

Danielle glanced at her pajamas and hotel robe. Ah, that would be a great big no. She snapped a picture of her feet in the too big slippers. It only showed the bottom of the robe and the television.

She sent the footie to him. Danielle laughed at her play-on-words. God, she was tired. She followed her sexy slipper shot with a text.

>No can do. Not dressed for the occasion.

>*Come over. I'm ordering for both of us.*

>I'll have to get dressed, and I'm too tired.

Whiney, but true. A knock at the door pulled her away from the bubbles percolating on her screen. Danielle rolled off the bed and shuffled to the door, trying to keep the size large slippers from falling off her size small feet. She leaned forward and looked out the peephole. Justin stood there and appeared to be texting on his phone. Her phone vibrated in her hand.

>*Open the door.*

Danielle rolled her eyes, dropped her phone into one of the robe's massive pockets, and cracked the door open, the security chain still in place. She scolded him, "Go away. I don't have any makeup on, and I'm in my pajamas."

"Come over and eat with me. I'm tired and hungry, and I don't care if you have any makeup on or not. Wear the robe, it looks big enough for both of us. Your modesty is safe."

Danielle scowled and scooted further behind the door so he couldn't see her. "That's so not the point."

"What exactly is the point? Are you hungry?"

"Yes." She was starving, at the point of getting a hunger headache.

"Then drop the coy routine and come on." Justin backed away from the door. "I'm waiting."

Danielle growled. Damn the man. Her brain was too foggy with fatigue to do anything but acquiesce to his orders. She shut the door and then released the security chain before she opened the door and held up her finger silencing anything Justin might have said. She shuffled back to her purse and grabbed her keycard before making the return shuffle to him. He stood directly in front of her and did not move. Danielle drew a deep breath and glared at him.

"I'm not sure why you think you need makeup. You're beautiful without it." Justin turned abruptly and walked toward his open door.

Danielle stood frozen to the spot trying to reboot her brain. *Did he just... No... Beautiful... Wait... Huh?...*

"Are you coming, or do you need me to carry you?"

Well, that got her attention, and the questions floating around her brain fell to the floor like lead weights. No, Justin was not carrying her. She could just imagine herself going all Scarlett O'Hara on him and swooning in his arms. *Nope, nope, nope.* Danielle reached back and shut her door, dropping her keycard into her pocket. The marble flooring accentuated the scraping sound of her slipper shuffle from the hall into the small living area of his suite. Like a beckoning lover, the luscious leather couch sent out an irresistible lure. After making sure the huge robe covered her completely, she ungracefully plopped into the welcoming cushions. A yawn she couldn't stifle escaped. When she finished with a full body shudder, she motioned toward the folders and computer open on the desk. "So, what fires were you putting out?"

Justin followed her gaze. "Just securing Chef Melvin's employment for the restaurant here. He agreed to our terms and is giving his notice tomorrow. We had a long discussion about the kitchen area and his vision for the menu. We've been working the particulars for both on Skype for the last two hours."

"Oh, so you can go back to New York when we are finished here?" Danielle slid the robe belt through her fingers and played with it as she talked.

"I'll travel back, but not with everyone else." Justin sat down on the couch with her and pointed the remote at the television.

"Why not? Oh, stop...go back."

Justin stopped scrolling through channels and reversed his path.

"Dude, we have to watch this."

"*Die Hard?*"

"Yeah, I mean, good guys, bank robbers and explosions. Bruce Willis and Alan Rickman." Danielle's concentration focused on the television. She loved the movie.

"Please, they aren't robbing a bank. They are breaking into a vault in the Nakatomi building. The entire concept is bogus. Seven locks, one consisting of a random code, five mechanical locks, and an electromagnetic seal as the last obstacle to the vault."

Danielle blinked and swung her head toward her boss. "That's a concise analysis. Did you see this movie one too many times, maybe?" She watched him carefully. Her fatigue took a backseat, replaced by curiosity.

"I grew up with five brothers. We owned the movie, and it played almost continuously for about four months." Justin leaned into the couch cushion landing on his elbow canted toward her. "I believe it was me who finally made the VHS disappear."

"Figures. So, you don't think they could break into that vault?" She pointed towards the television as Hans Gruber and the tech that was operating the equipment to break into the mechanical locks filled the screen.

"Oh, if there is a will, there is a way, but that vault is a Hollywood concept. One they didn't think through to a logical conclusion."

"What do you mean?" Danielle turned in the cushions, so she faced him. He swung his head toward her, now almost completely vertical, his head almost on her knee.

"Tell me that a company with six hundred million dollars in bearer bonds secured in a vault wouldn't ensure a random Los Angeles power outage didn't compromise their last line of defense?" Justin turned back to the television and dropped completely onto the couch, stretched out on two-thirds of it with his legs draped over the arm.

Danielle turned back to the television. "You're right. Anyone who would spend a million dollars on a vault would ensure a power fluctuation would trigger a failsafe. And now that I think about it, the drilling would take much longer, especially if the locking mechanisms were tungsten, titanium, or chromium. If I had that kind of money, I'd ensure the alloy was a combination of all three. A plasma drill would take..."

Justin abruptly lifted onto his elbow and stared at her, his forehead furrowed.

She paused at the expression he wore. "What?"

"Nothing, go on."

"I was just saying that a plasma drill would be the quickest way to defeat that type of metal, but I'm not aware of anyone building a portable drill that can sustain that heat and intensity for the duration required to break through a combination of the three hardest medals in the world." Danielle shrugged.

"How do you know that?"

Justin stared at her like she was a puzzle with about ten pieces missing. She wasn't. Her education in metallurgy was not her choice. Danielle shrugged. "I'm full of useless trivia. What can I say? I retain things." She turned back to the television. Justin never needed to know *how* she knew the information. That was something she would hide as long as she could. She could still feel Justin's gaze on her and dropped her eyes to his. The confusion from earlier was gone. What she saw took her breath away. Transfixed, she held his gaze. She didn't imagine it this time. Her eyes traveled down his long body splayed out over two-thirds of the couch. He was interested in being more than her friend if the stiffening reaction in a part of his lower half was any indication.

"Danielle—" Justin's voice had lowered at least two octaves, sending the air between them into an electrical maelstrom that sucked her breath away. A soft knock on the door shattered the moment and silenced whatever he was going to say. He rolled off the couch and walked towards the door. Danielle threaded her hands through her hair and dropped a drape of tresses in front of her face. She felt the simmering heat of that small moment spread through her.

Justin King wanted *her*. What should she do? Well, she *should* walk away. Pretend that moment never happened. She *should* go back to her room and go to sleep. Alone. She *should* value her career and position in the company more than she craved the idea of being with her boss. She *should* keep her distance because she had another life that he didn't need to get involved in. She could spew a ton of very rational ideas about what she *should* do.

The announcement of, "Room service," and the soft clatter of trays broke her spiraling thoughts.

"Just put it on the coffee table."

Danielle lifted her head and did a double take.

There were two servers, each carrying large trays laden with silver domed offerings.

"What did you do, order the entire menu?" She scooted back into the corner of the couch as if the movement would make more space on the table in front of her.

"I'm starving, and unless you ate while you were running your errands at lunch, you haven't had anything since this morning," Justin spoke as he was handed the folio. He signed and handed the leather wallet back.

"No, I had things to do and didn't have time."

"And you didn't eat earlier tonight, because?" Justin asked from where he stood watching the servers unload the trays.

"Because New York woke up." Danielle dropped her head back on the couch and closed her eyes. "There were several fires not actually fires, oh and one fire that was a three-alarm situation and nobody seemed to recognize it, let alone how to put it out."

"Ah, so a normal day."

"Basically. But done from Australia."

"Right." Justin sat down on the floor next to her position on the couch and started pulling covers off the platters.

The aromas sneaking around the room barreled

forward. "Oh, goodness, please tell me that is lebneh with feta." Her scoot forward to the edge of the couch happened in a blink of an eye. Justin handed her a small paper bag filled with warm pita bread.

"It is. The hummus is over there, dolmades, spicy potatoes, and beet salad." Justin started adding a small amount of each dish onto a plate as he uncovered the food. "I ordered the lamb tagine and the lamb shawarma, plus the scallops, because if the scallops are bad, I wanted to make sure we had enough."

"I think you have enough for a family of five." Danielle reached out and grabbed a dolma. The grape leaf was tender, and the rice inside exploded with flavor. She closed her eyes and moaned. Justin cleared his throat; at the sound her eyes flew open. He gave her a quick smile before he handed her the array of food he'd neatly arranged on a plate. As she set the china on her lap, her stomach gurgled loud enough for him to hear it.

"Good lord, woman. Eat!" His laughing command stole some of her embarrassment at the vicious growls emanating from her stomach.

Danielle stuffed the rest of the dolma into her mouth and ripped apart a large piece of warm pita. Justin got up and headed to the small bar. She hadn't noticed the open wine bottle before. He poured two glasses and settled back down on the floor next to her while she stayed perched on the couch.

"What kind of wine is this?" Danielle took a sip and savored the rich, full flavors.

"Generally, with a lamb tagine, one would serve Languedoc reds or a younger Riojas, perhaps a Cotes du Roussillon, but since we are in Australia, I paired it with an Australian Shiraz. The vintner is an upstart, but the outstanding flavors they are producing—especially considering the sandy soil and climate—make it a new favorite of mine." He nodded at her plate as he picked up another. "Eat." He didn't need to tell her a third time.

Danielle reclined against the back of the couch, full, and on her second glass of wine. The meal was good, but the company was exquisite. The conversation flitted from work to world news, to Australia and the climate compared to the cold New York winter. A companionable silence settled over them. Whether content from the food, wine or company, she found herself watching everything Justin did tonight. It was a liberty she wouldn't have taken a week ago.

Justin poured himself a portion of wine after he offered her more. She declined by putting her hand over the top of the stemmed crystal. As it was, two glasses of wine and less than four hours of sleep in forty-eight had her on the verge of a coma. Three glasses? She probably wouldn't make it back to her bed. He swirled the wine he'd poured into his glass and inhaled the aroma. He then sampled it. *Erotic.* That was the only word she could think of as she watched his eyes close and his head tip back after he swallowed the sample. His hair brushed against the robe she wore as his head came to rest on the seat cushion next to her thigh. His hair lay a fraction of an inch from her fingertips. The desire to reach out and feel the dark, thick strands was tempting. So very tempting. Danielle moved her fingertips and feathered through his hair. His eyes opened slowly, hooded and heavy.

Danielle swallowed hard and ran her fingers through his hair again. "This is nice."

His eyes traveled over her before a soft smile spread across his face. "Yes, it is."

"Justin?" She had to know what they were doing. They were risking their friendship…was it worth it? He turned and lifted to his knees, his body directly in front of her, his arms on either side of her. Soft mossy green eyes raked over her body. The robe had opened exposing the threadbare t-shirt she'd had since she was a teenager. It was an attachment and comfort that she wasn't willing to give up. She lifted her hand and tried to pull the robe shut, embarrassed.

"Don't, please." Justin dipped his head, kissing the area where her neck met her shoulder. She shuddered against the light, warm sensation. A gasp caught in her throat when his lips traveled up her neck and his mouth took the lobe of her ear, nipping it lightly. "Do you want me as much as I want you?" Justin's hand reached for her belt and worked the loose knot out. His hand slid inside the plush brushed cotton and rested at her side. His touch wasn't invasive or threatening. No, it was welcomed and wanted. He scalded her skin through her thin t-shirt. She leaned into his touch, seeking more, wanting more...God help her, needing more.

Her eyes rolled back in her skull when his lips traveled down her neck again. She couldn't breathe enough to speak. Instead, she wrapped her arms around his neck and scooted down enough so he was over her. Their gazes met and held. He lowered slowly, dipping almost far enough to press his lips against hers but pulled away at the last second. Danielle lifted and tried to follow.

He dipped again, giving her lips only the slightest touch. "Tell me you want me. Tell me you want this."

His whispered commands sent rivulets of desire through every nerve in her body. The cascading lust pooled deep and low. She snaked her hands through his hair. "I want you." She whispered the words and lifted up to him, demanding the kiss that had teased her. He wrapped his arms around her and pulled her from the cushion of the couch against his body. Her legs parted and wrapped around his hips as their lips met in a kiss that fed the hollow hunger that had lived within her for far too long. He nipped at her bottom lip before he licked the sting. His kiss wasn't a mere press of flesh against flesh, rather it was the very essence of everything she'd desired for years… the kiss *was* Justin. He wouldn't give her less than everything. Less wasn't in his genetic make-up. Justin King was meticulous—a perfectionist. He didn't rush into anything. He sampled, tasted, enjoyed, and gave her his entire focus and attention. The kiss embodied who he was, a master sommelier, and he treated her as if she were the rarest of vintages. It stole her breath, heightened her senses, and found her heart.

CHAPTER 7

*J*ustin pulled her closer savoring the soft sounds of pleasure, the tentative touches, and the flavor of wine mixed with her own version of sapid wonder. He could describe the nuances of every wine he'd ever tasted, but describing the marvelous palate that was Danielle Grant could take a lifetime to get right. Her hands found his bare skin and her touch sent a quake of desire through him. He had to pull away from her lips—to breathe. There was no other reason that would make him stop. One taste and he was enslaved to her unique flavor. He pulled away. Her jade green eyes had darkened, her pink cupid's bow lips were now red and swollen from their shared passion.

He reached out and pushed her hair from her face, cupping her neck. He lowered to her ear and whispered, "You are everything I dreamed you would be."

She froze under him, and he pulled back to make sure she was still with him. The look of wonder on her face made him pause. "What is it?"

"You've dreamed about me?"

The breathlessness of the question conveyed how important his answer was to her. He wanted honesty between them. Their friendship deserved it, and the respect he had for her demanded it. "I've wanted you for years. I didn't act because I didn't want to ruin us. What we have." He lowered and brushed a soft kiss against her lips, pausing to take the kiss deeper. His brain understood the magnitude of what they were doing, of the barriers they were breaching tonight, but his body, well fuck...his body was an impatient son of a bitch, and his little head was doing its best to overpower what his brain knew needed to happen. He needed to cool things down. He needed to give her a chance to think about the multitude of lines they were crossing before they went too far. But...God, his cock ached and engaged in combat against the absolute need to slow this attraction between them down so they could think.

Rationally. His hips pressed against her core, guided by instinct and need. They both groaned in the ecstasy at the friction.

"Sir, I just received a... Oh... I..."

Justin froze over Danielle at the sound of Max's voice. "Give me a minute, if you would Max?" He held Danielle's startled gaze as he spoke, pulling her closer into his arms, his back blocked Max's view of her. There was no way in hell he'd let what was starting between them become office fodder.

"Sorry, yes, of course. Absolutely." The hurried slap of Max's shoes against the marble tile preceded a quick open and shut of the hotel door.

Justin relaxed his hold on her. The dark rose hue climbing from her chest to her cheeks clearly displayed the extent of her embarrassment at being caught in a compromising position. "It looks like I need to have a talk with Max about boundaries."

Danielle pulled at her robe, closing the lapels. "I... I better go." She pushed herself up into a sitting position under him.

Justin closed his eyes and cursed silently in every language he knew. He released the tension in his shoulders and shook his head before he opened his eyes. "I'd rather you go into the bedroom and wait for me to deal with whatever Max thought was urgent."

She sent a piercing gaze toward the bedroom and then back at him. "I'm not sure that's a good idea."

Justin lowered and placed a kiss on her forehead. "I'll let you go, but you might want to wait in the bedroom. Considering his slight crush on me, Max is probably mortified, and I can almost guarantee he is pacing in the hallway."

"Oh, God...this was a bad decision." Danielle ran one hand through her hair as the other kept her robe closed. "What was I thinking?"

"The same thing I was thinking. That we are good together. There is chemistry here. What is between us is unique. At least for me. Don't let Max showing up scare you away. He doesn't know who I was with. There was no way he could see you. He'll get over his embarrassment. Give me some time to deal with whatever emergency brought him over here this late, and then you can go back to your room. No one will be the wiser."

"Okay." Danielle's gaze skittered around the room. She nodded without making eye contact. He lifted away, allowing her to escape to his bedroom. The door snicked shut before he allowed himself to swear softly. *Okay?* His brain obviously wasn't getting enough oxygen. What did okay mean? He scrolled back the words he'd just said. Hell, he'd have to deal with 'okay' later. Fuck, this *was not* how he was hoping the night would end. Through his disappointment, he conceded it was probably a damn good thing Max was hyper-efficient and an insomniac. Somehow, he couldn't find any enthusiasm for the idea.

He grabbed his wine glass and strolled slowly to the small bar. He poured a glass only to give himself a moment. A quick adjustment and a glance down ensured he was decent before he went to the door and opened it. Max stood across the hall, staring at his feet. "I'm so sorry, sir. I never thought...I mean..."

"Come in, Max." Justin stepped back and held the door open. Max pushed off the wall and glanced up. "I should have knocked. It's just that..."

"I've never had a visitor in my hotel room on a business trip before." Justin finished the thought for Max.

"Yes, sir." Max glanced around the suite.

"Ah, well, from now on in the evening hours, knock first?"

"Yes, sir. Absolutely." Justin took another sip of

the wine and lifted an eyebrow at Max. "There was something important that brought you here?"

"We just received initial notification of the Michelin Star ratings. You have two new three-star restaurants! Nido dell'Aquila and The Sabre! Public Relations in New York has sent press releases for review and approval. They have also sent a tentative schedule for the ratings reveal at each restaurant. The chefs need to be notified and I knew you'd want to do that personally. Sir, two three-star restaurants in one year. That gives you five three-star establishments. It is a wonderful achievement!"

Justin smiled at the excitement rolling off his assistant. His entire organization worked to provide a level of food and service that went above and beyond set in a unique and inviting environment. The Michelin recognition was the culmination of damn hard work by his entire team at each location. They deserved his attention now, and notification about their accomplishments as soon as possible. "Alright. Pull up the contact numbers for the chefs and the front of the house managers." Justin motioned toward the small desk and chair where they'd worked earlier in the evening.

"But sir, your guest?"

Justin glanced toward his bedroom. Danielle would understand the need to make the calls immediately. Besides, giving her time to think about what happened was wise. At least this way he could talk to her after she settled down and before she left for the night. He leaned forward in his chair and reached for his cell. "The contact numbers?"

OH MY GOD...HE wants me...has wanted me... Danielle paced the seventeen steps from door to window and back again. *He doesn't want to ruin us.* "Hell, *I* don't want to ruin us!" The words slid from her lips. She snapped her mouth shut and cast her eyes toward the door. She could hear the low rumble of Justin's voice and the faster more animated sound of Max's. Something had Max wound tight. She plopped onto Justin's bed and bounced off it again. *Justin's bed. Oh shit. They...she'd...he'd... Oh shit.*

Danielle dropped back down to the bed and pulled her feet up. She grabbed a large lock of hair and started twisting it, a nervous habit she'd developed at a young age. She'd been helpless when her mom went from a manic episode into the black pits of depression. She'd learned to make a mental list of what she could control and what she couldn't. The ingrained coping technique was one she hadn't consciously used in years, but the emotion connected to Justin brought the method to mind.

The thing was, there wasn't much she could control in this situation. She could control herself. At least hypothetically. Danielle snorted and dropped back onto the pillow. She turned to her side and focused on the door. Her phone vibrated in the pocket of her robe. She pulled it out and glanced at the face. She'd missed three text messages and had icons for numerous emails. The emails could wait. The texts could not.

>*Confirmation required on arrival date and time.*

Danielle sat up in bed cross-legged. She glanced at the door and pulled a strand of hair, twisting it around her fingers. Whatever was happening between Justin and her needed to take a back seat to the event she'd been planning for almost five months. She hadn't come to Perth by accident. She'd studied every possible aspect of what she was doing, and she was ready. God, she *hoped* she was ready. No. She was prepared, she'd practiced, and she'd prepared for every eventuality. The event that would happen in four days was something she couldn't reschedule. Danielle let go of her hair and replied.

>Confirming arrival date and time are still correct.

She closed the text and fell back onto the pillow again. Justin's low rumbling voice became white noise as Danielle closed her eyes and visualized the intricate preparation needed for the task she would be undertaking. She could see the equipment and feel the tension when it moved under her fingers. She was ready.

The door opened, pulling her from her visualization. Justin stood in the doorway, both hands thrust into his pockets.

"What was the emergency?" Danielle hadn't bothered to eavesdrop because she doubted Max had a legitimate reason for barging into Justin's room.

"We received our third star at both Nido dell'Aquila and The Sabre." A wicked smile spread across his face.

Danielle smiled wide. His news usurped any remaining awkwardness. "That is amazing. Congratulations. You deserve it."

"My people deserve it. It was a team effort." Justin leaned against the door jamb not coming into the room. The tension that vanished at his good news returned like a tsunami landing on shore. "We should probably talk about what happened between us."

Danielle nodded but held up a hand when he started to speak again. "For the record, what we were doing out there? I was onboard with everything."

"I sense a 'but' coming." Justin took his hands out of his pockets and crossed his arms over his chest.

She smiled and once again nodded. "Yes, the 'but' is I think we need to take this back to the States when we aren't slammed with meetings and jet lagged. I want to explore where this attraction between us will go, but I don't want to...I don't know...cheapen it to a business trip quickie?"

Justin dropped one of his arms and ran a hand through his hair. He blew out a long breath before he spoke, "I hope you know I would never consider anything with you as cheap or a 'quickie'."

"I do, but I also want us to talk about what is between us. The feelings I have for you aren't a sudden revelation." She stood and walked over to him. "Was it for you?" She lifted her hand and moved a finger between them pointing at him.

Justin wrapped his arms around her and held her loosely as he gazed down at her. "To be completely honest, the revelation about where I wanted to take us was sudden; the feelings I have for you weren't. I just didn't realize exactly how much I cared for you until recently. I didn't want to act on them. You know my track record."

"I would never hold that against you. Those women weren't me."

"True, but that being said, I have a tendency to repel women in short order." Justin pulled her a little closer, almost as if his action would delay what he felt was inevitable.

"The way I see it, we have a good foundation. Let's get this trip done. When we get back to New York, we can see where this goes." She lifted up onto her toes, pulling him down to her lips. Her kiss was soft and light because she didn't trust herself to hold to her own decree of slowing the sexual tension between them. As she pulled away, she stepped out of his arms. A quick pat of her robe made sure she had her phone and her keycard. She tipped her head indicating the outer room. "I should go."

Justin moved out of the way and let her pass. She padded across the room and stopped as she hit the small entranceway. Spinning around she motioned toward the couch. "I think we have some amazing chemistry. I really don't want to mess this up."

A half smile crept across his face. "Not messing it up would be a first for me."

"Excellent. I believe I would like being a first for you." Danielle wagged her eyebrows at him and headed to her own room.

CHAPTER 8

The wheels of the jet touched down at Hobart International Airport in Tasmania. The flight from Perth to Melbourne and then from Melbourne to Hobart took just over seven hours. Justin used the time to work. If he didn't, he'd be thinking about Danielle, which had become a habit. Since she requested a timeout, for lack of a better word, until they made it back to the States, he'd had more than enough time to think about her. Hell, he'd thought about her in the shower—three times. It did absolutely nothing to satisfy his need for the woman. He could not get her scent and taste out of his mind. The teasing smiles and looks she'd taunted him with the last two days had tested his resolve to honor her request. He didn't realize

Danielle was such a little minx...or perhaps he just hadn't noticed before. Damn, he'd been searching for someone when, quite possibly, that person had been right under his nose.

He waited for the aircraft to approach the terminal. The small airport meant there wouldn't be much, or in fact, any, wait on the tarmac for other aircraft to jockey for position. Thankful for the short taxi, he settled back into his chair and waited.

The only problem he could foresee in their relationship was his unquenchable desire for extreme adrenaline highs. They had a solid working relationship and friendship. Inevitably, the women he'd dated wanted things he couldn't provide. Stability, a home life, all wrapped in the cloak of respectability his money and businesses had given him. The thing they would never understand was while he was proud of his business accomplishments, the restaurants alone weren't enough. There would never be enough money, belongings or accolades to make him feel...alive. The hard, cold fact was he wasn't sure any woman could hold his attention like the rush of adrenaline did. Danielle was in a league of her own because he'd been obsessing about her, rather than the abseil he'd scheduled. Gordon Dam was supposed to be a quick abseil, not taking more than three minutes, but with over two hundred hours logged at rappelling, both on and off the night job, he'd scheduled a time slot so he could make a rap jump to the bottom. It was an extreme rappel. He'd drop off the dam face-first in an Australian rappel position and bound down the dam in giant leaps.

Those were the thoughts that should be on his mind right now, not wondering what Danielle was doing on her flight back to New York. The stairway lowered onto the Tasmanian tarmac. Justin was first off the aircraft. The heat from the summer wasn't the intense heat of Australia. He'd liken it to a nice spring day with temperatures in the mid-sixties to seventy. The walk through the small airport took only a couple minutes. Justin had to veer around a group of tourists taking photographs with a statue of three Tasmanian devils playing on luggage. He headed straight for the rental car agency, presented his credit card, international driver's license, and his passport and was on his way to the wilderness lodge near Gordon Dam within fifteen minutes of his arrival.

The drive to the lodge was uneventful, which didn't give him any relief from his thoughts of Danielle. He parked his car in the guest parking area and grabbed his small overnight bag out of the back seat. As his flight was the last one into Hobart, darkness had long since fallen. The lodge was sturdy and boasted exposed timbers, a cavernous foyer, and warm earth tones. The yellow jewel tones of the gas lighting and the roaring fire in the fireplace made the lodge feel warm and inviting. The chill from the outside night air stalled as soon as he stepped across the threshold.

"Good evening, sir. How may I help you?" The clerk behind the counter was dressed in what was no doubt the lodge's uniform—a black polo and khakis with cargo pockets. Justin glanced at the woman's name tag. Abbie smiled up at him.

"Reservation for King."

"Yes, sir, one moment." She started tapping on her computer and nodded to herself. "Yes, sir, right here. We have a note that states the package you sent ahead was placed in your room."

"Good, thank you." The crate held his rappelling gear. Not that he didn't trust the company he contracted through to abseil the dam, but his equipment was the best. He'd need to inspect it to make sure nothing had happened in transit. Justin handed over his black Am Ex and waited for his key card.

"Our restaurant is open until ten o'clock, after that there is limited room service. I see you are leaving us tomorrow. Will you require one or two keys?"

"One." Justin glanced over at the intimate dining area. There was a freestanding fireplace in the middle of the tables. He noted the time. He wouldn't be able to dine down here if he wanted to do a thorough inspection of his equipment. He'd had some spectacular food at small mom-and-pop type establishments and lodges were known for their use of local proteins, but he had equipment to check so a sandwich from room service would have to suffice.

THE SUN WARMED the top of the vast concrete expanse, but the breeze down the cut of the canyon that housed Gordon Dam was cool. Justin walked toward the middle of the dam carrying his rappelling gear. He noticed a small cluster of people standing around the abseil anchors and glanced down the sheer drop of the dam. The one-hundred-and-forty-meter drop guaranteed a good time. The hundreds of stairs leading back up to the top and his exit, not so much, but it would count as his cardio for the day.

His guide spotted him and waved him forward.

Not that he was hard to miss. At his height, carrying rappelling gear, he was an easy mark. Justin lifted his chin acknowledging the man and continued at his leisurely pace. He wanted whoever was on the anchor to start and finish their rappel so he was unimpeded in his descent.

His guide came over, extending his hand. "Mr. King?"

"That would be me." Justin took the man's hand and nodded over at the people gathered around the anchoring devices built at the middle of the dam. "I assumed I'd be alone." He'd actually paid so he would be.

"Yes, sir. As soon and my partner's guest finishes her descent we will clear the bottom, and you can go. I got your certifications. Impressive. Do you abseil for a living?"

"More like moonlighting. How much longer?" He moved his chin toward the people they were approaching.

"The woman is a little nervous, maybe a couple minutes. Or, if she is still working up the courage, you could go before her."

"First timer?" Justin knew the spike of fear and need to conquer it. He almost envied the woman her first rappel.

"At this level, yes. She has smaller abseils, but you have to admit our little descent is amazing." The guide threw his head back and laughed drawing the attention of the small group. Justin laughed along with the guide until he saw who was on the anchor. Danielle Grant. The woman's eyes grew wide before a radiant smile broke. "Funny meeting you in a place like this."

Justin swallowed hard. The sight of her in rappelling gear went straight to his cock. "I thought you were flying back to the States?" Justin's feet moved one in front of the other until he was beside her. His presence pushed back the smaller men who were working the anchor.

"I may have fibbed." She winked at him.

"Really? You think?" Justin laughed and reached to her gear, inspecting her equipment. "You enjoy rappelling?"

"I do. But this is the highest I've attempted." The pause and huskiness in her voice gave away her nervousness.

"Do you want me to go down it with you?" Justin's plan to rap rep solo down the face of the dam disintegrated. Reality as he knew it had been redefined as of ninety seconds ago. If he hadn't been infatuated with Danielle Grant before, he was now.

She snorted and shot him a glare of independence. "I don't need you to hold my hand."

"Fine, do it yourself, but wait for me at the bottom."

She lifted an eyebrow and smirked at him. "I have a flight to catch. I can't wait long."

Damn, that attitude when straight to his cock, too. If he wasn't careful, he wouldn't be able to wear his rappelling harness without flashing his hard-on to the entire staff. He watched as her handlers got her out onto the face of the dam. He let the staff give her last minute advice. Her intense concentration and determination as she nodded and gave them a verbal 'go' was a beautiful sight. Justin moved up onto the rail after she disappeared down the side. She had good form and steady descent. About halfway down he heard her laugh—a full, joyous, delightful laugh. He smiled and gripped the fence line, watching her to the base.

Justin turned and put on his gear. It was a practiced dance he could do in his sleep. The mandatory safety briefing completed, Justin stepped over the railing.

"Sir! You can't do an Australian rappel! It's against policy!"

The shock of his guide's voice made him smile

despite himself. He glanced over his shoulder and spoke, "It's a good thing I'm not doing an Australian rappel." A laugh from deep inside him emerged at the look of instantaneous relief on the guide's face. He leaned forward so he was at ninety degrees facing the ground. "I'm doing a rap rep." He yelled the words as he crouched against the wall, pushed forward and launched, letting the rope fly through his gri-gri. The ground sped toward him. The only sound he could hear was the hiss of the rope against his equipment and the buffeting of the wind through his helmet. The thrill of the rappel was quadrupled because the woman of his fucking dreams was waiting for him at the bottom.

CHAPTER 9

*D*anielle extracted herself from her harness. Her heart pounded against her chest; adrenaline coursed through her veins; she felt like she could crawl out of her skin with of the excess energy that danced through her system. *Justin King* was at the top of the dam, and he was going to abseil down it. She shook her head in disbelief and glanced up as she unclipped and stepped out of the rented harness.

A radio clipped to the waistband of the staff member who met her at the bottom of the rappel crackled. Words she couldn't decipher shouted over the airwaves.

"Shit, shit, shit!" The staffer straightened and looked up.

She did the same, shielding her eyes against the morning sun. She snapped her head up just as Justin leaned, squatted against the dam and launched into the air. She froze as he fell in an arc. His legs met the concrete base of the dam, and he flew out and down again. Awe spiked through her at the speed of his descent. *That* was what she wanted to be able to do. To let go, *to fly*. He landed against the vertical concrete face again and launched. As he approached the bottom, his speed decreased, and he straightened. As the bucket holding his static rope hit the ground before his feet, he landed in a crouch.

Wonder and amazement transfixed Danielle in place until Justin lifted into a standing position, looked toward her and grinned like a boy on Christmas. She sprinted to him, launched up, and wrapped herself around him, nearly knocking them to the ground. Justin recovered and swung her around as he laughed. He dropped her to her feet and grabbed her face holding her still. Dani swore she could see excitement swirling in the green depths of his eyes. He dropped his lips to hers and consumed her. Her body exploded with an urgent need to be as close to this man as she could get.

"Sir, excuse me…sir!"

Justin groaned and pulled away but kept her

close to him. She had to strain to turn her head toward the flustered guide.

"You can't do that! It is against policy. We have safety standards we must adhere to and uphold." He pointed with a waving arm toward the dam. His face was ruddy, and a vein bulged on his forehead.

She watched as Justin slipped into the professional businessman's veneer that he wore so well.

"You're right. I'm sorry, I promise I won't do it again." He kissed her one more time, hard on the lips, before he stepped back and started unhooking from his equipment.

"You are out of your mind! That was the stupidest, most awesome thing I've ever seen in my life. You have to teach me how to do that!"

"Not here. Never here. You will be banned," the guide sputtered behind her, but she didn't care.

Justin looked down at her with a broad smile. "We could do that, or we could do something else." He held his equipment in one hand and extended his other.

She took it without a second thought. "Like what?"

Justin shrugged as they headed toward the base of the stairs leading back up the one-hundred-and-forty-meter drop. "How about suit jumping off Mount Everest?"

Danielle stopped, pulling him to a halt. *Oh, my God*. The man could not get any more perfect. "You'd do that with me? I don't know how. You'd have to teach me, but God, yes! Let's do that!"

"It's a date." He turned and looked all the way up to the top of the stairs. "After we climb out of here that is."

She took his hand when he extended it, and they started up the stairs together. Adrenaline coursed through her veins. She couldn't keep the thrum under her skin from making her feel as if she could jump out of it, so, she tried to distract herself. "When did you start rappelling?"

Justin squeezed her hand. He drew a breath and shook his head. "Wow...it has been years now. I started out with smaller drops." He glanced down and winked at her. "What about you?"

Dani almost tripped when he winked at her, so she focused on the stairs as she spoke, "I guess it started after my dad got custody of me. I was a damaged teenager, and he was...well my dad is a driven individual. He's always been so busy. I acted out to get his attention. He took me to therapists and had me examined to make sure I didn't have a death wish." She laughed at the memory that had been tragically mortifying to the thirteen-year-old she was at the time. "Once he'd been reassured that my rebellious acts weren't suicide attempts, he made sure I had the proper safety equipment and coaches. He let me experiment. So, I've bungee jumped. I've done free climbs and snowboarded down a double black diamond run, which was terrifying and awesome. I started to learn to rappel just over two years ago. I've been planning to do this abseil since I read about it five months ago. When the purchase in Perth came to fruition, it was almost too good to be true." Her legs wobbled a bit as the spike started to wane. The muscles in her legs warmed from the climb up, but it felt good, made her feel alive. "What about you?"

"What about me, what?" Justin smiled down at her.

"Why do you do things like that?" She waved her free hand toward the dam. They walked up two levels of stairs in silence. She knew this side of Justin, too. The side that was private. She could practically hear the debate going on inside his head. If he didn't want to answer her, he wouldn't. She wasn't about to push him.

"I guess you could say I acted out when I was younger, too. I lost my dad. He was murdered."

"Oh, my God!" Her breathless words slipped out, unbidden.

Justin's hand squeezed hers. "It has been a very long time now, but it shattered me. I lost my anchor. I was the second oldest of eight. Dad knew I wasn't like my brothers. I didn't, and still don't, enjoy the Alpha macho positioning. I enjoyed things they didn't. Dad got that. I think a part of me died when he did. I guess I started doing things, taking risks and chances, to feel alive. I managed to get myself in a bit of trouble with the law when I left for college. A friend of the family somehow found out about it. He showed up at the jail where I was being held because I couldn't pay my bail and had refused to let my family know I'd screwed up so badly. He didn't say but maybe three words to me until he took me to my dorm room." Justin looked up at the sky and laughed. "That was a pivotal point in my life. He gave me an opportunity. Only one. If I screwed it up, he'd cut bait and toss me back into the ocean. I knew it was the opportunity of a lifetime. He paid for my tuition, and in return, I worked for him during the summer months. A part-time job, but it was something he demanded I do. After I graduated, I apprenticed for him and was sent around the world to some of the best restaurants. I studied what worked, what didn't and why. He and my brothers put up money for the first restaurant I purchased. I made him a shareholder of the next three, to pay him back for what he had invested in me. I channeled my energies into the business, but it wasn't enough. Since I had the money, I invested what downtime I had into events like these."

"Was that friend in the restaurant business?"

"Gabriel? No, he has other business concerns. He used to manage a massive corporation. He's semi-retired now."

Dani stopped and looked up the stairs. They were only halfway up. She leaned back against the handrail and pulled a refreshing hit of cool air into her lungs. "What did you do for him in the summers he made you work for him?"

Justin smiled and pulled her forward up the stairs. "Gopher stuff mainly. I…went and got things that he needed…most of the time."

"Most of the time?"

"Yeah, when he didn't need me to retrieve things for him, I was free to work on improving my skills and abilities."

"For business? That's cool."

Justin's chuckle reached her ears. "Yeah, I enjoyed learning things from him. What about you? How did you come from being an obnoxious teenager to a brilliant businesswoman?"

"Oh, well that is really boring. After my dad started noticing me, I realized he wasn't going to flake on me like my mom did. So, I started trying to fit in. It was different than when I was with my mom. Having a set schedule, three meals a day, clean clothes and electricity all the time, you know? I don't blame her for how we lived. She has mental issues." Danielle refused to let her mind call up the horrid images from her childhood and focused on the times her mom was manic. She was so happy and full of life at those times. There was always an adventure, always fun, but far too soon, Dani learned that the good times were followed by dark times. So very dark. Dani pulled back from the memories and cleared her throat. "Dad's a workaholic. Kind of like you, but I see you go out and have fun. Although I didn't know how much you let loose. Dad never does. His work is his only focus now that I'm out of the house."

"What does your dad do?"

They continued to trudge up the stairs. The weight of their boots scraping on the metal steps were the only sounds while she debated what, exactly, to tell him. Justin was rich in his own right, surely her father's money wouldn't matter to him, and if it did, it was best if she knew sooner rather than later. "He owns Phoenix Armament."

Justin stopped and looked down at her. "Paul Greenfield is your father?" Justin tried to collect his thoughts, but they scattered to all corners of his brain as if a pool shark had shattered the set on a billiards table.

There was very little that Justin could not tolerate. But he hated weapons. Weapons. Unnecessary, unneeded and in his mind—poison. His father was killed by an act of violence perpetrated by a person on drugs who had a weapon. The fact his family made their living the way they did was one of the reasons he maintained a distance. He loved his family, but he fucking hated weapons. He'd worked on this point with his therapist, and while she believed they were making progress, Justin wasn't so sure.

She let out a sigh and nodded before tugging on his hand getting him started up the stairs again. "Yeah."

"Why do you use the name Grant?"

"My mom's name. I had her maiden name until

the age of thirteen when she was institutionalized. She had an envelope in a lockbox. The cops found it after they... Anyway, it had my birth certificate, and Paul W. Greenfield was listed as my father. The city welfare people tracked down the only Paul W. Greenfield they could find. A DNA test was done and presto, I was whisked away to live in a house the size of my high school."

"You kept your mom's last name." Justin prompted.

"Yes, because once anyone found out I was Paul Greenfield's daughter I became...hell, I don't know...an asset I guess. It wasn't like they were seeing me, it was more like they were dating Phoenix Armament."

"I can guarantee you, I have zero desire to date Phoenix Armament. I want nothing to do with your father's business." Justin squeezed her hand and tugged it a little, getting her to shift her attention up to him. "I don't like guns, but I do like you."

Danielle bumped into him with her shoulder. "I don't like guns either, but I seem to know an inordinate amount about them. Are you really going to take me suit jumping off Everest?"

"Do you really want to try?"

"Oh hell, yeah. Don't you?"

An angry shout from above them diverted his attention for a moment. He laughed and shook his head. "Yes, I do. Besides, I don't think the good people at Gordon Dam will ever let me come back."

"There are other places to rappel. Maybe we should research those while we look into an Everest climb and suit jump?"

"That sounds like my kind of date."

Danielle melted even further as Justin lifted her hand and kissed the back of her leather glove before he let it go. The manager of the company was heading down the stairs, yelling and waving his hands, anger pulsing around him. Dani kept quiet as Justin met the man and spoke with him. She watched her boss, her friend, and God, she hoped her lover, work his magic charm. The people had no idea with whom they were dealing. He was a business Rasputin. Everyone he dealt with succumbed to his will and fell under his spell.

CHAPTER 10

*J*t took Justin five minutes to settle the manager down enough to accept an obscene tip to smooth out any lingering hard feelings. He kept Danielle in his line of sight the entire time. Not that he thought she'd disappear on him, but because he couldn't take his eyes off her. Over the course of his extreme adventures, he'd met a few women who sought the same thrills he did, but there was never any physical attraction. But with Danielle? She'd somehow filtered her way into damn near every facet of his life. Someone with whom he could work, play and possibly love? The woman was priceless, and he was damn sure going to make sure she knew it. Her moratorium on sexual contact wasn't going to last past the time it took to drive them back to the lodge, get a room, and close the door behind them. He wanted, no…he *needed* to be with her.

"Hey! Would you slow down a bit?" Dani skipped alongside him to keep up with his long legs. He shortened his stride, but not his pace. She pulled their joined hands. "What are you rushing to, big boy?"

Justin unlocked his rental and opened the passenger door. He helped her into the vehicle and leaned down to take her lips. He took possession of her mouth the way he wanted to be with her, passionately and completely. Her lips opened, and he delved into her, drawing her into the same state of arousal he was in, before he broke the kiss. "I'm rushing toward you, Danielle. I have been my entire life, I just didn't know it."

"Oh, God. How fast can you drive?" The words were breathless and almost prayer-like.

Justin leaned forward and gave her a kiss. "I've driven race cars at speeds of over two hundred miles per hour." He watched as her already blown pupils expanded farther, relegating the green to a thin border.

"Do that. Drive like that again." Her low, sexy command went straight to his cock.

"Yes, ma'am." He shut her door and hustled

around the car to the driver's side door. He was in and out of the parking lot in a blink of an eye. The rented Mercedes flew down the roadway heading back to the lodge. A trip that should have taken twenty-five minutes took less than fifteen. They bolted out of the car at the same time. Dani laughed. It was a beautiful sound—carefree and filled with life. He grabbed her hand, and they jogged into the lobby. They stopped at the desk where he had to ring a bell for the desk clerk.

When no one showed immediately, Danielle pushed the button again. "Don't they know we're impatient?"

Justin couldn't help the smile that spread across his face as he pushed and held the button down. "If they didn't, they do now."

"Ah, Mr. King? What can we do for you?"

"I'll need a room." Justin pulled out his wallet and presented his black Am Ex. The card always got the attention of the businesses he frequented.

"One night, sir?" The clerk asked as she worked the computer.

Justin glanced over at Danielle. She lifted an eyebrow before she shook her head and mouthed the word 'two.'

Justin's cock jumped behind his jeans. He swore

it screamed and did a happy dance. Instead of grabbing himself to stem the party going on in his pants he swung his head back to the clerk. "Two nights, please."

"Of course, sir. Unfortunately, the only thing available is the Grand Suite, the rate…"

"I don't care, I'll take it." He interrupted her before she could prattle on about the fee associated with the room. He didn't care if he had to give blood to get the damn place, any cost would be more than worth the price. Dani chuckled and leaned into his side. He dropped his arm over her shoulder, anchoring himself in the knowledge that he hadn't imagined the events of today. They were real. Dani was beside him, and God help him, he was fucking happy. Truly happy, as in jumping off a dam happy, but he had both feet planted firmly on the ground. The euphoria he'd felt since he saw her on the anchor equipment on top of the dam hadn't abated. Not. One. Bit.

He vaguely registered the presence of another man behind them. The clerk handed the keycard to him, but Danielle grabbed it and spun toward the hallway slamming into the middle-aged man behind her. She lost her balance and Justin grabbed her arm. Dani laughed as she stood up, an apology on her lips as she rose. "I'm so sorry, sir…" She stopped her apology and cocked her head at the man. "I'm sorry, have we met?"

The man groused, "Other than you running into me just now, no."

"Oh…so sorry." Dani did a double take as the man shouldered past them to the counter.

"Guess who doesn't have a sense of humor?" Justin grabbed Dani's elbow and propelled her toward the hall.

"Well, he doesn't, obviously. I could have sworn I've seen or met him before." Dani's steps faltered as she swiveled her head to look back at the man.

Justin turned down the hall severing her opportunity to gawk at the stranger any longer. "For the record…" Justin pointed to the left when the hallway branched out. "I'd much rather you pay attention to me."

"Oh, I plan on paying attention to you. Over and over and over again." Danielle sprinted ahead of him, turned and ran back at him launching herself. He braced as she hit and lifted her so her legs wrapped his hips. "See," she announced playfully. "You have my full attention."

He stopped in the middle of the hall. A revelation hit him like a Louisville Slugger connecting with a ninety mile an hour fastball. "I've known you for years, and you've never let me see this side of you."

As if a shadow passed over the sun, her happiness lessened and dimmed to the point of disappearing. "Are you disappointed?"

"Only that it took so long for you to trust me enough to be yourself." Justin held her wrapped around him in the middle of the hall and lowered his head to kiss her.

She leaned back and stared up into his eyes. "Then let's stop wasting time, Mr. King." She let go of his neck with one arm and waved the keycard under his nose. "Giddy up."

Oh, no she didn't! Justin hiked her up, freed one hand and swatted her ass right before he tipped her over his shoulder. Her squeals echoed down the hallway. He grabbed the back of her knees, and she went insane. Her laughter peeled through the lodge. Two maids who were in separate rooms popped their heads into the hall when Danielle's laughter turned into shrieks. Justin couldn't help laughing. Who knew the back of a person's knees could be so ticklish? Well, he did now, and he tormented her while she was draped over his shoulder. He spun when he got to the door, and upside down, she inserted the card into the reader. Somehow, they managed to open the door, and Justin bypassed the small kitchenette, the sitting area, a large bathroom and headed to the bed. He bent at the waist and dropped her onto the bed a split second before he dropped on top of her and wrapped himself around her. He caught his hands in her hair and held her still, moving his kiss from her lips to her ear, then to her neck.

"Too many clothes." Her words sent them both into a flurry of movement.

Hands, hers and his, pushed, pulled, tugged and unhooked, bringing her soft, warm skin against his. Justin had enough sense to grab his wallet and pull the one and only condom he carried out of the side pocket. He was going to have to find a pharmacy, but not until later.

She pushed him onto his back and straddled him. Her brown hair fell around her face and down her shoulder, caressing the top of the swell of her breast. His hands lifted, palming her and running his thumbs over the light brown nipple that had tightened into a hard pebble. She braced her arms on his shoulders and moved lower, bringing delicious, hot friction against his cock. "Oh my God, you're big."

Justin laughed and rolled her onto the bed under him. "Wanna see how big?" Granted not his best line, but he was having fun while having sex, and that was a novelty.

Danielle nodded. "I do. I want to taste you."

Justin grabbed the root of his cock and squeezed. Hell, the rate he was going a teenage boy would have more staying power. He grimaced and shook his head. "Not this time. I won't last if you put your mouth on me."

"Then I want your cock in me. No foreplay. I've waited so damn long." Danielle lifted her hips toward him.

Justin dropped down onto his elbow. "I'm not going to fuck you, Danielle. I'm going to make love to you because you deserve my best."

Her breath caught at his words. She raised a hand to his jaw and stroked his bottom lip with her thumb. "If this isn't real…"

Justin tipped his head to the side and kissed the palm of her hand. "I know. Me too." He lowered onto both elbows and started a slow, detailed worship of her body. He nipped at her collarbone, laved attention on each of her breasts, found the spot on the top of her hip that made her squirm under him. He traced the 'v' of her legs with his tongue until he reached the softness between. She opened herself, giving him room to settle between her legs. Her hands, no longer able to touch him, grasped his hair as he dipped in for the first taste of her. Her scent and taste were everything he'd imagined and somehow, more.

"Justin." Like a chant, his name spoken over and over floated around them. Her hands in his hair pulled, and he lifted. "I need more." Her words pulled him up to her lips. He reached for the condom, but she put her hand over his. "Not needed. I promise I've got that covered."

Justin tossed the foil packet, not caring where it landed. He lifted her leg, and she wrapped it around his hip. He centered his cock just outside her heat. He waited until her eyes met his before he entered her. Their gazes locked. The sensations of coming together fused with the vision of beauty below him. He stroked in as far as her body would allow and held himself still for a moment before retreating and thrusting forward again. Her body was the heaven he'd always longed for, but never knew for sure he'd find. The rightness of the two of them, together, washed over him. Not the furious lashing of tumultuous waters, but more like the surf lapping the sands on a tropical beach. Clear, beautiful, warm and inevitable. He lowered for a kiss but stopped when he noticed tears welling in her eyes. He stilled his hips immediately. "What is it? Am I hurting you?"

She shook her head. "No, God no."

Relief rained down on him. Justin pulled out and stroked back inside her. "Why are you crying?" He bent and kissed the path a tear had just taken toward her ear.

"You overwhelm me." She wiped at her tears and smiled up at him. "Don't stop."

Justin lowered his lips to hers. His kiss mimicked the motion of his hips, and his tongue explored, danced and dueled with hers. He pulled away to breathe, but he couldn't go far. A mere hair's breadth separated them. He stared into her eyes and knew that there would never be another for him. Something profound had occurred between them in the last forty-eight hours. He'd found the missing piece of the puzzle that he'd been searching for and he'd fight to keep her close. She was the mate to his soul.

Her body tensed under his and she bowed up under him. She clenched around him in her climax. Justin dropped his head to her shoulder and allowed himself to rut his way through the orgasm that obliterated him. He saw white and red spots behind his eyelids and damned if he didn't come close to passing out. He had enough mental acuity to keep up on his elbows so he didn't suffocate her.

They held positions for a moment, struggling to control their breathing. With a kiss dropped on her shoulder, he pulled out and rolled to his side, bringing her with him. Exhaustion, from the adrenaline spikes of the morning's descent and the mind-shifting sex, blanketed them with a soft cover of languid bliss. They lay together, her wrapped in his arms. To him it was perfect. He felt her kiss his collarbone before she drifted to sleep. His eyes closed as he followed her over the edge into oblivion.

CHAPTER 11

*D*ani woke to the sensation of Justin's finger tracing its way down her arm. She turned towards him and blinked the sleep away. "So, it wasn't a dream?"

He smiled at her. "I thought the same thing when I woke up." He lifted onto his elbow and looked down at her. "At the risk of sounding needy, were you serious about Mount Everest?"

"Absolutely. I'll need to train and get conditioned for the climb, but yes, one hundred percent, yes." A sudden rush of relief passed over his features, and he visibly relaxed. She studied his face. "That's important to you, isn't it?"

Justin nodded. Once. The seriousness she'd come to recognize in the boardroom found its way into his eyes. "Finding someone I care about that shares my interests was a pipe dream before yesterday." He leaned over her; his eyes roamed, scanning her face. He lifted his hand and ran a finger down her neck. "Why didn't I know this about you?"

Dani leaned into his touch and tried not to purr in her contentment. "There is a lot about each other we don't know. Our time together has always centered around work."

"Then how did you become so important to me?" Justin lowered for a soft kiss.

"The same way you became important to me. We respect what each other has accomplished, and we enjoy each other's company. You became my constant. Other than the job, I don't have that."

He lay down on his side and Dani mimicked his position. They stared across the pillow at each other. "I think you're right. I have a huge family, but I'm never around them for any length of time. My fault, not theirs. What about your father?"

Dani sighed. Her father, well, she needed to broach that subject, didn't she? "I talk to him all the time. I actually moonlight for him. He has been having a problem in his inner circle. He believes there is someone siphoning off information on the new ideas he is developing. He has some outside security firm doing an investigation. My dad is a stickler for accountability and making sure his product is sold and used within the dictates of the United States government's regulations. His biggest client is the Department of Defense, and he wouldn't do anything to jeopardize that."

"What kind of moonlighting do you do?"

"Nothing in competition with JK Holdings. I made sure of that. He was looking for a new manufacturing location, and I helped him with that. From there, I somehow got roped into helping him source his materials. They have to be legitimate businesses recognized and approved by the government, but Dad has found quite a few of those have shady business ethics. He has me vet each of the companies. We've eliminated two of his major suppliers recently and gone with smaller companies that were more in line with his business ethics."

"I wasn't worried about you not doing your job for my company, I was just curious what kept you busy at night." Justin's open smile settled around her heart. The man was not real. He couldn't be.

"Well, that only takes a few hours a week. When I'm not at work, I work out, train and keep my body in condition for whatever event I'm planning. I also date."

Justin's easy smile disappeared from his face. "Dated. Past tense. We are exclusive."

Dani lifted an eyebrow because she couldn't resist teasing him. "When did we make that decision?"

"When you were sleeping. You agreed with me."

She grinned at Justin's immediate response. "I did?"

"Yes. I told you that you were mine and I was yours, and the rest of the world didn't matter." He winked at her.

"I think we made a smart decision."

"I concur. Now, what shall we do today, Ms. Grant?"

Dani rolled onto her back, closed her eyes, and stretched, pulling the sheet down, exposing her body as she enjoyed the pull of her muscles. She felt him move over her and wound her arms around his neck without opening her eyes. "Mmm...this. We could do this all day, Mr. King."

He lowered and kissed the side of her mouth before dropping to her ear, nibbling on the lobe. His hips ground against her core. She was delightfully sore. His cock was long and thick, and when he made love to her, she felt like the center of his universe. She spread her legs allowing him to settle between them as they kissed. He could put her on the edge of orgasm just by kissing her. She arched up into him, wanting more. "Please." She needed him inside her, needed to feel the connection that was new, wonderful, and so damn right.

His hands traveled her body as he rose to his knees. What a picture he made. His thick, heavy cock stood away from his body, the large mushroom head held a pearl of clear liquid at the tip. He sat back on his heels and used one hand to stroke his cock. His eyes closed momentarily before they snapped open as if he was afraid she'd disappear. "You are so damn beautiful." His voice had a scratchy note in it and was lower than she'd ever heard it.

"I was just thinking the same thing about you. Care to show me what you can do with that impressive erection, Mr. King?" Dani waggled her eyebrows at him.

"I'm trying to decide what position I want you in." He gave himself a languid stroke, enlarging the clear pearl that escaped from his flushed cock.

"Why do you have to decide? We do have two days, I'm sure we will get to most of them eventually."

Justin smirked at her and rolled her onto her stomach before bringing her onto her hands and knees. His body folded over her as his cock found its way to her center. His girth made the initial penetration slow going, but God, the wait was worth it. They worked together, him thrusting and her pushing back, meeting his movement. He held her shoulders, and she loved the possessiveness of the clutch. The frenzy of their union took nothing away from the meaning. They were together and exclusive. Dani gasped as her orgasm detonated throughout her body. She vaguely heard Justin shout her name before she felt him release inside her. He held still within her for several long seconds before he moved back and slid out. He pulled her up so her back was against his chest. "I just came inside you, and already I'm trying to decide if now is too soon to make love to you again."

Dani twisted her head around and pulled him down for a kiss. "It would never be too soon. I am as hungry for you as you are for me. Why don't we take this to the shower?" She lifted off him and made it five steps from the bed before she heard him moving and seven steps before he snatched her off her feet. The surprised squeal that erupted from her would probably have the staff coming to the room to ask them to keep things down, but she didn't care. She was happy.

CHAPTER 12

"If you don't hurry, we aren't going to be able to eat before we need to drive to the airport!" Danielle yelled the words from the kitchenette where she had made them both a cup of coffee. They'd lived on questionable room service food for the last two days. Well, questionable food but unquestionably fantastic sex. They'd talked for hours, about everything and nothing, the way friends do. She sighed in complete contentment as she stirred his coffee. Too bad they had to leave today. Business waited for no man and Justin had already nearly given Max a heart attack with the unannounced extra day of being incommunicado in Hobart, Tasmania.

Justin padded out to the kitchen wearing nothing

but a hotel towel. The damn thing was barely knotted around his waist. His Adonis belt and happy trail on prominent display, she couldn't help ogling. He stepped in front of her and tipped her chin up, lifting her eyes from the wet terrycloth and his rising desire hidden beneath. "My eyes are up here." He leaned down and kissed her as he reached around her for his coffee.

Suddenly food wasn't important anymore. Well, not the protein she imagined before he walked out. Right now, she wanted to eat him. She dropped her hand to his towel and flicked the tucked material, dropping the damp terry cloth to the floor. "Your eyes are gorgeous, stop fishing for compliments." She dropped to her knees and ran her cheek up the soft skin that covered his hardening shaft. His cock was long and thick with dark blue veins that crisscrossed under the velvet-soft skin. She licked around its large mushroom head before she pulled him into her mouth. There was no way she could deep throat him. She worked her hand from his base to her mouth as she took him as deep as she could. Gagging at his head at the back of her throat, she pulled away and went down on him again while stroking the lower portion of his cock. He sucked air through his teeth as she swirled her tongue around his head when she lifted. Danielle added that tongue movement to every stroke. She could feel the muscles in his thighs quaking as his hands reached down and gently cupped her head. His hips flexed the smallest amount as she lowered. He tapped her cheek. "I'm going...pull off." *Oh, hell no.* Dani sucked him down and moved her free hand to his balls. They were high and tight against his body. She gently tugged on them, and that's when Justin shattered, spilling into her mouth. She swallowed everything he had to give to her and held him in her mouth until he pulled free with a hiss. He helped her up before he kissed her. There wasn't a portion of her mouth he didn't devour.

She pulled away and glanced over at the clock. "Go, you've got five minutes." She handed him his coffee. "I still want breakfast."

"I think I found the perfect woman." He turned away, leaving the towel on the floor. She cocked her head to the side and watched his wide, strong back, tapered waist, gorgeous ass, and muscular legs disappear into the bedroom. There was no "thinking" required on her part. She knew she'd found the perfect man.

Her phone vibrated, dragging her attention away

from the naked body beyond her sight. She glanced down and answered the incoming call.

"I need you to get some information for me. A person of interest. I have heard through unreliable sources he may have ties to Libya."

"Hi, how are you?" She chirped the question.

A long silence followed her question before her father answered. "Why the change in the status quo?" They didn't usually share details of their existence. He loved her, she knew it, but still, it was difficult for him to verbally express it.

"I don't know. Feeling happy, I guess. I am actually leaving for the airport soon. I can research that when I get back to the States. Libya is a failed state, now. There is no recognized government. Anyone having contacts over there is shady at best."

"Which is exactly the reason I need the research, and I need it from someone I trust implicitly."

"Thank you." She took the compliment for what it was. The people he trusted could be counted on one hand.

"You're welcome."

"Is this a big supplier?" Danielle took a sip of her coffee and listened to Justin whistling in the bedroom.

"It isn't a supplier. He is someone in the organization."

The smile dropped off Dani's face, and she
concentrated her stare at the countertop. "You have
someone on the board that has ties to Libya?" The
ramifications of that could shake the foundations of
his company.

"No, in R&D."

"You think he is the one stealing your design
information?"

"Makes sense, but I won't bring in the big guns
until I know for sure he is the one."

"Funny pun."

"Not intended. Can you get this information for
me when you get back to the States?"

"I can, and I will. It will be forty-eight to seventy-
two hours. Is that going to be alright?"

"Yes. I've taken covert action to prevent him from
accessing the proprietary inventions that would
cause catastrophic repercussions, and I have hired
people to watch him."

"Sounds like you are convinced this man is the
one conducting industrial espionage."

"My safe was broken into five weeks ago. There
was no documentation that could be acquired, but I

hired people to ensure it didn't happen again. If this is the man, he will be dealt with, swiftly and with prejudice." There was no change in his tone. The bombshell was dropped as if he was talking about the weather.

Fear spiked a rod of electricity through her at the comment. "Why didn't you tell me?"

"How does it affect you? I handle my concerns at this end. You take care of the company you work for and feed me a bit of unbiased research when you can. I'm more than capable of safeguarding Phoenix." Again, the even concise delivery. No accusation or incrimination, just her father stating facts.

"I didn't think for a moment you weren't capable, Dad, but I still worry about you." He didn't let anyone close to him. To her knowledge, he had no one to whom he could voice his concerns to or to discuss his fears. She'd been his only exception.

"And I you."

"Be careful. I know you don't like it when I say it, but I love you, and I worry about you."

A long silence punctuated their conversation before her father replied, "Ditto, Dani." She drew a shaky breath. That was as close to saying he loved her as he ever got. He cleared his throat and said, "I like it when you say it, I just don't know what to do with it," before he disconnected the call.

"Is everything alright?"

Justin stood beside the counter drinking his coffee. She'd been so engrossed in her conversation with her father she didn't hear or see him come back into the room. She drew in a deep breath and shook her head. "Yes? No? I don't know?" She laughed and took a drink of her cooled coffee. "Dad is having issues and wants me to do some research for him."

"Do we need to rebook the flight?" Justin grabbed his phone and started typing.

"No." She put her hand over his phone and gently pushed it to his side. "He said three days wasn't going to matter. From what he told me today, this situation has been brewing for a while."

"Alright. Let's get some breakfast, make our way to Cambridge and the airport. We have several long flights ahead of us." Justin grabbed his keycard and held out his hand to her.

DANI'S HEAD rested against his shoulder. They'd been flying forever. Tasmania to Perth to gather both sets of luggage, Perth to Sydney. Sydney to Los Angeles and now on the last leg of the trip, Los Angeles to New York.

They'd talked, laughed and learned about each other. It was the first flight where he hadn't poured over documents or immersed himself in learning a new language. A novelty to be sure but concentrating on his business when there were so many things to find out about Danielle was unthinkable. The stewardess made the landing announcement, and Danielle rose off his shoulder.

"Is it wrong of me to be worried that when we land that this bubble will burst?"

He grasped her hand and put his other on the top of their intertwined fingers. "I'm not going anywhere. We are going to your apartment to get some clothes and anything else you need, and then you are coming to mine. We'll figure it out from there."

Dani smiled and dropped her head onto his shoulder again. "As easy as that?"

"There is no need to make it difficult." He wasn't going to give her the opportunity to second guess their relationship.

"We will need to do some paperwork for HR. We can't break the company's policy on employees dating." A small smile tugged at the corner of her lips.

"I set the policy. I'll have Max file the appropriate forms."

Dani groaned, "Uggg...God, Max. He hated me before. He's going to despise me now."

"Just let him do his job. He's good at it. Besides, if I didn't have him, I wouldn't have as much free time to spend with you." Justin relied on Max for all the minor administrative tasks that would drown him in cyber paper. He paid Max well enough to at least be civil to Danielle. The fact that Max had always had a crush on him was probably the real reason Max didn't like his acquisitions manager. Justin made a mental note to talk to his assistant about that.

"I know, I get it. I'm invading his territory."

"The only one who has a claim to my personal time is you." Justin had reaffirmed his position about exclusivity several times during the flight home. It was important to him that she knew he wasn't interested in dating anyone else.

"And the only one with a personal claim to me is you." She tipped her head up, and he placed a soft kiss on her lips.

"So, it's settled. Your place for clothes and necessities and then to my apartment."

"Funny, I didn't think I argued that point."

"You are definitely the perfect woman for me."

The trip through baggage claim where his driver met them seemed to take forever. He wanted to get Danielle to her apartment, grab enough to last a couple days and then head to his for an hour-long shower, sex, and then sleep. Maybe they could condense that into shower sex and sleep. He escorted her up to her apartment, and thank God, she took exactly five minutes to grab several days' worth of warm winter clothes, pull her toiletries out of her suitcase and pack a smaller bag. That, along with her briefcase, and they were back down heading to his apartment.

He'd originally purchased one unit in his Central Park West Apartment, but when his neighbor put his apartment on the market, Justin snapped it up. The wall between the units came down, and everything expanded. The work took over a year to complete, but now it was his home and a haven, although he wasn't often there.

His driver opened the car door for them. "I'll get the bags, sir."

Justin nodded and clasped the man on the shoulder. "Just set them in the entryway?"

"Of course, sir." Paulo had been with him for the last six years and would have normally taken the bags to his bedroom while Justin was showering. He didn't want that to happen today.

Justin reached back to assist Danielle out of the car and headed into the building. The security detail at the foyer's main counter nodded to him as he walked toward the elevator and punched in his code. He pulled Danielle into him and lost himself in a kiss while the elevator climbed to his floor. When the door slid open he backed her out, still kissing her. She wrapped her arms around his neck and walked backward until they reached the door. She continued to kiss him as he reached into his pocket and pulled out his set of keys. It took five or ten kisses longer to open the door. He pushed it open with one hand while backing her into the apartment. He kicked the door closed with his foot before he reached under her jacket and cupped her breast.

"Ummm...this is rather embarrassing."

"Speak for yourself, this is fucking hot."

"Gross, that's your brother!"

"Girls!"

The burst of almost simultaneous feminine comments layered each other, one on top of the other. Justin froze. Both he and Danielle swung their heads toward the massive living room where four variously curious, amused or shocked faces observed them. His mom and all three of his sisters, Jasmine, Jade, and Jewell sat on the couch with an explosion of bridal magazines spread out around them.

"What are you doing here?" He sucked in air but didn't loosen the hold he had on Danielle.

"Ummm...*you* said we could stay here while we shopped for dresses." Jewell retorted.

"Yeah, on the twenty-eighth!" It was Justin's plan now to divert them to a hotel so he and Danielle could have privacy. Hell, he'd pay for the presidential suite at any of the five-star hotels in New York to be alone with Dani right now.

"Duh, dude." Jade snorted and then laughed. "It *is* the twenty-eighth." She stood up and walked over to where they stood. She extended her hand. "Hi, I'm Jade." As Danielle extracted herself from Justin's grip and took Jade's hand, his sister continued, "That is my mom, Amanda. The one in the pink is Jasmine, and the one in the green sweater is Jewell. Who are you?"

"Jade!" Justin, his mother, Jasmine, and Jewell shouted her name at the same time.

She dropped Danielle's hand and raised both of hers in the air. "What? Don't tell me y'all don't want to know, too!"

Justin drew Dani back into a hug and whispered

in her ear, "I'm so sorry for everything you are about to endure." Danielle's shoulders moved and then shook. He released her and looked down.

Her eyes danced with merriment and she broke into a fit of laughter. "Heck of a way to meet your family, isn't it?"

"Oh, honey, we are only a small portion of his family. Just you wait until you meet his brothers, their kids and the rest of the extended mess we call a family!" Jade grabbed Dani's hand and pulled her into the living room. "You too, mister," Jade called over her shoulder.

Justin dropped his head back and closed his eyes, knowing the inquisition that was coming.

"Dude? You coming, or you going to let your woman face us alone?" Jewell threw a stack of magazines onto his antique coffee table making space for Danielle and him on the dark brown leather sectional.

"So, who are you?" Jade asked again.

Justin regained his senses and moved, quickly. "Everyone, this is Danielle. Danielle, the inquisition known as my mother and sisters. The chief brat is Jade."

His mother reached over and put a hand on his hand. "I promise to make Jade behave."

"Since when has that ever happened?" Jewell laughed at her mother.

"Yeah, right." Jasmine snorted and dropped back into the soft leather.

"Good luck." Justin's reply landed on the heels of his sister's quips.

"Hey! Keep that up for another hour or so, and I might take offense." Jade flipped her ponytail off her shoulder and twisted to face Danielle. "So, how do you know my brother?"

Justin helped Danielle take off her coat while she answered, "I've worked with Justin for four years."

All four women snapped their head toward him.

"You've been dating someone for four years, and you haven't introduced us?" Jade spit out the shocked accusation.

"No, that is not what she said. We've worked together for four years. Our relationship is new." Justin pulled off his own jacket placing both his and Danielle's on the hall tree. He stepped back down into the living room and veered toward the bar. He and Dani deserved a drink, especially since his family had descended. Damn, he'd forgotten all about them coming to New York to look for Jewell's wedding dress.

"How new?" Jade probed.

"Jade." Her mother admonished her daughter.

"No, that's alright. Very new. We've been friends for a long time, but things have evolved recently. We found we had similar interests outside of work." Danielle accepted the snifter of brandy he handed her.

"Hey? Where's ours?" Jade glanced at Justin's glass to the bar and back to him.

"It is ten o'clock in the morning. We've been flying for the last two days. We are going to have a drink, go take a shower and hibernate for at least a day." Justin directed his comments to his mother. He sure as hell hoped he hadn't offended her.

"I understand completely, sweetheart. We will be out of your hair soon. Our car will be here in about fifteen minutes. Do you want us to make accommodations at a hotel for tonight and tomorrow?" Amanda placed a hand on his arm when she asked. Well, fuck...it seemed wrong when she said it.

"Is anyone camping out in my room?" Justin swirled his brandy, warming it in his hand. He noticed Danielle was doing the same thing. Damn, he loved the fact she knew how to properly enjoy the expensive alcohol.

"No, there are enough guest rooms here with one

to spare. Although Jade wanted to take your room." Jasmine lanced a mock glare over at Jade.

"Not true." Jade stuck out her tongue at Jasmine. "I *had* your room until they said it was a violation of your privacy."

"Please stay. You just won't see us until the jetlag lets us out of its grip." Justin spoke before he took a sip.

Danielle took a small sip of her brandy before she spoke, "I'll just go back to my apartment."

"That's not happening." Justin's automatic response came out just a little sharper and more possessive than he'd intended.

Jewell snickered and stood up. "Well, that tone I recognize. Zane gets all growly, too."

"Ditto. Nic also seems to think he needs to do the Neanderthal thing." Jade made a face.

"Yep, been there still doing that. Chad is possessive as hell, especially now that we have Chloe." Jasmine agreed.

"Frank, too." Amanda stood up. "Come on girls. We have dresses to find."

"Okay, but there is no way I'm doing a hoop skirt. I want something sexy. If I have to go to a wedding, I want to look hot." Jade was the last off the couch.

"Classic and conservative." Jewell threw out the words like they'd had this argument before.

"Classic and conservative is boring. *Mom*, you have to make them listen to me." Jade grabbed her coat and handed Jasmine hers. Jewell handed Amanda her coat and put her arm in hers as the front door opened and Paulo walked in.

"Mrs. Marshall. Good to see you again. Ladies." Paulo dipped his cap towards his sisters. "Are you in need of a ride?"

"Oh, we hired a car. We didn't want to bother you."

"It is no bother! Mr. Justin, will you need me anymore today?" Paulo looked at Justin for the first time.

"No, I'm not going anywhere but to bed." Justin took a sip of his brandy watching the gaggle at the door.

"Well then ladies, your chariot awaits! The limo is in front of the building. Please go down. I'll be with you shortly." Paulo ushered all the women out the door and closed it behind them, while he remained in the apartment. "It could take a very long time, sir. I'm sure they will want dinner out, and I have a hook-up for tickets to *Hamilton*..."

"Tell the concierge to bill them to me and take

them to The Sabre. I'll call ahead for dinner reservations. You'll have a meal waiting, too."

"Thank you, sir." Paulo opened the door.

"One last thing?" Justin called out to his driver.

"Sir?"

"Your Christmas bonus just tripled." Justin raised
his brandy snifter in a salute.

"It is my pleasure sir." The smile he shot Justin
could rival any lights on Broadway.

CHAPTER 13

*D*ani downed the small amount of brandy left in her snifter and stood up as Justin's driver shut the door. "Looks like we have a window of opportunity. Care to take a shower with me?"

Justin tossed back his brandy and put the glass down. "At this moment, there is nothing I want more. I'm sorry about my family." He took her hand and headed toward the back hall.

"Don't be. I've never experienced a large family, and I've always wanted brothers and sisters. I think you're extremely lucky."

"They are insane. Each and every one of them." He pulled her into his bedroom where he promptly shut and locked the door behind them.

Dani glanced behind her at the lock and then

reached for her shirt, pulling it off and dropping it as she approached the bed. She unbuttoned her slacks, shimmied them to her ankles, and stepped out of them as she passed the bed. Her bra trailed off her fingertips onto the floor as she approached the bathroom, leaving her thong the last bit of clothing to be shed as she entered the massive en suite. The shower stall was a six-foot by six-foot square of clear glass, exposed patina brass piping, and countless showerheads. The effect was visually stunning. She glanced over her shoulder and watched as Justin walked into the bathroom, naked and hard. His dark chest hair swirled down to the thin, happy trail that ended at that magnificent cock.

He smirked at her and flicked several toggle switches on the wall to start the water. He slid a thermometer bar to a position just the other side of the blue and red combination and steam started pumping into the shower chamber. With practiced ease, he opened the shower door and flicked another switch that turned on soft jazz music. She glanced at the walls and ceiling unable to see where the speakers were located.

"They are installed around the showerheads. Justin answered her unasked question. He pulled her into his arms and walked her backward under a waterfall showerhead drenching them both in warm water. He grabbed a bottle of body wash and poured a line across her shoulders and chest. Closing the top and setting the bottle back, Justin traced the soap line with his hand. He watched the suds run as he spread the soft lather over her entire body, paying special attention to her breasts and lower to her sex. Danielle was a puddle of goo in his hands. He could ask anything of her, and she'd comply. Instead, she reached for the soap and, using her hands, washed his entire body. His cock and balls received an inordinate amount of attention.

"You need to stop, or I'm going to come."

"You know what they say, right?" She held his balls in one hand and gently squeezed them pulling a groan from him.

He swallowed hard and shook his head. "No, what do they say?"

"Cleanliness is next to godliness."

"I'd rather be dirty and next to you." Justin pulled her into him and lowered, kissing any coherent thought from her brain. She had no idea how long they stayed in the shower, kissing and touching. Eventually, they washed their hair and got out. She used his toothbrush after he did because she wasn't leaving the room in search of her toiletry bag. It took only a couple minutes to comb out and braid her hair. She used a small leather tie to fasten the tail.

When she walked out into the bedroom, lights along the crown molding were illuminated and low, bathing the entire suite in a golden hue. Justin lay on his back on the bed; his hand circled his hard cock. He extended his other hand toward her.

Danielle walked to him. "I want to ride you. Like this." The words came before rational thought processed, but she wouldn't take it back. She did want him.

Justin let her straddle him but pulled her down for some more of those delicious, mind-blowing kisses. Her vision reeled when she sat up, whether from the lack of oxygen or the desire that ravaged her, she didn't know. She didn't care. Lifting up, she grasped his thick cock to center it under her, before she worked herself down his shaft. Her hips found a rhythm, and her desire danced to that beat, growing and swelling until the melody that spurred her forward took on a of life its own. Danielle grasped his shoulders and leaned forward. She opened eyes she hadn't realized she'd closed and found him staring at her. "Please."

The word was no more out of her mouth than

she was on her back and he had one of her legs pressed toward her shoulder. His thrusts were strong, sensual and carried the power to annihilate her very being. What they had was so much more than the type of sex she'd experienced with others in the past. He leaned down and kissed her as he moved. His one free hand reached between them and fingered her clit with slow, languid swipes. Danielle broke free from his kiss, inhaled sharply, and climaxed so hard she saw a blanket of white blast behind her eyelids. Her body shuddered in rhythmic waves.

"Look at me." Justin's growled command forced her eyes open. "I want you to see what you do to me." He snapped his hip up and thrust two, three more times. His body clenched before he growled out an unintelligible shout as he lost himself inside her. He was spectacular. Straining muscle covered in a deep crimson flush held over her. His chest heaved with the exertion of his climax and sweat trailed down the side of his face. He was breathtaking–and *hers*.

Danielle closed her eyes and only opened them briefly when they changed positions. He pulled her onto his chest, and she settled there. The business trip to Perth had been successful. Completing the excursion to rappel down Gordon Dam, an event she'd been planning for months, gave her more than a sense of satisfaction. It had given her Justin. Sleeping in his arms, in his bed, gave her peace.

A DOZEN EGGS, cream, a pinch of cayenne powder, some salt, a touch of cake flour and baking powder whisked up in a second. Justin added some chives, ham, and cheese into the bakeware and then poured individual portions of the egg mixture over it. The eggs went in the upper oven above biscuits that were baking in the lower oven. He was starving when he woke up, and he knew Danielle would be, too. Plus, he had to provide for his sisters and mother.

He poured some honey into a small saucepan and added a tablespoon of unsalted butter stirring it until blended. He added a couple drops of cream to the mixture as his mom came into the kitchen.

"Good morning." Justin stopped stirring long enough to hug his mom and receive a hug in return. He hadn't seen her in over a year. There were a few more strands of gray in her hair, and her laugh lines were deeper, but she looked good.

"Good morning. You know you don't have to cook for us, right?"

"I know, but you know I love it." Justin winked at her. She'd taught him how to cook, but the passion for it was honed by watching world-class chefs create works of art.

"Are you sure we aren't in the way?" His mom held his gaze as she searched his expression.

"Not at all. Danielle would have met you eventually. This way she knows some of you before the horde descends." He kissed his mom on the forehead and pointed toward the refrigerator. "There is a tray of fruit in there, would you pull it out?"

"Coffee. Gotta have coffee." Jade padded into the kitchen as his mom headed toward the refrigerator. She stumbled toward the wrong wall wearing a pair of men's athletic shorts and a t-shirt that had to be five sizes too big. Jade was nothing if not original.

"Sit down before you burn yourself." Justin grabbed her hand just before she put it on the burner he'd just turned off. He pushed her toward the island and a barstool.

"Bossy." Jade pouted but plopped down on the stool on the other side of the counter.

"How was the trip to Australia?" His mom was the only one in the family who knew his travel schedule. He called her at least once a week. Not that there was much to talk about on his end, but she was his touchstone as far as the family went. She filled him in on all the events and happenings of his siblings and their children.

"Great. We found out while we were down there that we received our third Michelin Star at Nido dell'Aquila and The Sabre."

His mom stopped pouring Jade's coffee. "Oh, Justin that is wonderful news. I know your teams work so hard to make each of the restaurants perfect. I'm so happy for you!" He got another hug.

"That's really cool. So, what's for breakfast?" Jade reached for the pot and finished pouring her coffee.

"Jade, this is big news for Justin. You have to know that." His mom took the pot back from his sister and poured him a cup. Danielle walked into the kitchen looking beautiful in a pair of jeans and a dark green sweater. Justin pulled her into his arms and gave her a respectable kiss. Not at all the type he wanted to give her, but it would have to do until he got his mom and sisters out of the house again.

"Good morning, Danielle." His mom spoke when they broke the kiss.

"Morning Mrs. King." Danielle headed for the coffee mugs.

"Oh, sweetheart, I haven't been Mrs. King for several years now. I remarried. But just you never mind about titles and last names. The only thing you need to remember is my name is Amanda. I answer to just about anything."

"Yeah. So, what's for breakfast?" Jade asked again.

"Did you get your coffee, Justin?" Danielle grabbed the honey, cream, and sugar from the counter and looked around for his cup.

"Mom just poured me a cup, I haven't fixed it yet." Justin opened the lower oven and pulled the biscuits out. He slid one off onto a plate and poured a small vessel of his honey concoction, setting both in front of Jade. "That's hot."

She picked it up and dropped it immediately, fanning the air with her fingers.

"Stubborn girl."

Danielle handed him his coffee and went to sit beside his sister. God help them all if Jade opened her mouth again.

"Mom, go ahead and sit down. I'll get the eggs out, and we can eat."

"Jasmine and Jewell can fend for themselves," Jade said as she dipped a piece of the biscuit into the honey. "I'm not sharing."

"Not even with Nic?" His mom teased as she took a sip of her coffee.

Jade lifted her eyes and narrowed them in a

squint. "He's still sleeping. I'd say I'd let him fend for himself, but then he'd pout. I hate it when he pouts."

"Nic's here?"

"Where Jade is, Nic is." His mom laughed the response.

"What about Chad and Zane?"

"Nic, Chad, Zane?" Danielle's head ping-ponged between Justin and where his mother and sister sat.

"Nic DeMarco is my man. Jasmine is married to Chad Nelson, and Jewell is marrying Zane. That's why we are here." She pointed at Justin. "He's catering Jewell's wedding. Didn't he tell you?"

"God, no I didn't tell her. I was trying not to scare her off. Eat your food. I'll make some more biscuits and eggs after we eat. There will be enough for everyone." Justin pulled the egg cups out of the oven and set two on each plate along with a biscuit and a honeypot. He moved the fruit to the countertop and sat down facing three of the most important women in his life.

"They won't be up for hours." Amanda laughed as she took several strawberries and grapes from the fruit platter. "Jewell is a night owl. She and Zane work strange hours, but it works for them. Zane had to stay in D.C. to work, something big going on that involves Jacob and Jason, too. Chad took Chloe, his and Jasmine's daughter, to his mom's house to visit. He's heading back to the ranch today. He uses the airfield at the ranch, so he doesn't have to fly into Rapid City. The last time they were there he got mobbed at the mall and had to hide out in a ladies' restroom until security came."

"Ha! That was funny." Jade snorted into her coffee.

"Be nice." Amanda sent the quiet reprimand causing Jade to roll her eyes. "Anyway, Jasmine doesn't have to wake up to take care of the baby, so she's taking advantage of the vacation to recharge her batteries."

"Mobbed?" Danielle asked.

"Chad Nelson is a country singer. Rather famous from what Jasmine says." Jade shrugged. "I don't listen to that kind of music, but he has a slew of platinum records and awards in his man cave." Jade mopped up the honey out of her small pot and looked at her mom's plate. Amanda smiled and shook her head while handing Jade the honey.

"Oh." Danielle seemed to take in the information and consider it. Justin wished he could have prepared her to meet his family, especially Jade, but she seemed to be taking it in stride. The woman adapted well to any business setting. He should have known she'd be able to roll with the punches of meeting his family.

"Did you find a dress you liked?" Danielle asked Jade as she took some fruit. Justin smiled when she put fruit on Jade's plate without asking his sister if she wanted any. Jade swung a glare her way before she forked the fruit and devoured it.

"We narrowed it down to two dresses for Jewell. She wants to go back today and make a final decision. As far as the bridesmaid dresses..." Amanda lifted a shoulder.

"No," Jade spoke between mouthfuls of food.

Justin set his coffee cup down. He had to ask. "Why are you eating like a starving lunatic?"

"Because we went out to dinner at The Sabre last night." Jade said the words as if to say 'duh.'

"And?" Justin lead her for an answer.

"And it was one of your froo-froo restaurants with little dishes of food. Not enough to feed a real person."

"You could have ordered more." Justin laughed his response.

"No, I couldn't! They were done. I was still hungry, and Paulo wouldn't find a drive through."

"Dresses?" Danielle asked again putting the conversation back on track.

His mom smiled and winked at Justin, mouthing, *I like her.* He was glad because he was falling a little bit harder every minute.

"Jewell made her selection. I don't like it." Jade pulled her coffee cup toward her and wrapped her hands around the mug. "The skirt and the color are okay, but the freaking neckline. Do I look twelve to you?"

Danielle glanced over at her. "Nope. I know a great seamstress here in the city. She could work the neckline of each dress, so they are all different, reflecting each of the bridesmaids' personalities but staying similar enough to make the bridal party flow."

Jade set her coffee cup down and swiveled in her chair. She cocked her head at Dani and blinked. "You are my new best friend."

"Awww...shucks." Danielle's response got a round of laughter, the hardest of which came from Jade.

Jade got off the bar stool and grabbed another biscuit and her coffee cup. She raised it in the air. "To Danielle, you two have my blessing." Jade winked at Justin and headed back to the opposite hall from where his master suite was located.

"Well dear, you've passed muster." Amanda chuckled. "But, I'll tell you a secret. You're the only woman Justin has ever introduced to us, so you were immediately a winner in my books. He's very private, so I know you are special." She lifted off the stool. "Now, you two go do whatever it is you have planned for the day. I'm going to do the dishes, get my daughters into a group and go finish this bridal expedition. I need to get back to South Dakota before the blizzard that's forecast makes it in from the West Coast."

"Do you have a flight booked?" Justin drank the last of his coffee after he asked.

"No, Dixon and Drake flew Jasmine and me in. Jade came up with Nic and Jewell. Dixon called this morning and said they wanted to leave by six tonight to make sure we didn't run into any weather that would cause us to divert."

"You have your own pilots?" Danielle blinked. Her gaze bounced from Justin to his mother.

"Oh, sweetheart, no. My other sons work for a company who maintains a plane on my husband's ranch. Believe me, I'm nothing special."

"I beg to disagree." Justin smiled when his mom swatted his arm.

"You can disagree, but that doesn't make it so." His mom laughed.

"It was a pleasure meeting you, Amanda." Danielle extended her hand.

His mom grabbed her up in a hug. "You'll learn. We're huggers. Just don't let his brothers hug you. They might break you."

"The hell they will," Justin growled.

"Yep... just like Frank." His mom laughed and headed into the kitchen.

He and Danielle walked hand in hand back to his office. "You needed to do some research for your father, right?"

"I do. I was going to head downtown to his office. He didn't give me the name of the individual involved, and I can use his computer systems to access the DoD databases he's allowed to use. It could trim some of the research time, which gets me back here sooner."

"Give me a second, and I'll call Paulo to take you."

"No, don't worry about it. I can take a cab; besides he was out late with your family. Let him rest." Dani moved into him and laid her head on his shoulder. "I'll work as fast as I can. You realize tomorrow is going to be difficult?"

"Tomorrow?" Justin had no idea what she was talking about.

"When Max files that paperwork with HR, the rumors are going to spin out of control."

"I don't care about the rumor mill. The only thing I care about is you." He'd fire anyone that spread any gossip about them.

She beamed. "That was the right answer. Now, let me go so I can come back. I'll be ready to crash again by mid-afternoon. Jetlag hits me in waves."

Justin took her lips and delved into her, tasting the woman that he'd suddenly found irreplaceable on too many levels to count. "Call me when you're ready to come back. I insist that Paulo picks you up and brings you home."

"Deal." She lifted onto her toes and kissed him again. "See you soon."

CHAPTER 14

*D*anielle walked out onto the blustery city sidewalk and lifted her arm. A cab immediately swooped to a stop in front her. She gave the address of Phoenix Armament's headquarters and opened her phone to sort through her emails. It was customary to take the day after an overseas trip off to recover from the inevitable jetlag. Everyone did it, and everyone checked in, ran through their emails and made sure there were no fires that needed to be extinguished. The forty-block cab ride was spent doing exactly that. She swiped her card and paid the fare before shoving the door open and stepping out onto the sidewalk. Her father's offices were on the fifteen, sixteenth and seventeenth floor of the building. Dani pocketed her cell phone and swung her purse over her shoulder, turning just enough to catch a glimpse of a profile. She stopped and turned with a frown and visually searched the throng of people clogging the sidewalk. She could have sworn she'd seen the same man who was at the lodge...and the pharmacy! *That* was where she'd seen him before. The gentleman at the lodge in Hobart was the gentleman who'd entered the pharmacy in Perth at the same time she did.

A cold chill walked its way up her back. There was no way the three men could be doppelgangers. She needed to talk to her father. There was no reason for anyone to follow her because of her work with JK Holdings. She made her way upstairs to a glorified holding cell aka the reception area. People could not enter the Phoenix Armament offices without a badge, pass code and fingerprint recognition. She had no idea what the man at the reception desk did all day long, other than watch people enter and exit the offices. Her father said he was an additional security measure. Probably an armed guard, although she'd never seen a weapon. She smiled at the most current version of the door guard before she pulled out her identification, swiped it, entered her pass code, and placed her thumb on the pad by the door. A series of clicks sounded before the door opened. She'd always thought the security measures were overkill until her father told her about the industrial espionage that occurred in the weaponry business. She made her way through the maze of halls to her father's office. It was the same small size as the rest of his staff's. The only perk he'd given himself was a corner office with a wonderful view.

She stopped at the door and watched her father work. His reading glasses perched on his nose as he compared the documents in front of him with what was on the computer. He was a handsome man. Lonely, but handsome. She often wondered why he never dated. Maybe he did and kept it from her, although with the hours he worked, she doubted it.

"Are you going to stand in the doorway all day or are you going to come in?" He spoke without lifting his eyes in her direction.

"I was waiting for an invitation." Danielle chuckled as she pushed off the door jamb. "I came in to do the research you wanted."

"Good. I need to validate my assumptions or put them to rest." Her father leaned back in his chair and nodded to a small desk partially obscured by the open door. It was where she'd done homework during high school and occasionally when she'd come home during college. She'd worked in his office over summer vacations and learned useless information about metallurgy, weapons specifications and other things she'd never use, but she'd spent time with her father and that was important—to both of them—even if neither acknowledged it.

Danielle dropped her briefcase and purse next to the desk and settled in. She powered up the computer and was just starting to get into the meat of her research when her father interrupted her.

"Did you make your rappel?"

Danielle glanced over her shoulder at him, surprised that he'd asked. He hated the fact that she engaged in dangerous pastimes, but they'd agreed long ago that adults made their own decisions.

"I did." A smile she couldn't prevent spread across her face. "I really did."

Her father's eyebrows rose. "Care to elaborate on that?"

"I met someone, or rather I discovered I shared similar interests with a person I've known for years. It was probably one of the best days of my life."

Her father tossed down his pen onto a stack of paper and leaned back in his chair. "Who do I have to intimidate? I do have a rather impressive collection of weapons."

Danielle laughed, not sure where the parental

posturing came from, but enjoying it nonetheless. "Don't worry, Dad, besides, I don't think you could intimidate this guy. He has his own money, says he doesn't like weapons, and is going to take me suit jumping off Mount Everest."

Her father palmed his face and scrubbed his hands down his cheeks while blowing out a lungful of air. "You will be the death of me, yet. Who is this man? I need to make him go away. Mount Everest? Please."

Dani threw back her head and laughed. It was rare for her father to engage on a personal level, and she was really enjoying his lightheartedness today. "I don't believe you can make Justin King go away."

"Your boss?" The incredulity in his voice resounded around the small office.

"Yes, my boss, but he's more than that; he always has been. We just...I don't know. We fit. We always have, at work and now."

"Isn't that going to cause problems when whatever is between you dissolves?" He dropped his eyes to the stack of papers next to his computer.

"Dad, I don't know where this is going, but in my heart, I'm hoping it doesn't dissolve. I care about him. I have for a long time now. The side of the man I discovered on this last trip only intensified those feelings. I mean who would have thought he enjoys rock climbing and rappelling. Oh, Dad, he did a rap rep off Gordon Dam! Can you imagine?"

"What the hell is a rap rep?" Her father cut his eyes to her, a frown bringing his brows together.

"A forward-facing rappel straight down a one-hundred-and-forty-meter dam in three leaping bounds."

"Wonderful. You're dating someone who should be institutionalized." They both froze as the specter of her mother invaded their playful exchange. He shook his head. "I'm sorry." Dani gave him a sad smile. He put his glasses back on and squinted at the computer screen. "Does he treat you well?"

"He does, Dad. He's pretty amazing. I'd like you to meet him."

Danielle chuckled at the grunt she got in response. That was more like her father. The open window for father-daughter time had closed. She rolled her eyes at him and turned back to her research.

It took another four hours, but the information folder she handed her father held the most complete data she could find. "I don't feel good about this, Dad. You should hire someone who can dig deeper. Everything I found points away from the fact your employee is involved, but..." Danielle sighed, she couldn't tell what was wrong with the documentation in the folder, but something wasn't right.

"Your gut telling you something is off?"

Her father encapsulated her feelings. She nodded, still staring at the folder. Her eyes tracked from the papers stacked between the manila cardstock and met his. "I'm not usually a suspicious or nervous person, but with the guy that keeps popping up and–"

"What guy?" Her father whipped his glasses off and snapped forward in his chair.

"I may be paranoid, but I saw a gentleman in Perth, maybe mid-fifties. He walked into the drug store after me. I don't know why I noticed him, but I did. I could swear the same man was at the lodge in Tasmania where Justin and I stayed. Then this morning, coming into the building, for a moment I thought I saw him again. I don't know. When I say it out loud, it sounds stupid."

"Did he approach you? Listen to any conversations you were having? Make any movement that would make you think he was a danger?"

The rapid-fire questions pulled her from her musings. "No. I just noticed him, you know?

Nothing to make me think I was in danger, but you've got to admit, that's strange."

"Strange indeed." Her father pulled out a pad and paper. "Write down everything you can remember about the man at each occurrence."

"Why?" The more they talked about her fears, the more she believed they were unfounded.

"I don't think it was anything but coincidence or maybe some gentleman that happened to look like the man you first saw, but why not collect as much information as possible. If the guy shows up again, do not make contact with him. We'll call the police. You could have a stalker."

"Really, Dad, a stalker? I'm not a celebrity, and there are, maybe, ten people that know I'm your daughter. Why would anyone want to stalk me?" Dani grabbed the tablet he was holding out to her and started scribbling, now confident that her imagination had been working overtime.

"I'm not willing to take a risk. Just put down as much information as you can. Unfortunately, I don't think we can take this to the police as the guy hasn't made contact or threatened you in any way. But I want you to be hyper vigilant. Try not to go anywhere by yourself for a while. You can come back home and stay with me. The house has a solid security system. The apartment you live in doesn't even have a doorman."

"I don't need a doorman, Dad, I have my Glock 43 in the hall bureau and a forty-five in the bedroom. If someone came into my apartment, they wouldn't leave unless it was in a body bag. I mean, you taught me how to shoot, and I'm pretty damn good if you do say so yourself."

"True." He sat back in his chair and studied her. "Even though I don't tell you often, I worry about you."

Danielle stood and went behind his desk. He tensed up, like always, but she hugged him anyway. "I love you, too, Dad."

"Yeah, yeah." Her father cleared his throat and leaned away from her. She'd long ago become accustomed to the fact his aversion to touch had nothing to do with her. "Go. You're here on your day off, and I don't want to take you away from your new relationship. I appreciate you pulling this information for me. I'll look through it and stew on it for a bit. If there is nothing solid for me to take to the people I have on retainer, then I'll keep looking. I don't know why, but I don't trust the man. I can't fire him because I don't have cause. I can't let him work on the new weapon because my gut is telling me the guy is stealing design information from me. I'm in a Catch-22 position here." Her father spoke more to himself than her toward the end.

"You can claim downsizing."

"He has seniority. I'd have to lay off a third of my workforce to get to him. I can't do that to hard-working men and women who depend on this company to live." He looked up at her and gave her a half-hearted smile. "I'm probably just being overly cautious, but keep your eyes peeled and let me know if you see that man again."

"Sure." She gathered her coat, purse, and briefcase.

"Do you have a way home? I could get you a car." Her father lifted his phone.

"No, that's okay. I texted Justin before I gave you the files. His driver should be downstairs by now."

"Don't go outside if he isn't waiting." Her father rose and walked with her to the door of his office.

"I won't. Let me know what happens here?"

"That is a certainty." Her father glanced up and down the hallway before he smiled at her. "Tell that man he better be damn good to you; your dad has an arsenal at his disposal."

"I'm doing no such thing. I'll call you later this

week. We are having dinner. I want you two to meet. You'll like him; I promise."

"I promise I'll try." Her dad winked at her and turned on his heel, heading back to his desk. She shook her head and turned, making her way out of the office maze that snaked through the entire floor. She didn't get to go upstairs to research and development this time, but the next time she was here, she wanted to go through the labs. People who watched the *James Bond* movies thought Q had a lot of toys. They had no idea.

She made her way downstairs and crossed the lobby. Paulo waited for her in front of the building, double parked. She held her coat at the neck, hoping the freezing temperatures wouldn't invade the warm cocoon of her wool coat, but that wish was in vain. Icy winds swirled around her as she made her way across the sidewalk. Paulo was out of the car and around the vehicle by the time she reached it. She smiled at him and gladly slipped into the warmth of the black limo. She glanced out the window and at the faces of the people who scurried along the frosty sidewalk. She shook her head and pulled out her phone to check on her other job. She was an over imaginative fool. There was no way someone was following her.

CHAPTER 15

"There are four properties that initially caught our attention. The first of them is located in the southwest sector of the downtown area. While the pricing is competitive, our analysis of the area shows there isn't a customer base to make the venture successful unless we bring other businesses in with us." Danielle hit each talking point on the slides as she stood in front of the panel. Justin watched with pride as she sized up the assets her teams had located for the next possible location. He wasn't sure about expanding again. Quite frankly, he had other interests that seemed to fog the clear vision for the future he used to have. Danielle continued to present her findings. Justin already knew which building she'd settled on and why. The meeting today was to get the rest of the team's input. He had people who were exceptional at their job, and he wasn't going to mess with the process, although he agreed with Dani's assessment.

"Are there any questions?" Dani flicked the presentation off and started fielding questions.

Justin followed along but focused on Danielle more than the questions heading her way. It had been like that since he'd seen her on Gordon Dam. His heart hadn't settled into the same old dull thud. His mind hadn't gone off in pursuit of the next grand adventure because he knew what it would be. He was climbing Everest with Dani, and they were suit jumping down the slope. They'd been doing research about the camp levels, the guides, and requirements to make an expedition up the mountainside. The climatology and topography were also details they were taking into consideration. When they weren't planning the event, they were training. Justin shifted in his seat. Danielle was the last number of a combination on a mechanism he'd been trying to crack for as long as he could remember. With her, he was...Justin glanced out the window. With her, he was complete. That sounded sappy as fuck, but it was true. He didn't feel the itch to fill every waking moment with movement. He could be at peace. Justin glanced at the faces sitting around the conference table. They were fully engaged in the question and answer phase of the briefing. Did they have any idea the monumental shift that had occurred within him? Could they see the feelings he had for Danielle? Did he care if they could? The answer to the last question was a resounding no. She calmed the turbulence inside him. She vanquished the incessant thrum of restlessness that used to entomb him. She was his oasis, the thing that let him rest and, yes, he loved her.

He'd admitted that fact to himself over a week ago, although he hadn't told Danielle. It was way too soon in their relationship to lay the "L" word out there. Or at least, that's what he assumed. Who knew? He was winging his way through this rela-tionship anyway. They'd been back from Australia now for three weeks, twenty-one days of being more than the friends they had been, and twenty-one nights of sex better than he'd ever imagined. He shifted in his seat when his body reacted to the memories that flashed through his mind's eye. He caught Danielle's eyes as she swept the room when she spoke. Her voice faltered for a moment, and a light blush rose to her cheeks before she continued on with the briefing.

Max let himself into the conference room, redirecting Justin's attention from Danielle. He carried a now familiar packet of paperwork. There was little doubt the bound and sealed envelope was from his brother Jason, at Guardian. His gut sank as he took the sealed envelope and placed it beside his tablet. Max exited as quickly as he'd entered. His eyes moved from his assistant to the woman at the front of the conference table. For the first time since Gabriel had bailed him out of jail all those years ago, he was not looking forward to another assignment. He pulled himself out of his thoughts when Danielle started to sum up the meeting.

"So we agree we will pursue the Bowman building *if* we can validate the zoning requirements and local laws are within our tolerance."

Justin watched as everyone's head went north and south. He stood and dismissed the gathering. "Thank you for your time. We have a finance meeting at three, for those of you who will be attending, there are spreadsheets that I want updated. I need a cost ratio breakdown on the quarterly reports." He picked up his tablet and the sealed envelope while waiting for the room to clear.

"Hey, you," Danielle spoke to him as the last person left. "You looked distracted today."

"Only by you." Justin bent down and pressed a quick kiss against her soft lips.

"Stop that. Remember our agreement, no kissing at work. We've proven we can't trust ourselves to behave."

Justin barked out a laugh. More than once the first week they were back, Max had nearly caught them in a compromising position. The no kissing mandate sucked, but it was needed.

"Are we on for lunch?" Justin put his hand on her back as they walked out of the conference room.

"I have a meeting, remember?" She bumped into him with her shoulder.

"I do, but I was hoping *you'd* forgotten." He stopped outside his office. Danielle paused before going on to her section at the other side of the building.

"You'll have to live with the fact that my boss is a slave driver." She winked at him and walked away and damned if he didn't blatantly watch her every step as she walked away. The tight skirt and high heels showcased her athletic body. He was so fucking relieved he had the right to watch her without trying to be discreet. She turned the corner and moved out of his sight before he headed into his office.

On his way past Max's desk, he stopped. "I'm not to be disturbed, by anyone for any reason, unless Ms. Grant calls or comes by. If that happens, buzz me first. I have some personal business that needs my attention."

"Yes, sir." Max acknowledged his words as he typed with one hand and held his messages out to him with the other. As always, the multi-tasking miracles Max could perform were impressive. "What would I do without you, Max?"

The man blinked his eyes up at the question. "Good God, sir, I hope you never have to find out."

Justin laughed and tapped the envelope on Max's desk. "Me, too."

He closed his door and locked it behind him. Once at his desk, he hit the remote to make his glass walls opaque. He took off his jacket, loosened his tie and opened the envelope. Madrid. He glanced at the blueprints and schematics. Damn, what a challenge. The familiar electric energy started to arc under his skin. This assignment wasn't as time sensitive as some of the ones that had been handed to him previously. He glanced at his calendar. He needed time blocked off to prepare. He examined the blueprints of the high rise and the location of the safe. The type and manufacturer were new to him. He needed more information. He took out the sheet of paper included in the courier's packet and started making notes. Guardian usually provided him with all the information he needed, but there were a few instances where he required specific facts, measurements or intelligence. This was one of those times. He used the chemically treated paper and the specialized pen included in the packet. After he listed his concerns and questions, he would contact Guardian's courier and send a sealed packet back to Jason. If someone intercepted the communication, they'd have to figure out how to see what was on the paper without ruining it. It was probably overkill, but Jason insisted on the requirement.

Justin spread the blueprints out over his desk and stood up so he could see the entire floor. He scanned the information, pausing to take in the nuances of the security system. Whoever installed it knew what they were doing. His lips lifted in a sneer. Challenge accepted.

A tap at his door pulled him away from the documents and notes. He glanced at the clock on his wall in surprise. He'd spent four hours working the new assignment. "I'll be right there, Max."

He was going to be late for his financial meeting. Damn it, he hated being late, but he wasn't going to rush putting the packet together and possibly miss something. Justin folded the blueprints, made another note on his sheet and placed all of the documentation he'd received into his old-fashioned safe located under the faux leather mat that protected the floor under his desk chair. He'd made a few personal modifications to the safe. It could be cracked, but it would take someone with exceptional skill, and they'd have to find it first. He closed and locked the safe. It took a minute to replace the floor mat and chair. Justin grabbed his suit jacket and slipped it on, fixing his tie and adjusting his sleeves before he placed his questions in the provided courier envelope and sealed it. A quick text to the service would have someone here to pick it up within fifteen minutes. Justin carried the sealed pouch out to Max and handed it off. "The courier will be here within fifteen minutes. From your hands to his."

"Of course, sir." Max took the envelope with one hand while he handed Justin the paperwork he needed for his three o'clock meeting.

"Remind me to give you a raise." Justin spun on his heel as he spoke.

"You already did, sir, but I'll remind you again around bonus time." Max's laughter chased him down the hall to his meeting.

CHAPTER 16

"Why are we working rappel now and why only three floors at a time?" Danielle was harnessed up and ready to go. Guardian had found him a vacant building with almost the same dimensions as the one he'd be entering in Madrid. The windows were wider here; he'd have more space to hold and hide if necessary, but he needed to practice. Danielle waited for his answer while perched on the edge of the building.

Justin smiled and played it off. "It is called technique. We are going to work on the small things. Today I'm teaching you how to Dülfersitz in a modified form. We are still harnessed in, but the rope is ours to control because there is no one below or above to belay us. It is difficult, but necessary if you are serious about learning some of the more extreme aspects of climbing."

"Okay, I get that. Will we be using this technique when we climb Everest?" She positioned the rope around the leather insert on her leggings. Justin had the clothing they both wore specially made for this training, except he'd use his again next week.

"I hope not. This is a safety rappel that you will need to know how to use in case something drastic happens. We need to work on dropping in measured and distinct distances. I want you to control your descent so there is zero swing or movement other than your body dropping straight down. Trust your belay device but keep a firm control on the speed of your drop through the tension of the rope. You control how fast you descend. Don't go so fast that you can't stop where you want to stop or so slow that you're not making headway. You'll become exhausted. Stop every third floor, but make sure you stop on the right side of the window, not on the window, below it or above it. The right side."

"So, you are teaching me how to rescue you if you fall?" Danielle's eyes were huge as she faced him.

"I'm teaching you a method I hope you'll never have to use. Something to keep in your bag of tricks just in case. Trust me, building your skill will help you on future rappels." He checked their anchor equipment and double checked her set up before he stepped to the ledge. He nodded and kicked back dropping at a measured pace. Danielle dropped after him, her descent steady and true. Damn, the woman was everything he'd ever wanted.

"How long are we stopping?" Danielle asked as she held her weight against the belay equipment suspending her about sixty feet above the ground.

"For a few minutes." Justin glanced at the window. The ledge on the Madrid building was seven inches wide. The glass would be double paned. He glanced at the view from where he was swinging above the ground. The southeast side of the Madrid building was sitting on a feeder street to the main avenues of the entertainment district. He glanced up. The roof was almost an exact duplicate of the one in Madrid. Unless he was able to rig some device to keep him closer to the side of the building, the rappel would be risky. Even factoring in darkness, he'd be too exposed. No, this entry needed to be scrapped. He'd work option B of his plan. Dangling this far from the side of the building would prevent him from securing himself without an anchor. Additionally, the exposure of swinging eighty feet in the air on a well-traveled street that could have light to moderate traffic would make it too risky to use. The more he examined the process, it became clear entering the building from the roof would be wiser. It would take longer, and he'd have to travel through four floors before he reached the main offices where the safes were located, but...slow and steady won the race and all that shit.

Justin glanced over at Danielle who was looking up at the roof. "Okay, we will go down four flights now." He watched as she looked down, nodded and released some tension on her rope, and dropped steadily. He kept parallel with her as she descended. They stopped only momentarily before he told her to drop another six flights. She was a strong woman, and the determination on her face was a thing of beauty, but this was a draining rappel.

When they landed on the ground, she laughed, which turned into a groan as she crumpled onto her ass. "Oh, my God, I'm shaking like a leaf. That was terrifying and awesome, and I never want to rappel like that again."

"But you know you can if you have to, right?" Justin unwrapped from the line and unbuckled his harness.

"You better not fall off of Everest. That rappel scared the shit out of me."

"And yet you did it."

Dani collapsed onto her back looking up the wall of the building. "Holy shit. I did it."

Justin extended a hand to her, but she waved him off. "I'll just lay here and try to stop freaking out. You can have the honor of going back up there and getting our equipment."

"I'm not leaving you in the middle of a construction zone by yourself. Sorry, but you're coming with me. You need to walk off the adrenaline spike anyway." Justin extended his hand again.

"Ugh...okay, but only because you're right." She followed him back into the building, and they trudged up the stairwell. "So, there is no one here today at all?"

"Nope. They closed up for the day. Mandatory safety training session." Justin held her hand as they ascended.

"And you got the key to the area, how exactly?"

Dani's open smile brought a happy laugh from him. "Connections. My brother knows a guy who knows a guy."

"The building is almost done?"

"I believe so." He peered through the windows as they were rappelling. It looked like the contractor was almost done. There were several floors that still needed finishing, but all in all, they were probably a couple months from finishing the work.

"It has heat?"

"It should. Why?"

"So, we are completely alone?" Dani pulled his hand and pushed through the fire escape door on the fourteenth floor.

"What are you doing?" Justin followed her through some hanging plastic that was protecting the finished area from the painting going on beside the fire escape.

Danielle laughed and kept walking toward a corner office with an expanse of windows. Justin glanced around and couldn't help comparing the two buildings. This interior was nothing like the Madrid building. She turned around and started to peel off her gloves and coat. "I may have had an idea while I was descending."

Justin followed her at a slower pace. He watched as the layers of clothing came off. His cock stiffened behind his fly. "And what was that idea?"

"I wondered what it would be like to have you make love to me while we both looked out on the city. We are far enough up that nobody from the street should be able to see us unless they are voyeurs and have binoculars."

"What about the buildings over there." Justin came up behind her and cupped her breast stroking the nipple through the lace of her bra.

"Those buildings?" Danielle purred as she arched back into him.

"Mmmhmmm." Justin acknowledged as he lowered his lips to the place where her neck joined her shoulder. She shuddered at the small bite he placed there.

"What buildings?" Her breath caught as his other hand snaked across her stomach and angled down toward her sex.

"You like the thought of someone seeing us, don't you?" Justin kissed along her shoulder.

"Yes." The full body shiver gave him his answer before her whispered admission.

He walked her forward to the window. "Hands on the glass. Don't take them off for any reason." He felt her moan against his chest before she complied and braced herself against the window. He kissed his way down her back, licking the ridge of her shoulder blades and tracing the feel of her ribs as he descended. His lips glided along the lace of her thong before he lowered it to her thighs. He pulled off his gloves and traced the swollen lips of her sex with his fingers. Danielle's legs shook as they braced against his sensual assault. He licked the dimples just above her ass and kissed each one as his fingers found her clit. Her gasp of his name dropped like kerosene on a fire. Heat roared through him. He stood up and pulled her back onto his chest. "You want them to see me take you?"

"Yes."

Justin reached down and undid his zipper pulling himself out. "You want me to take you like this? Make them jealous of what I have?" Danielle moaned and pushed back against him. "You ready for me?"

"Yes, please, Justin!" Her hands were still planted against the glass.

"Watch that building across from us, Dani. They're watching you. Do you see them watching you?" Justin didn't know if anyone was looking, but he wanted to ramp up the game they were playing because he wasn't going to last. He'd gladly help her with any fantasy she had, unless she wanted him to share. He wouldn't do that. Ever. Rage at the thought of someone else putting their hands on her coursed through him as he buried himself in her. "They can watch, but they can never have you." He thrust up into her and held deep. "Do you know why?"

"Because I'm yours." Dani's breath pushed out of

her as he withdrew and slammed into her with a possessive stroke.

"That's right. You're mine. Nobody touches you. Nobody but me." He leaned down and bit her shoulder as his hand snaked around to her clit. He did nothing more than apply pressure as his cock pounded into her.

"Nobody but you. Justin...so close...please."

"You'll wait. Do you know why?" Justin pulled her off the glass. Her arms snaked up around his neck, her back arched in a delicious dip.

"No."

"You'll wait because I asked you to." He pinched her nipple. Her cry echoed in the empty walls of the building.

"Please."

"No." Justin pulled out, spun her around and tore off her thong. He lifted her up and braced her back against the glass. She wrapped her legs around him, and he found his way back into her. "Look at me." He stared at the beauty he held as she opened her eyes. "You are mine."

"Yes." Danielle managed to say the word as he pounded into her, branding her as his, making his claim known. She. Was. His. Danielle bowed off the glass pushing him back. Her core spasmed, and then clenched around him. She wrapped herself against him and mewled as he chased his own release. He held her entire weight as he drove into her. He tightened her to him as lightning lacerated his spine and exploded through every cell in his body. His shout echoed as he continued to thrust through the climax that threatened to stop his heart. He moved forward and braced Danielle against the window while they caught their breath.

"Should I be embarrassed?"

The whispered words made him lift his head up and look at her—all beautiful and disheveled by their sex. "Why would you be?"

She rolled her eyes. "I'm not into anyone actually watching, but..."

Justin kissed the tip of her nose. "I'll fulfill any fantasy you have."

"Except sharing." She smiled up at him.

"I won't share you." He let her feet slide down his legs, still holding her to keep them both steady.

"I don't want to share either." She lifted a hand to his cheek. "You make me feel safe, so I can say things like this." She motioned toward the window.

"I can't wait to find out what else that mind of yours dreams up." Justin brought his lips down to hers and feasted until they had to pull away to breathe. "We need to get your clothes on and get our equipment."

"But I worked off my adrenaline spike." Danielle pushed her bottom lip out in an attempt at a pout.

"And so did I, so if I have to suffer, you have to suffer, too. Remember that climb up Everest. We need to be in condition." Justin tucked himself away and helped pick up her clothes.

"I have a feeling that line will get old before too long." Danielle slid her boots back on after pulling up her leggings, sans underwear. Justin pocketed that piece of lace.

"It may, but if we have sex after every training event?" Justin wagged his eyebrows at her.

"Then we will be the happiest climbers Everest has ever met." Dani grabbed his extended hand, and they headed to the roof.

CHAPTER 17

"So, you have everything you need?" Justin paused at Jason's question. He clicked off a mental checklist.

"Yes. I'm traveling out tonight on the red-eye, landing in Frankfurt, Germany. I have two days in the Rheingau areas purchasing Rieslings and some new Pinot Noir. From there I travel to the Bordeaux area in France. I'll be there for three days for purchasing and a day off for sightseeing. The trip to Madrid from Toulouse is eight hours. I'll leave about noon to get there after dark. Do you have my equipment pre-positioned?"

Jason nodded and crossed his legs. It wasn't often his brother came to New York. He and his wife Faith were going to see a Broadway show this weekend. Fortuitous that it happened to be the day he was leaving...or not. He could never tell what Jason really had on his mind.

"Any complications that I need to know about?" Jason lifted an eyebrow when he asked.

"None that I haven't detailed. I'd like to have more time with the mock-up of the new locking system on the XR device, but I have the mechanics and the tools, plus I have a workaround if need be. We do not want them to know I was there, correct?"

"Correct. If our intelligence is accurate, there is hardcopy accounting in that vault. We have a team in place to take custody of the property. Sierra team will be in the local area during the op and will meet you at the location we agreed upon."

"Five guys to bring back some numbers? Must be some important information." Justin leaned back in his chair.

"Sierra team just happens to be in the vicinity. You'll meet with Van Wheeler. He's the skipper of the team. Gunner, Rico, Scuba, and Harley make up the rest of the team, and they are hell on wheels. You could do worse than have them on your six during this op."

Justin lifted his chin and narrowed his gaze.

"What am I extracting?" He'd seen his brother hedge before. He'd become extremely proficient at reading people, and his brother was no different.

"Ledgers we believe will document actual dona-tions to terrorist organizations." Jason looked up directly into his eyes. "They will have guards and countermeasures. That is another reason for Sierra Team to be close. If shit goes bad, we want a way to get you out."

"I won't get caught. I will back out before that happens." Justin did a mental shuffle of the secondary and tertiary fail safes on the new system and how he was going to neutralize them. "So once again, breaking and entering on a nationally approved level."

"I can neither confirm nor deny the existence of any alphabet soup approval." Jason gave him a shit-eating grin.

"So, no DoJ, DoD, FBI, CIA or secret entities I'm not aware of, going after this one is there?"

"No. The Mossad was the organization there before you on that last operation. Their female specialist was effective, but her operation wasn't sanctioned by the Counsel. The Mossad has been...talked to... about the situation. Sometimes they are rather headstrong and take matters into their own hands."

"They could have caused both of us to be exposed." The fact that a specialist like him was already on the premises in Perth still made him pause.

"Noted. But there is nobody involved in this except us. The national agencies that I can't confirm approved this mission, approved this mission. We are alone, and we work better that way. Besides, what are you worried about? A little competition? To hear you tell it, you're an excellent cat burglar."

"As I have told you a hundred times before, I prefer the term 'information extraction specialist'." Justin loathed the term cat burglar. It made him seem like a thief. That was another term he despised. He wasn't a thief. He provided a service for Guardian and his nation, and thief implied he was breaking the law for his own benefit. Justin suppressed a chuckle. Well, he was, but it was on an emotional level, not a monetary one.

"Thief." Jason winked at him as he said it. They'd had this conversation too many times to count.

"High priced, high tech, high risk, information extraction specialist." Justin puffed on his fingernails and brushed then against his coat.

"I know, and I'm damned glad we have your services. You have your secondary passport?"

"Yes, between the lining of my suitcase in the x-ray shielded molding." He had money and a burner phone in there, too. It wasn't his first rodeo. He glanced at the clock and stood. He needed to get Jason on his way, or his wife Faith wouldn't get dinner before her show. "I'm sorry you couldn't have come in yesterday. You could have met Danielle." Justin walked with Jason toward his office door.

"Mom really likes her, but beyond that, Jade and Jewell haven't stopped singing her praises. I'm glad you finally found someone." Jason pulled him in for a hug. "You're the last of us to find someone to fill the broken places. Hold on to her if she's the one. Don't let anyone or anything get in the way of taking care of her."

"She is the one, and all the damned souls in hell couldn't keep me from taking care of her." He hugged his brother once more before opening the door. He waved one last time as Jason hit the outer office door before he headed back to his desk, gathered his phone and keys, and called for Paulo to come get him. If he was lucky, he'd have an hour with Danielle before he had to leave for the airport. If traffic cooperated.

Of course, traffic didn't cooperate. Justin palmed the phone and hit Dani's profile under favorites.

"Hey, I thought you were going to come home before you had to fly out. Did you get busy at work?" Danielle's voice immediately calmed the anger that the traffic in New York City had induced.

"No, traffic is at a standstill. It isn't looking good. How about you come downstairs and take a ride with me to the airport?"

"I can't. I'm supposed to do a video conference with Roland about the problems we found with the Bowman property. With the time difference and the crunch on the proposal for purchase if we don't meet now and find a way forward, it may be too late, and we could lose the property." She blew out a breath of air. "Maybe you could postpone your wine buying trip?"

"I can't. I have all the vendors lined up." Justin dropped his head against the leather seat. "I'll be back home in eight days."

"Well, I'm sure we will survive a week without each other." Danielle chuckled. "Did that sound convincing?"

"No. Not in the slightest." Justin laughed with her. "I'll call when I can." He hated leaving her and would have taken her with him if they could have made their schedules work, but with a major acquisition in the works, it wasn't in the cards.

"I'll miss you. Take care of yourself and don't let any vineyard owner swindle you and give you bad wine."

"I don't think that will happen."

"I know it won't." Dani's voice softened. "I'm going to miss you."

Justin nodded, fuck there was so much he wanted to say to her, needed to say, but on the phone wasn't where he needed to be when he said it. He had a perfect weekend planned for when they traveled to Jewell's wedding. No work, just the two of them. He'd made all the arrangements, and he'd even been looking at rings. Not that it was time to pop the question, hell he had to tell her he loved her first, but asking her was inevitable. He cleared his throat around the emotion. "You know how much you mean to me, right?"

"I know. I feel the same way. Be safe. Until then."

"Until then." Justin echoed before he hung up. Danielle refused to say goodbye. Ever. It seemed when her mother finally went over the edge of sanity for the last time, she looked at Dani and told her goodbye. Since then, Dani'd never said the words. It was irrational, but Danielle's fear was that if she ever said it, she'd never see the person again. Justin ran his thumb across the face of his phone. He smiled down at the selfie he'd taken of them at the gym. He needed the next eight days to fly by. He'd get in, get out and get home.

CHAPTER 18

Danielle leaned back in her office chair. The leather creaked as she closed her eyes and yawned. The Bowman property had been a nightmare from the initial proposal onward. But, it was the best possible location. If the new legal strategy didn't work, she'd have to throw in the towel and let Justin know it was time to cut their losses. She wasn't ready to put up the white flag just yet, however.

The cleaning crew had come and gone. The building was quiet. Danielle should've gone home hours ago, but Justin's apartment was so big she tended to wander aimlessly at night. She glanced at her schedule for tomorrow, or rather today. Two meetings—both in the late afternoon. She sent a quick interoffice memo to her administrative assistant to let her know she wouldn't be in until her three o'clock meeting. It was almost time for the city to start waking up. She'd go back to her apartment, grab a shower, some food, and a little bit of sleep. No doubt all three would go a long way to clear up her mind for whatever tomorrow brought.

She gathered her coat, purse, and briefcase while her computer shut down. Two more days until Justin came home. He hadn't called today, but he'd told her he might not be able to. She understood. Business was business, but it still left a little hole where longing and self-pity grew. She loved him, but they hadn't reached the point where they'd declared that to each other. She kept the words tamped down because she didn't want to terrify Justin into running away. *Hi, we were friends, now we're lovers and oh, by the way, I'm in love with you. As in, I love you in a desperate, obsessive kind of way that makes me crazy when you aren't here and makes me long for your touch.* Yeah, if she was Justin, she'd be running away from that kind of crazy. They were still new, but their past made it seem like they'd had been together so much longer.

Tired and brain dead from the day and night's worth of work, she let her mind float around Justin on the way down to the lobby and gave a quick nod to the security guard who was unfortunate enough to pull the midnight shift. He nodded in return and watched her leave. The city was remarkably quiet at this time of the morning. She extended her hand and watched a cab parked down the street turn on his fare light and head her way. A sharp, cold wind cut through the wool dress and coat she wore. The cab pulled up, and she got in.

"West 87th and Central Park, please."

The cabbie grunted something in response. His jacket collar was pulled up and it shielded most of his face. Probably protection from the cold although the cab seemed warm enough. For once, Danielle didn't pull out her phone. She'd gone through every email before she'd left the office. The only distraction in the vehicle was the meter mounted at the front of the cab. The cabbie turned heading east. "Excuse me, I said West 87th."

"City always works on the sewers this time of morning. They had all the holes open. I'm taking you around it. Won't charge you any more than the short route."

Dani narrowed her eyes and glanced at the road signs for several minutes. No, they were going way out of the way. She palmed her phone.

"Take it easy, miss."

Dani snapped her head up. The cabbies voice sounded like he was talking into a tin can. He held a mask over his face and pushed down the top of an aerosol spray. Her eyes watered, and she choked on a horribly sweet smell. Her phone slipped from fingers that were suddenly numb. Her eyes went from her hands to the man driving. He wore a mask over his mouth and nose, but she'd seen him before, in Perth and in Tasmania...and outside her father's building. Dani blinked back the fog that consumed her and watched as he picked up her phone and threw it out the window. "Go to sleep. If you're lucky, your father will deal. If you're not? Well, you're a little too old for the slave trade, but someone might find you attractive enough to keep around. I know they would if they saw the performance you put on at that vacant building a couple weeks back. Your man gave it to you good. I'll give him that much."

Danielle's mind spun out of control. She reached toward the man. "Don't. Please." Her speech slurred and sounded slow even to her ears.

"Ha, too much money not to, and I'm really tired of following you around. Thought we were going to be able to get the information in other ways, but best-laid plans and all that rot. You understand, don't you? Nothing personal. We just need to give him a reason to comply."

Danielle blinked at the man as her vision tunneled. Her hand dropped into the melted snow on the floor of the cab. It was a sharp contrast to the warm fuzz that surrounded her. Her body tipped following the path of her arm. Down. God, no. She fought to breathe deeply, to get her lungs to expand and her body to move.

"Ah, see, there you go. Go to sleep. If your father cooperates maybe they'll actually let you wake up." The man's laugh chased her down the spiraling darkness.

CHAPTER 19

*J*ustin took in the expanse of lowered faux ceiling between him and the air duct he needed to reach and disassemble. The only supported iron beam he could use to cross was no more than three inches wide. He tested the wire that suspended it and the fireproof ceiling tiles. It was a high tensile braided cable. It would hold his weight, but if he walked across the beam, his weight could cause it to sway. No matter how solid his balance was, if the beam swayed, the ceiling tiles would dislodge. If the tiles dislodged, the motion sensor would activate, and he'd be caught. He had three feet of clearance above him and a new alarm system below him. The information Guardian had provided was outdated...by about four days if the dates on the panels he'd found were accurate. Who the fuck changes out a state of the art alarm system? Justin could only draw one conclusion to that question. Someone who believed their old alarm system had been compromised. But how would they know? More importantly, how the fuck was he going to get across the expanse?

Justin lifted and waddled in a crouch to the beginning of the beam. He'd have to crawl across. His hands would be protected by the gloves he wore, but that metal would make mincemeat out of his knees. He sat down on the end of the supported area below him and took off his soft suede-soled shoes. He stripped off his socks and put his shoes back on. A couple quick flips of his pant legs rolled up the material to his knees. The sock wrapped around his pants, where he tied them at the outside of his knees so he could move without impediment. Sweat dripped down the side of his face, and he brushed at it with an irritated swipe.

Justin made sure all his pockets were sealed or zipped and that his backpack was secure before he regarded the bar again. Fuck, this was not what he'd planned, but thank God he was damn good at breaking into places. He placed his first hand out onto the bar and followed with the second. His knee slid out onto the bar as he slowly and carefully made his way toward the wall twenty feet away.

Huge drops of sweat landed on the tile with audible splats. Justin moved in microbursts keeping his center of gravity over the bar. The hard angle iron dug into his knees, and the pain was distracting, but Justin pushed through it. He had four feet left to go when he heard voices below him.

He drew a steadying breath and froze, focusing on the bar and keeping his body from shifting. The muffled voices laughed during their conversation. Great, it sounded like they'd settled in. Justin slid his hand along the bar and moved his knee. The small space amplified the slight scrape of his improvised knee pads. He waited, ensured there was no swing to the bar and moved again. The sweat from his brow dropped again and again. His hands reached the supported area around the air duct. Lifting from the narrow, suspended beam to that area would be where shit could go wrong. The release of weight, if not done in a smooth, concise fashion could cause the bar to shift.

One hand secure on the supported area, he moved the second up. His knees slid up, inch by inch until he could shift his weight to his shoulders and lift through his arms. The pain of blood returning to his damaged knees made him grimace and puff air through his lungs. He couldn't move quickly. He couldn't let the bar swing. Once all his weight was on his elbows and shoulders, he pushed up while applying pressure through the tips of his toes onto the center of the beam. The sweat ran freely down his face and onto his neck. Justin inched one foot forward and off the beam. He planted his knee on the hardened surface of the supported area and choked back a groan of pain. He'd fucked his knees up, of that there was no doubt. He shifted his weight onto his knee and lifted his toes off the beam, staring at his foot over his shoulder the entire time. Justin folded up onto the supported area and rolled onto his back. He glanced back from where he'd come. A huge smile split his face. *What a fucking rush!* Damn, he hadn't even made it to the safe, and this was already one of the best missions he'd been on. He glanced at the air duct and followed the metal back with his eyes. There. A juncture. That meant access. Not to the office. Hell, dropping down through air returns was all Hollywood, although Tom did make that shit look good. No, he had a failsafe for times just like these. There was no way anyone wouldn't know he'd been here because he was about to knock out the entire building. Night, night. Sleepy time.

Sorry, Jason, but if you want the information, you'll deal with the fact that the extraction will be discovered a little sooner than anticipated.

The enclosed ventilation system that made this building a fortress also made it vulnerable. It offered a way to get in, get the documentation, and get out without going across that damn bar again. Justin carefully assessed the air handler. Fortunately, there were only two balanced magnetic switches set at the access point—one at the vent cover itself, and one attached to a thin filament connected to the vent cover. It was an old-school redundancy most people would overlook in the fiber optic enclosed systems that existed today. Whoever set up the system was good. Not great, but Justin would give them props. He neutralized the switch on the grid and cut the filament. The other BMS dangled uselessly on the thread. If he'd pulled the cover without seeing it, the device would have triggered alarms in the security center.

His backpack came off, and he opened the bottom left pouch on his vest and palmed two small rolls. One was plastic sheeting; the other was a Kevlar infused tape. It was cut into inch strips and set on a wax paper backing. He taped the edge of the plastic down around the air handler until only a small corner remained open. Justin pulled a canister out of his mesh pouch. It looked like a hand grenade, but it was knockout gas. It was an aerial version of Diethyl Ether. From what Jason told him, it had been chemically altered to be more concentrated and guaranteed to knock out anyone who breathed it in for at least an hour. He set the canister down and pulled a scaled-down version of a gas mask out of the back pouch of his backpack. It fit over his mouth and nose leaving his eyes unobstructed. While he occasionally wore glasses when he was working with the clientele in his restaurants, he didn't need them for this. The hooked nozzle of the ether "grenade" fit over the lip of the air handler, and Justin taped the plastic closed before he depressed the tab dispensing the chemical. Once the dispenser emptied, he retrieved it and strapped it back in. There were no prints on the tape or the plastic, why leave the container so someone could back track the manufacturer. From there they could see who purchased it. No, he'd leave nothing to identify him or his organization. Sloppiness wasn't his hallmark.

With his backpack strapped on, and all the pockets of his vest secured, he headed back to the drop ceiling. The crouch he maintained kept his knees bent, and that strain felt amazing. *Not.* Justin approached the area where he'd previously heard talking. Nothing but silence. He glanced at his watch and gave it three more minutes to allow the chemical to make its way through the entire facility. Justin put on his ski mask. It was fucking sweltering in the area he was in, but if he ran into difficulties with the safe, he wouldn't have time to make it out without having his image snagged by a security camera. He hated cameras. Videotapes and digital recordings were a bane to his existence when he worked for Guardian. Several times he'd wondered if it would be worth it to go straight to the prize and double back for the digital proof. Yeah, like that would happen. He wouldn't know what the fuck he was looking for anyway. But it would be a rush to try it. Wouldn't that be a trip? The smile he wanted to bust out with was hampered by his gas mask. Maybe he should study up on digital storage of security camera systems.

Justin sat down and dropped his feet onto the ceiling tiles suspended by the bar. He glanced at his watch before he lifted his leg and punched out a ceiling tile. The thick fire-retardant material snapped and crumbled to the floor. Justin waited, listening for any indication of movement. When all was quiet, he lowered himself down out of the ceiling. Two men in janitor's uniforms were slumped over a small table. Employee break room. That meant he needed to go right when he reached the door. Justin zipped soundlessly through the halls of the building, his mind referencing the blueprints he'd committed to memory.

The outer door to the suite of offices he was targeting was locked. It took less than ten seconds to extract his picks and open the lock. He repeated the process again and again until he reached the office he required. The security center would be receiving motion detection, door, and thermal alarms. He'd rerouted and spoofed the copper telephone lines from the exterior of the building to the local police and fire departments, so no alarms were going out of the building. That meant nobody was awake to hear them. Justin marveled at the fact a fiber optic, state of the art security system depended on the antiquated telephone system for redundancy. Hell, it made his job easier, but what a waste of money. The guy he was taking the ledgers from could stuff his stolen goods under a mattress for all the good the redundancy of his expensive system did for him.

He moved into the office and dropped the painting behind the desk, chuckling to himself. How stereotypical, but hey, not everyone had imagination. The safe he faced was a bitch to open on a good day. He popped the digital panel and rewired the power source to a battery. Then he cut the power while the panel believed it was still active. If the panel read a tamper it would send an additional five-inch bar into its resting place as a failsafe. The only way to open it then would be the key code. There was one, and only one, key code per safe. Justin worked quickly to trick the tumblers into thinking the pad entered the correct key. It took precision, practice, and patience. At the twenty-seven minute mark, he opened the last tumbler. A thrill skittered up his back. It always did when he defeated the system. He opened the door and... There was nothing in the safe. Not a damned thing. Justin stepped away from the vault and searched the room. Where would he hide documents that he didn't want anyone to obtain? Well, hell, since he didn't have much time, he started with the basics. The desk took three minutes to search, only because he had to get his picks out again. Next, the books that lined the wall were taken down one by one. He opened them to make sure there was nothing hiding between the covers. When he was done, he turned over both chairs before he grabbed the end table and tipped it over. Bingo.

Justin slipped his knife out of his pocket and cut the tape holding the small book to the bottom of the table. He opened it and thumbed through about twenty pages of numbers, names and dates before he stuffed it into his vest and headed to the rear of the building.

There were street cameras on both the exit and entrance of the alleyway, so he'd need to keep to the shadows and time his movements. The back door opened. He could hear the alarms wailing behind the closed door of the security room situated on the ground floor. He glanced at his watch. He had five minutes to clear the area before the gas would no longer be effective. He ghosted into the alley and found the shadows. He lifted his ski mask enough to take off the gas mask and drew a deep breath of fresh air before he lowered the mask again and moved to his right, down the alley. According to the documentation Guardian gave him, the camera at the end of the alley would only catch his back as he rounded the corner. He moved out and hid his face from the camera. A quick twist of the ski mask and he was wearing a skull cap. He kept his head down and rounded the next corner averting his face radically to avoid another street camera. He walked briskly up the three blocks where pedestrian traffic exploded around the bars and restaurants that lined the avenue. Justin walked into a bar he'd selected earlier and headed to the bathroom. He received several long looks but paid them no mind. The establishment didn't have cameras, and people wouldn't remember enough about him to identify him. He locked the bathroom door and stood on the toilet to remove the ceiling tile and pull down his change of clothes. Black slacks, a black button down, a heavy black button-up sweater, and Italian leather shoes mimicked the outfit he wore in, at least in bulk. His wallet with fake identification and passport plus the canvas envelope were tucked away. The little ledger was tucked inside his thick shirt, under the sweater. His gear was bagged and placed in the ceiling. One of Sierra Team's people would retrieve it after he left. Justin flushed the toilet for effect, washed his hands and left the restroom.

He ordered a drink while standing at the bar. A tall man, muscular with brown hair and a neatly trimmed beard took his place next to Justin and ordered a whiskey. Justin took a drink of his beer, because, fuck it, he was thirsty. "You caused one hell of a stink." The low rumble of his drinking partner's voice was just barely loud enough for him to hear.

"There were complications." Justin took another

long pull from his beer. He set the glass down and walked to the door. He knew the man, Wheeler, would follow him. Justin strolled casually through the people on the sidewalk.

Wheeler caught up with him about three minutes later. "Were you successful?"

Justin stopped walking and someone behind him bumped into him. "I'll pretend you didn't say that." Because really? "Was your team successful in retrieving my equipment?"

"Please." The man rolled his eyes and Justin raised his eyebrow. "Alright, I get it, we are all good at what we do. I need the package and Archangel wants a SitRep. They are monitoring the police radio, and like I said, all hell busted loose about a minute after you got to the club." Wheeler placed his hand over his ear, and that is when Justin noticed the earpiece. There was no way he'd ever work with someone in his head like that. "He says if you are alive, he's going to kill you." Wheeler glanced over at him and laughed. "I never want to hear those words come out of Archangel's mouth directed at me. The dude is massive. Have you ever seen him?"

"Once or twice." Justin hid the grin that wanted to erupt. "Take me to dinner, Mr. Wheeler, and I'll give you what you want."

"Ah, sweetheart, I'm sorry, but my heart was broken not too long ago. I'll settle for the package."

"And I need to get it out of my shirt, so unless you are willing to let the traffic cameras see me disrobe and pull out the book you require, you will take me to a restaurant and buy me dinner. You can get what you want from me, but I'm starving, and I'd prefer a sit-down restaurant rather than a police cell. Your choice."

"Not much of a choice. You're a bossy motherfucker. Anybody ever tell you that?"

Justin laughed and followed Wheeler as he stomped down the sidewalk. "Not once."

The restaurant Wheeler chose was tucked back in between two larger clubs, down an alleyway and out of the main district, literally a hole in the wall. Justin sat down in the back booth with Wheeler and glanced around. "You must have been here before. There is no way you just stumbled upon it as we were walking"

Wheeler waited, nodding at the waiter. Justin glanced at the menu and ordered for both of them in perfect Castilian Spanish. When he was finished, and the server left, he glanced back at Wheeler and lifted an eyebrow.

"My second in command eats. A lot. He found

this place a couple years ago. They have good food. Now, if you don't mind, I need to put my hands on that package. The voices in my head are mad and getting madder. My team has checked in, but I haven't. My boss's boss's boss is pissed and yelling in my ear. I'd do just about anything to make that stop." A sheepish grin spread across the man's face.

Justin understood. Jason could go on and on when he was spun up. He hadn't heard that happen since he was a teenager, but he didn't figure it had lessened over the years. The waiter reappeared with their drinks and silverware. Justin couldn't help but notice the water spots on the knife and the people at the door who'd been waiting for almost the entire time they'd been seated. He hoped the food was good because the front of the house was abysmal.

He saw their waiter head to the front of the establishment and used the time to slip his hand inside his shirt, retrieve the book and hand it to Wheeler. Justin watched as Wheeler tucked it inside his jacket. "I'm going to use the restroom, send a message, and come back." Wheeler excused himself as Justin scanned the front of the building. Several police cars careened past the front door, lights and sirens blazing. Nobody stirred or gave them any undue attention. Madrid was a big city, and emergency vehicles were commonplace, but they got Justin's blood pumping. He imagined law enforcement was scurrying. He'd finish his dinner, walk the ten blocks to his rental vehicle and head back to France, to his true identity and a flight home. That thought put a smile on his face. He couldn't wait to hold Danielle in his arms.

CHAPTER 20

The third time his phone call went unanswered, Justin became concerned. The fourth, fifth, and sixth time scared the fuck out of him. In all the years he'd known Danielle, she'd always answered or called him back within minutes. Always. Justin glanced at his watch again. Four hours since he'd last called and still nothing. He palmed his phone and moved to the farthest corner of the gate at the airport. He'd be boarding soon. He couldn't endure a transatlantic flight not knowing what was wrong, and he knew in his gut something *was* wrong. He hit the switchboard number and stood facing the glass, watching the people behind him in the reflection.

"Good Evening, Mr. King. Please stand by while

we locate your brother." The same voice, steady, calm, and reassuring. This morning the delay in being put through to Jason ground against his last nerve.

"What's wrong." Justin could hear the sleep in his brother's voice. He glanced at his watch again. Five in the morning here, shit that was midnight in the States.

"She isn't answering her phone. Something is wrong."

"Dude, who isn't answering?"

"Danielle. She always picks up or calls me right back, even before we became involved. It has been four hours since my last call and over eight hours since I called the first time. Something is wrong."

"Alright. Hold on. I'll need an address." Justin could hear Faith mumble in the background. "It's Justin, he's overseas and needs some help. Go back to sleep."

"I'm sorry for waking you up, but this shit is wrong. She's staying at my place, but she has her own apartment." Justin rattled off her address and drew a breath that didn't quite fill his lungs.

"I'll get on it right away. I got your back."

The announcement sounded overhead calling his flight. "I'm about to board."

"We'll have her, or answers, when you land. You're landing at JFK?"

Justin nodded, vaguely realizing he needed to speak. He cleared his throat. "Yeah. Jason, I'm not overreacting."

"I didn't say you were. It isn't like you to sound the klaxon when there isn't an air raid. Let me get some people on this. I've got you." Jason disconnected the call. Justin picked up his carry on and headed toward the gate. He'd missed first class boarding and had to stand in the line for economy. He didn't care, his mind ran in circles. Something was wrong.

Justin called Max as he waited in line. "Sir?" The croak in the man's voice told him once again how late it was in New York.

"I need the emergency contact number for Danielle Grant. Immediately." Justin clutched the phone tightly.

"Of course. I need to boot up my computer. May I text it to you in a couple minutes?"

"Please hurry, Max." Justin couldn't keep the concern out of his voice.

"Is Ms. Grant alright, sir? She didn't show up for her meetings today. Her assistant called your office looking for her."

Shit! He knew it. Justin clamped his eyes closed and ground out, "I don't know."

"Right. I'm on it. Give me two minutes."

"Thank you."

"Sir, I know I haven't been the nicest person to Ms. Grant, but I'd never want anything to happen to someone you care so much about."

Justin swallowed back the emotion boiling inside him. "Thank you, Max. I understand, and I appreciate it." He hung up the phone, swiped the face and called up his boarding pass. He held the phone over the scanner and breezed through the gateway but ended up stalled in the middle of the passage. His phone vibrated in his hand. Paul Greenfield was Danielle's emergency contact, as he suspected. Jason pushed the number and put the phone to his ear. The phone rang through to a voice message. "Sir, this is Justin King. I'm worried about Danielle. She isn't answering her phone, and she didn't come into work yesterday. I'm in Paris about to board a flight home. If you have information concerning her whereabouts, would you please call my brother, Jason King. Tell the switchboard operator I asked you to call him." Jason rattled off the number and ended the call. The line stutter-stepped forward while he sent a text to Jason letting him know

Danielle had failed to come into work and he'd asked Danielle's father to contact Jason. Once inside the plane, he took off his suit jacket and handed it to the stewardess. His phone vibrated, and he glanced at the face.

> *Log onto airplane internet when airborne. Communicate through email dead drop. I'll leave word when we have information.*

He stood again and grabbed his tablet. The elderly woman in the seat next to him smiled and pulled out a thick romance book. Thank God, she wouldn't want to talk. He sat down and waived off the mimosa the attendant tried to give him.

Granny next to him grabbed two, "Since the young man doesn't want his." She winked at him and downed one glass in a single effort.

Justin faced forward and closed his eyes. His mind thrashed against the confines of the aircraft. Every fiber in his being wanted, no needed, to be in New York. He felt useless and he raged at his inability to do anything. *Where was Danielle? Why the hell wasn't she answering her cell?*

Justin leaned forward and bowed his head. Praying had never been his thing, but when you are forced to acknowledge you don't have any control over a situation, a higher power needed to be called in. He breathed out his anger and slowly inhaled before he said his first prayer since the day his father died. *Dear God, I don't deserve anything from you, but I believe Danielle does. She's...she's the other half of me and I...I don't know how to do it, but I'm asking you to watch over her. Whatever is happening, please be with her. Protect her...until I can get there.*

He lifted his eyes and blinked to focus. The plane took off, and Justin leaned back into the seat. This was going to be the longest day of his life.

Three hours. Three damn hours and all he'd been able to do was to stare holes in the back of the seat in front of him. His head ached from the mental warfare raging in his mind. If something happened to her, he would hunt down whoever caused her harm and he would kill them. A visual picture of his brother, Joseph, flashed to his mind. His brother had tracked down and killed the bastard who had murdered their dad. At the time, Justin didn't understand how he could do it. He had no concept of how a switch could flip and allow his brother to feel that type of anger, especially when all Justin could feel was grief and remorse. In this minute, however, he understood. He knew exactly how Joseph must have felt.

CHAPTER 21

*J*ustin glanced at his watch and then at his tablet. He'd driven himself insane refreshing the browser. Still nothing. They were on final approach, and Jason hadn't given him a thing. His brother wouldn't leave him hanging if she was alright, so there was something wrong. Of that he was certain.

"Sir, you need to power down the tablet in preparation for landing," the flight attendant casually commented on her way past.

He knew he needed to, but it seemed like he was severing an anchor rope. The freefall to the bottom of whatever was going on with Danielle could quite possibly end his life as he knew it. He jabbed the button and powered it down.

As soon as the wheels touched the tarmac, Justin powered up his phone. There were no missed calls or texts. His gut dropped. He made his way down the gateway and into the gate area before he dialed. He weaved through slower people and headed towards customs.

"Have you landed?"

"Yes, what the fuck is going on?" Justin ignored the irritated look a mom with two kids sent his way.

"Get through customs. Jared will meet you there. You're coming to D.C."

"Jason, tell me what is happening." Justin cut off a gaggle of school-age kids as he hooked right to get into line at customs.

"I can't go into it over the phone. For now, Danielle is alright. That's all I'll say over an unsecured line."

Justin murmured string of curse words, something he rarely did because he seldom felt this fucking useless. He presented his passport and customs declaration forms to the guard when he reached the head of the line. And yes, he snapped his answers to all the mandatory customs questions. The guard lifted an eyebrow at him and regarded him quietly. Justin drew a deep breath and let it out slowly before he apologized, "I'm sorry, I've received some bad news, I didn't mean to take it out on you." The guard nodded and looked again at his information and well-worn passport. He slid the magnetic stripe through his scanner and waited for the screen to clear. In reality, the act only took a few moments, but the inordinate amount of stress Justin was under made the simple task feel like it took hours.

Once he was cleared, he bolted out of the customs area and damn near fell over his brother Jared.

"Come on. We are heading to the other side of the airport. Guardian has a jet ready to go."

"What the fuck is going on, Jared?"

"Nothing I can tell you now. Let's go." Jared grabbed his elbow.

Justin stopped and jerked it out of his hold. "No! Fuck that. I want to know what is going on, right now. I have a right to know what is happening." Justin had reached the end of his rope. It had stretched all the way across the fucking Atlantic Ocean, and he was damned if it would go one inch further.

Jared grabbed him in a hug and pulled his ear close to his mouth and hissed, "She's been kidnapped. Stop wasting time. We need to get to

D.C. and work this situation. Now find your balls, man up, and get your ass in gear."

Justin pulled away from his brother and glared at him. "Don't ever doubt I have enough balls to man up. Lead the fucking way."

THE TRIP to D.C. and the drive to Guardian Headquarters was accomplished in stilted silence. Jared wouldn't share any information other than to say Guardian was working it, and he couldn't disclose sensitive information to people who weren't cleared. Justin's pissed off meter pegged in the molten lava zone on that comment. He had the clearance, but he couldn't fucking let his brother know because of the nature of his work with Guardian. Talk about a fucked-up mess. The only thing that kept him sane through the plane ride to D.C. and the time it took to process into Guardian's headquarters was that Jason would know he was cleared for the information. Jason would tell him what was going on. He'd said she was alright...for now. Fuck. Who would want to kidnap Danielle? There was no reason...except...her father was an arms manufacturer. Granted a legitimate one, but...

"Justin?" Jason's voice brought him out of his spiraling thoughts.

"Tell me what is going on," He demanded as he walked down the hallway toward his brother.

"I will. Come with me. Jared, you'll need to be brought into this." Jason headed down the hallway in front of them.

"Do you need Nic, too?"

"He's already in the theater."

Justin followed his brother through a maze of hallways until they entered a James Bond-esque type of room. The lights were low, and there were at least seven different screens flashing on the wall at the back of the theater. He walked down the steps. His brother Jacob and his wife Tori were at one huge console, their heads together whispering and motioning towards a screen. Jewell and her fiancé Zane were at another. Jade and Nic sat in the front row where Jared dropped down beside them. Jason motioned for Justin to take a seat. He shook his head and stood, arms crossed over his chest. He wanted answers, and he wanted them now. Nobody was going to dictate another fucking thing to him until he got them.

"Alright. This is a classified briefing at a Uniform Victor level." Jason's voice was loud and stopped all conversations. At Jason's declaration, every head in the place snapped toward Justin. He threw his hands up in a frustrated gesture.

"Justin has Uniform Victor clearance. He's had it for longer than most of you have been in Guardian's service."

"Say what now?" Jade spoke the words that no doubt everyone was thinking.

"Justin's code name is The Magus."

"Holy fuck. You're the magician? The cat burglar?" Jade blurted.

Justin swiped his forehead. "Information Extraction Specialist." He put his hands on his hips and glared at Jason. "What the ever loving fuck is going on?"

"Jewell, bring up screen one."

Justin glanced up. His heart stopped, and his lungs constricted. There was a grainy video feed of Danielle. She was lying on her side on a concrete floor. "Is she..." Justin couldn't bring himself to ask the question.

"She's alive. They come in every so often and wake her up. She's obviously drugged."

"Where is she? Who the fuck did this?"

"That is what we are working out," Jared

answered. "By the way, I'm pissed I didn't know you were a world class thief."

"Amen," Jade commented.

"Ditto," added Jacob.

He ground his teeth together. "I'm not particularly interested in what you're pissed about. Any of you. I followed orders the same way you have." He threw his arm out and pointed at the screen. "What I do for this organization has nothing to do with what is happening now."

"Hey, Justin?"

He spun toward Jewell. "What?"

"I have some information I need to tell all of you. If you and Jason could sit down and stop yelling, I'll be able to walk you through it. I know you're hurting. I've been on this end when Zane was on the other end of that video feed. I know what you're feeling, but we need to work this issue, not indulge in a pissing contest."

Fuck me standing. He dropped his head and rubbed the back of his neck.

"We are the best at what we do, you included. Let's get this figured out and get your woman. Okay?" That came from Tori.

He nodded and dropped into the chair at the end of the row. Jason sat between him and Jared—his usual position—as he and Jared were always butting heads over something while they were growing up.

Jewell raised her eyebrows in a silent question and he nodded—once. "Okay. The feed is being routed through...oh, about a gabillion different IP addresses, and being bounced around the globe. They are good, but not good enough."

He watched as Zane put a hand on Jewell's shoulder. She glanced up and smiled softly. His heart felt as if it had been lanced. Danielle looked at him that way. His eyes darted up at the video feed. He torqued down on his jaw again. He needed to be part of the solution, not the problem. His hands shook, so he clasped them together and leaned forward placing his elbows on his knees and watching the floor. He focused on one point between his feet and listened.

"What is the location?" Tori's question followed on the heels of Jewell's announcement.

"Misrata Province."

"Libya?" Jacob's outcry echoed in the quiet room.

Justin tore his eyes from the floor and flicked his gaze to Jason. The man had assumed almost the same position as he had.

Jason closed his eyes for a moment and nodded. "Jacob, what teams do we have available?"

Jacob pivoted on his heel and called up a screen. All eyes read the easily deciphered information. Red dots by each team indicated none were available. All were currently engaged in active operations.

"Fuck." The whisper from Jason held more impact than a damn explosion. "Zane? What about your assets?"

Zane rubbed his chin and then shook his head. "I can recall Thanatos. Rescues aren't our strong suit."

"Damn it. I know that." Jason took off his glasses and rubbed his eyes.

Jacob cleared his throat before he spoke. "I may have a solution."

Every eye turned his direction. He glanced at Tori and shrugged. "The old Alpha team is all in town. We could go."

Tori blinked at him and then glanced at Justin. She dropped a hand to her husband's forearm and gave him a soft smile. "Alpha team hasn't been on a mission together for years."

"Granted, but we are damn good at what we do. We lived, ate, slept and breathed the same air for years. All of us have passed the PT requirements. We can get in and get her out."

"Ahh...boys...looks like there are some gnarly

complications." Jewell stopped typing and looked up at the screen that flashed onto the wall.

"Is that a fucking moat?" Jared leaned forward as if proximity to the screen would bring the satellite picture into better resolution.

"Yes. This is the origin of the feed. They've masked the hell out of it, but this is where that video is coming from."

Soft mutterings of "shit", "fuck" and "damn" trailed off into silence. He gazed at the screen in sick disbelief. All his adult life, he'd pursued actions that made brave men turn and walk away. He did it because he *craved* overcoming the hit of sheer terror that accompanied any threat of death; he was *addicted* to the adrenaline spiking through his veins as surely as any heroine addict to his crack. He fed on knowing he could master the panic and threat and still perform with precision—he could outwit death. But this? Some monster abducting Danielle for God only knew what reason? He'd been struggling to get his mind right—do what he'd always done: use the fear to sharpen his wits and performance. He couldn't. For the first time in his life, he couldn't do anything but lock the emotions down and not feel *anything*. If he didn't, horror would paralyze him. It wasn't a threat to *him* that brought him to his knees and made him cry for help. It was the death threat to *her*. His eyes scanned the room and settled briefly on each brother and sister in that room—each of them assembled and ready to move heaven and earth for *him*, for Danielle. Thank God for his family. When Danielle got home safely—he couldn't contemplate any other outcome and remain sane—he had some fences to mend.

"Tori, we need intel on that compound. Get with your counterparts and get us some answers. Jacob, call in your team." Jason stood and motioned to Justin. "Let's go to my office. I'll fill you in on the kidnapper's demands and why this situation went from a simple kidnapping to an operation monitored at the POTUS level."

"POTUS?" He lifted from his seat and echoed the word. "Her father."

Jason stopped and nodded. "Paul Greenfield received the ransom demand five minutes before you left your voice mail. I sent Ross Stapleton from the New York Office over to make contact with him. Greenfield was huddled with his security team trying to figure out the best course of action. We took that out of his hands. He's waiting in one of the conference rooms."

"What do they want?"

"A new prototype weapon."

Jared, Nic, and Jade had followed them out of the door and trailed as they walked down the hallway.

"What kind of weapon?"

Justin twisted so he could see Jared, who'd begun to answer his question.

"It is a variation on the Thunder Generator. That weapon concentrates energy into a shockwave which can incapacitate a crowd of demonstrators. But Phoenix Armament has used microtechnology to make the weapon shoulder-carried, not much heavier than a grenade launcher."

"They want a crowd dispersal weapon?" he stopped in the middle of the hall, but Jared kept his mouth closed and leveled a look toward Jason.

Jason glanced both ways to make sure there was no one else was listening and shook his head. "No, the shockwave has been concentrated. It kills. Effectively, at extreme distances and the barrel is flexible. It can be fired from around the corner with 99% accuracy. There is no need for ammunition. The weapon is a sniper's dream. The Daesh, the group we think is holding Danielle, is a terrorist group that operates out of the Mistrata Province. I'll know for a fact as soon as Tori and Jewell finish the background."

"Terrorists." He rubbed the back of his neck. Fucking terrorists had taken her.

"That is my belief. We will work a plan, and we will do everything within our power to get Danielle back. Alive." Jason dropped a hand on his shoulder. "I promise you, we won't stop until we have her back. Now let's go talk to her father, get the intel we need and make a plan."

CHAPTER 22

*H*e sat alone in the darkened theater. The only active screen was the live video feed. Two bastards had come in and shaken Danielle awake. They forced her to drink and slapped her when she refused. Now, she cowered on the floor in the corner of the bare cell, her arms clenched around her knees, awake and terrified. She startled frequently. Obviously, there were sounds that were terrifying her. He couldn't hear them, but he could see and feel her terror. He could taste her desperation.

He floundered in desperation, too. He'd fought to be included on the rescue mission. He'd had to be physically restrained at one point. Jason and Jacob had adamantly refused to let a "thief" go into a war zone, and Paul Greenfield had agreed. Justin didn't remember much after hurling a metal chair across the table at his brothers. Jared, Nic, and Zane had manhandled him back to the theater, shoved him into a seat and shouted, "Do. Not. Fucking. Move."

He stared at Danielle. His fucking heart was sitting in the corner of a dark cell, and he was being told to sit here and wait. The bitter vitriol in his gut rolled and grew with each passing beat of his heart.

The door behind him opened and he heard footsteps, but he didn't look up. He knew by now Jacob and his team were gearing up. They'd be leaving, without him. Justin would have to endure being an impotent spectator relegated to sitting in front of the monitor, watching the woman he loved suffer.

"There's been a complication."

Justin lifted guarded eyes to Jason and Jacob. He steeled himself. If the men he'd thrown a metal chair at were here telling him there was a problem... "What?" His gut sank to levels he didn't know existed.

"From the intel we've just received that compound is the Daesh headquarters. They've pumped money into the security system. We've run all possible scenarios. No matter how rapidly they deploy, when Jacob's team breaches that fortress, the alarms will sound. Danielle will be moved—or more likely—killed." Jason extended the familiar courier's pouch to him. "I need a miracle, Magus. Get inside that compound and deactivate the alarm system, undetected. When the system is deactivated, notify Jacob. Alpha team will breach the fortress and rescue Danielle."

Justin stood and reached for pouch, surprised to see his hand trembling. "My equipment?"

"I have it waiting on the aircraft. Wheels up in thirty minutes. Get going." Jason cuffed him on the back and motioned toward Jacob who'd already reached the theatre door. Justin jogged up the steps and turned one last time to put his eyes on the grainy image of Danielle curled in on herself, her head resting on her knees. Justin gripped the door and swung it open. *Hang on, baby. I'm coming.*

THE ROAR of the C-17s engine's drowned out most of the conversation that Jacob was having with his team. He watched as Alpha team poured over the blueprints, the same way he had. The drawings and information were lacking, and the location sucked. Four rifle pits at the top of the building had almost three-hundred-and-sixty-degree coverage. Answers to questions about the lighting and a backup power source went begging. The wiring for the security system would run true to most schematics, but he didn't know if it was fiber optics, copper wired or a point to point microwave shot. He could defeat them all, but not knowing what he faced going in put him at a serious disadvantage, exponentially multiplying his chance of exposure. There was no thrill to this mission. No underlying sense of satisfaction. He faced death if discovered, and not only was his death assured, but Danielle's, Jacob's and every member of Jacob's team. The irony of *who* trusted him with their lives—he, the man who worked so hard to keep his family at arm's length—wasn't lost on him.

He glanced at his brother. He knew each of Jacob's men, albeit in passing. He believed Chief ran the business end of the complex in South Dakota. The twins, Dixon and Drake, were the training gurus, and Doc Cassidy, well, he worked at the hospital on the ranch.

Chief walked over to him and sat down in the jump seat next to him. He handed him an earpiece and a small box. "The earpiece will be turned on only if we need to communicate with you." He nodded towards the twins who were laughing at something

Jacob had said. "Having those two in your head while you work is a learned skill. This box is your transmitter. When you've neutralized the alarms, you flip it open like this and activate it by pushing down on the button. Throw it away or keep it, it doesn't matter, we'll be coming in."

Jacob moved over and sat down on the other side of him. "From what we can see of the cement construction of the walls and floors, we believe she's being kept in the lower level. The satellite photos show a sandstone structure, so we are confident she's in a basement."

Justin nodded. He'd surmised the same thing.

"We've got eighteen hours until the ransom is due to the Daesh. Greenfield was able to convince them he needed the time to get the specs from the government quality control inspector. It was a good stall tactic, but we will be pushed to get there, get in and get her out before the time elapses. You'll need to keep up. Are you in decent physical condition?" Jacob glanced at him.

Was he as bulky as his brothers? No. But he'd had cardio for days, and he was strong enough to free climb the side of a mountain. "I won't slow you down."

Jacob nodded. "Try to get some sleep. We are

doing everything we can. Rest so you can do what you need to do when we land." His brother nudged him with his elbow. "So...a fucking cat burglar. One that can chuck chairs like a Nolan Ryan fastball."

He rolled his head against the plane's vibrating bulkhead and returned his brother's amused expression with a glacial stare. *Cat burglar*. He hated that fucking term. "High priced, high tech, high risk, information extraction specialist."

Jacob laughed and slapped his leg as he stood up. "Right. Whatever you say, man. Whatever you say."

Thank God for the roar of the aircraft's engine. At least it drowned out Jacob's laughter. He closed his eyes and concentrated on breathing. He needed to rest so he could do what he needed to do. That's what Jacob had said, and for once he agreed with his little brother. When he closed his eyes the image of Danielle shot across his memory like a photograph. A snapshot of her fear. He held that image as he slowed his breathing into measured lengths. *Hang on, baby. I'm coming.*

"DUDE, WE ARE ABOUT TO LAND."

Justin blinked his eyes open and glanced around

the cabin of the aircraft. Jacob, Chief, and the Doc were strapped in across the cargo bay from where he sat. One of the twins, he didn't know which one was which, sat on either side of him.

"So, you're like a thief?" The one on the right asked.

He glared but didn't respond. He wasn't civil when he first woke up, and that shit wasn't helping.

"Seriously, you steal shit, right?"

He groaned and leaned forward, scrubbing his face. He glanced at Jacob. A big ole smile split the man's face. Yeah, Jacob knew exactly what the twins were doing.

"No, I don't steal shit. I'm an information extraction specialist."

"Huh, fancy name for a crook, ain't it, Dixon?"

"Yep. I can list ten names for a thief that aren't that fancy." The one on his left spoke.

"Only ten? I bet we can come up with more. A thief is a thief after all."

"Seriously?" He glared from one to the other. They were never getting reservations at his restaurants. The jerks.

"Oh yeah, let's see. There is mugger."

"Prowler."

"Housebreaker."

"Wait, isn't that like for an affair?" the one on the right asked.

"Nope, that is a homewrecker."

"Oh, yeah, true. What about swindler?"

"Yep and then there is looter, robber, and filcher."

He dropped his head to his hands. He knew they were trying to lighten the atmosphere, but seriously? They were obnoxious pricks…in a little brother type of way.

"Oh, you forgot pickpocket, heister, bandit."

"And cat burglar."

"No, we said that."

"No, we didn't."

"Damn it, Dixon, I know I said that."

"Bullshit," the one Justin assumed was Dixon responded. "We started with thief then we listed and, I might add this is in order because *I* don't forget shit two minutes after it happens: mugger, prowler, housebreaker, swindler, looter, robber, filcher, pickpocket, heister, and cat burglar."

"You forgot bandit," Drake interjected.

At the thud of the aircraft landing gear and the sudden jerk of a full reverse engine stopped their diatribe, or at least Justin assumed it did. Thankfully it was too loud in the cargo hold of the aircraft to hear if they kept going.

He unbuckled his harness as soon as the plane stopped shuddering. He crossed to the bag that contained his equipment and lifted it. Raising his head, he met Jacob's amused look. The bastard. In the future, he was going to ensure O'Malley's was out of 2009 Tor 'Beckstoffer To Kalon - Clone 4' Cabernet Sauvignon every time his brother showed his face.

The ramp opened into nothing but darkness. Several of the men around him, loaded down with packs, headed down the ramp. He adjusted his bag in his hand and followed. They crossed the tarmac with only the strobing lights on the aircraft breaking the perfect black of the night.

"No landing lights for the pilots?" He asked Chief.

"They were on. They are turned off immediately so we can unload without any satellite imagery. If unfriendlies have infrared, we'll be seen as a heat source, but they won't know what we are unloading."

The two black jeeps that had been strapped into the cargo bay roared to life. When they rolled down the back ramp, several packs and his bag went into the rear one. Jacob and the Doctor were in that vehicle, and thankfully, his brother motioned for him to climb in. The twins and Chief were in the other. Jacob got in, put on a pair of night vision goggles and started the engine. As Jacob put the vehicle into gear and pulled away, Justin looked back and caught a glint of moonlight off the other jeep that shadowed their movements.

Doc's arm rested on the front portion of an M4. He knew what the weapon was because Gabriel had forced him to qualify with several different types of guns. He glanced over at his brother armed with three handguns, that he could see, and a knife that would make *Crocodile Dundee* envious. All he had was his brain and his skill. It would be enough. It had to be. He settled into the seat and gazed out the window into the darkness. They had a long drive ahead of them.

CHAPTER 23

*D*ani startled awake, not realizing she'd fallen asleep. She pulled her legs back toward her trying to conserve body heat. She was so cold. Her shoes and coat were gone. The cream-colored wool pencil skirt she wore was filthy and damp. She glanced around her cell noticing for the first time the plastic bucket in the corner. Her mortification didn't stand a chance against her body's needs. She quickly made use of the pail and returned to her corner. She pushed into it even though the cement wall was cold and leached body heat from her. She wrapped her hands around her knees and leaned forward just until her back and shoulders were off the wall. There was a loud shout of laughter outside her door. She heard people out there occasionally. Once, someone pounded on the door and sent her terror spiking, before a laugh echoed and the sound of their footsteps faded away. She dropped her cheek on top of her knees and stared at the side wall.

They wanted something from her dad. Danielle knew him well enough to know he'd give any amount of money to get her back, but if they wanted weapons? She closed her eyes tightly. She'd heard her dad's lecture about weapons falling into the wrong hands. He was a stickler for government regulations and compliance. He would never knowingly allow a criminal to illegally possess one of his weapons. No, if they wanted weapons, she knew he wouldn't pay.

She straightened and shoved more tightly in the corner when footsteps halted outside the door. She blinked as bright light flooded her six by ten cell. A rusty, dented, metal bowl hit the floor along with a plastic bottle of water. Half the food in the bowl fell onto the floor.

"Eat," a man grunted, before the door shut again. Danielle crawled to the center of the room and grabbed the water bottle. She could tell the cap had been opened. She unscrewed the top and sniffed the water. If they wanted to drug her again, it would probably be easiest to do it at meal time. She took a sip of the tepid water and recapped the bottle. If there were drugs in it, she wanted to mitigate the magnitude of the effect. The bowl contained a broth with beans. Danielle balked at the smell. She needed to eat, but she wasn't going to eat that. At least, not today. She pushed back into the corner. It was getting darker. The small window at the very top of her cell no longer illuminated her cement prison. Danielle dropped her head back. She wondered if her father had called Justin or if work had called him when she hadn't shown for her scheduled meetings. How long had she been gone? Where had they taken her? She didn't hear any city sounds, so probably somewhere upstate? Maybe? Wherever it was, it was quiet. No aircraft or vehicle sounds. There was no distant wail of emergency sirens or the erratic punctuation of horns and with a window at street level, it should. No, she was outside New York City, and that wasn't good. She could be anywhere upstate or maybe they took her south towards Virginia? There were a lot of places they could hide her out of sight, fairly secluded areas not more than a long car ride outside of the city.

A quick flash of red caught her attention. She stood and walked over to the far side of the cell.

There it was again. The tiniest flash of red. She got close to the wall and stared through the darkness. A camera. She immediately glanced at the pail. Maybe it wasn't a wide-angle lens. Her captors were watching her. Not that she could escape. The only way out was through the ceiling, and that wasn't an option. The walls were smooth and even though she could free climb proficiently, getting up these walls and being able to work her way into the ceiling was next to impossible. Danielle inspected the corner under the camera. She might be able to crabwalk her way using the side walls as support, but without equipment, she'd fall before she could remove the ceiling tiles and figure a way out. Not only that, but there was a little problem called a camera. Danielle scurried to her corner at the sounds of a person walking. She waited, but the person outside the door lingered. There was no sound for several moments and then she heard the sound of footsteps echoing as they left. A chill of fear ran down her spine. Of all the things she'd been through, that pregnant pause outside her door scared her the most. Why did they stop? Why had they left? What had they wanted? Her mind chased thoughts down terrifying rabbit holes. She wiped away a tear that escaped. She wanted to go home. She wanted to be with Justin. She prayed her father had made the right choice and knew if he did, the right choice wouldn't result in a happy ending for her. At least she'd had happiness for a little while. She closed her eyes and hugged her legs. Justin's chiseled features and dark hair filled her mind's eye. She should have told him she loved him. Tomorrow is never guaranteed. She knew that, and still she hadn't told him her truth. Her mother's maniacal laugh ran through her memories. At least they hadn't said goodbye. She'd cling to that.

JUSTIN CRAWLED up to the edge of the wooded area behind the flat-roofed fortress comprised of smooth forty-foot-plus walls of concrete block covered in beige plaster—typical middle eastern construction. The sun was just starting to set, and he could see the guards walking on the top of the sandstone structure. The walls were smooth without handholds and the moat circled the entire compound. But he didn't care about that. He held Jacob's binoculars and examined the construction and angles of the outside walls. The team had moved as close in as they dared so he could look for a way in. There was only one option and that was a chimney climb. There was a jig in the wall making a three-sided rectangle of the sandstone. If he could reach that jig, he could get up the wall. He'd drape over the top when Jacob gave him the all clear, then the earpiece would be turned off. He didn't need or want help beyond that point. Jacob's team would take their places after he'd cleared the wall and then he'd find a way to neutralize the alarm system. His eyes swept the building one more time. No visible power lines meant a generator or underground power. Both were easy to ascertain and depending on what power source they used, he'd know where to go to nullify the alarm system.

"You can climb that?" Jacob's hand extended asking for the binoculars again.

Justin passed them to him. "Yes. No problem." He wasn't concerned about the climb. He'd make sure his equipment was secure, so it didn't make any noise, and then he'd scale the forty-foot walls.

"How are you going to get across the moat?" Dixon, or Drake, whichever, had bellied up beside them.

Justin pointed toward the far corner. "There is a rock halfway and a log on the other side that I'll use."

"Dude, you do realize the expanse of that jump, right?"

He whipped his head toward whichever twin was talking to him. "I know how to do my job. What about you? How are you crossing the damn moat?"

"Oh, hell, that's easy. When we get your word the alarms are defeated, we take out those four guards and cross the bridge. The gate is opened, and we traverse to the main building, go through the front door, taking out anyone in our way, and then we head downstairs, get the lady and get out. You make your way out while we are inside."

Justin swiveled his head toward Jacob who nodded in agreement. He rolled onto his back and closed his eyes.

"You going to sleep, dude?" That came from the twin on the opposite side.

He shook his head. "Running the blueprints through my mind. I have two possible power sources, and I need to determine the most likely place for the panel to be positioned. If I have a primary, secondary and tertiary location selected for both, I'll find the panel faster."

"That wall is at least fifty feet high." Doc sat with his back against the tree, blocked from view by a large outcropping of branches.

"I'd estimate forty to forty-three feet," He replied.

"Where do you think the power will be?"

"In a compound this size, I'd have a structure to house the incoming electrical and fiber or telephone cables. If the main structure has an UPS, it could be there also."

"A UPS?"

"Uninterrupted power supply or maybe a secondary generator." He kept his eyes closed. He knew what he had to do, and he knew how to do it. The wildcard factors here were numerous. Personnel, power, positioning, type of alarm, type of triggering system, redundancy and most of all, where were they were keeping Danielle.

"Let's pull back. We'll break open some MREs, grab a bite and rest before we begin. We have at least four hours before it's dark enough for you to scale that wall without being seen.

CHAPTER 24

*J*ustin braced himself against a rock in the copse of trees where the team had been earlier. He'd made sure there was no tripping hazard and waited for Jacob to give him the all clear. The guards on top of the wall weren't exactly precise with the time of their patrolling, and it was making it difficult to judge when both would be facing away from the far corner of the wall.

"Go now." Jacob's voice triggered all his pent-up energy. He flew towards the bank and launched himself toward the rock in the middle. His forward momentum landed him on the far side of the outcropping. He hit the rock on the ball of his foot and sprang forward, landing on the dead log. The ground was flat in front of him, so he drove his weight forward and down, onto his hands, where he executed a front flip into a cartwheel and then a forward roll into the shadows of the wall. He pushed his back against the wall and regrouped. Jacob would never let him live that down. He'd added tumbling to his workout routine about ten years ago. It was an extremely effective tactic to keep your forward momentum going while traveling a wide distance quickly.

"Shit son, that was fucking impressive." Jacob's voice in his ear freaked him out for a moment. He made his way down the shadowed recesses of the fortress wall and to the chimney-shaped jig. He switched his backpack around and put his arms through it, so it hugged his chest. Bracing his back against the sandstone, he lifted his legs until he was suspended between the two walls. He slid his arms down and pressed back lifting his back away and up about six inches. His feet followed. Arm press, back up, feet follow. The process repeated over and over until Justin was below the lip of the top of the wall. He was drenched in sweat, and his legs and arms were shaking. He braced himself and waited for Jacob to send the all clear.

"Standby."

Justin got ready to move.

"Now. Go right. The guards are talking to your left."

He flung his left arm over the top of the wall and pulled himself over, dropping to the walkway the guards used. He crouched low and ran across the rampart to a stairway. Justin ghosted down the stairs until he reached the first landing. He pushed into the shadows and observed the inside of the compound. There were old military vehicles and battered pickup trucks. A doorway on the right was open and light spilled into the courtyard. Justin descended the stairs and found the deep shadows behind the trucks. He listened for any indication of a generator. The silence in between the bursts of laughter told him the electric was underground. That meant the panel would be...he reoriented himself. *That way.* He pushed off and made his way to where he would put the exterior alarm panel. The weeds behind the building came up past his knees. He moved slowly, not sure what lay underneath. He used his hand to trace the back of the building. A water pipe. That was a good sign, it meant utilities. But there was no alarm panel or electrical box. The same for his secondary selection. He glanced at his watch. He needed to find that fucking panel. He made his way to the main structure, which was more or less a mini-mansion.

There were no bursts of laughter from the guards this far inside the compound. A soft hue of gold flowed from the windows. He crossed the lawn activating a floodlight on the back of the house. He sprinted across the lawn and slid into a rose bush. The razor-sharp thorns tore at his arms, the thin material of his shirt caught and ripped as did the skin under it. His gloved hand snapped away the branches that dug into his arm. He planted his back against the darkest corner of the exposed wall. Holding still and trying to remain as quiet as possible Justin turned his head to examine the eaves of the house. The floodlights illuminated everything. There were no exposed camera ports. He lowered his gaze and continued the examination of the exterior of the structure. Nothing. The floodlights went dark causing him to close his eyes tightly to try to regain his night vision.

Doubt crept into his mind. There was *no* indication of an alarm system, no state of the art alarms to trigger an armed response because of his move across the lawn. He heard and saw nothing. No guards other than those posted above and the ones in the small outbuilding. He lifted carefully keeping tucked tight to the wall expecting the lights to cascade the yard in illumination again. Nothing happened. He glanced up at the floodlights. The sensor must be facing outward only, nothing below it. He glanced at the window beside him. There was a soft golden hue, but indistinct, as if an interior light was casting through a darkened room. He stepped over the majority of the rosebush and dealt with the jabs and tears of the branches he couldn't avoid while maneuvering himself up to the window.

As he'd anticipated the room was dark, but the light from the hall partially illuminated the interior. He examined the double hung window carefully while still keeping his situational awareness on high alert. There were no wires or balanced magnetic switches that he could see. That could be good, or very bad. If the sash had been drilled and the wires were run through the casing, he wouldn't be able to see them. He glanced at his watch. He had little time to find and deactivate the alarm system before the timeline Greenfield had initiated with the terrorists passed. He closed his eyes briefly and pulled in several breaths while he ran everything through his mind again. He had to go with his gut. There was no alarm system for the house itself, but there could be one in the area where they were holding Danielle.

He weighed the magnitude of his decision. If he set off an alarm now, he and Danielle were dead. If what his gut was telling him was true and there was no alarm, he could get in, deactivate any alarm system to the basement area and get Danielle out without putting Jacob and his team at risk.

He glanced at his watch again. There were only minutes until the deadline passed. The decision made, he pulled out his knife and inserted it between the sashes. He quickly applied a sturdy pressure and the lock released. He pocketed the knife and zipped the pouch closed before he pushed the bottom sash up a fraction of an inch. Nothing. A fraction further. Still nothing. He lifted it two inches and waited thirty seconds. A minute. Nothing. Justin lifted the sash and slipped in. Landing lightly, he visually searched all corners of the room looking for motion detectors. Nothing.

He made his way across the room and studied the dead-end hallway from the open doorway. The doors that lined the hall were open, with only one room being lit from the inside. Justin slid down the door casement and closed his eyes, listening for any sounds. The soft tapping of a keyboard and the low sounds of music emanated from the same lighted area. He stood again, and slipped out of the room, and moved down the hallway where he held at the end. A quick glance back to the lighted space ensured he'd made it without alerting anyone. The continued light tap of keys played like a back note as he studied the flow of the house that he could see. The front foyer and formal living area were to his left. That meant the kitchen would most likely be to the right. He peeked around the corner making sure there was no one in that area before he rounded the corner and headed toward where he hoped the stairs to the basement would be.

A door closed and he ducked into the kitchen. A male voice called out, and the person, a man, in the office responded in one of the few languages Justin didn't know. Naturally. He heard solid, heavy steps coming towards him and then turn off down the hall. He took the opportunity to open the first door in the kitchen. A pantry. The second was a broom closet. The third went into a hallway and towards a formal dining room if the chandelier he could see was any indication. He squatted down. *There had to be a stairway*. His eyes caught on the braided oval rug just to the right of the island. Fuck...maybe? He moved over and pulled the rug toward the island. There it was. A trap door in the floor. He searched the sides of the door. No wires. There were two deadbolt locks. Child's play.

He pulled out his picks. He worked on the lock while debating his next step. If he signaled he was in and the alarms were neutralized, he sentenced four men on top of those walls to death. If he got downstairs and was trapped? He and Danielle were dead. The locks opened with only the small sounds of tumblers turning. He put his picks away and took out the transmitter. He might be a selfish bastard, but Danielle was a victim of these men and their desire for a horrible weapon. He flipped the lid open, pushed the transmit button and, out of habit, pocketed the device. Nothing would remain to indicate he'd been here.

He lifted the rug back over the door and prayed it would lay flat after he went down the steps. Holding the rug to the door, he gripped the door handle and lifted. A low creak and a groan of a spring reverberated through the kitchen. It was probably much louder in Justin's brain, but he froze, waiting to hear if the noise had drawn attention. After several seconds, he pushed it open far enough to start down the steps, bringing the door down after him—slowly and carefully.

Total darkness entombed him. He unzipped a

pouch and produced a small LED light. He flipped the switch and attached the light to a patch of Velcro on his vest. A large pantry area and wine cellar were immediately visible. He cautiously stepped down the ladder-like stairs and took the light off his vest to shine it against the walls. There were two doors. The first one was unlocked and led to a storage room. The second was locked. The light was slapped onto the Velcro, and the lock was picked with proficiency. He examined the door to make sure there were no alarms and then pulled it open. A short hallway led to one door. Justin moved quickly. There was no key lock on the door only a thumb-driven deadbolt. He popped the lock and pushed the door open, slowly.

"Danielle?"

"Justin?"

"Don't move. They have a camera on you."

A small sob punctuated the silence. "I'm so scared."

"I know you are. I need you to be brave for me. I know you're strong enough to do it. I've seen you rappel off buildings and down a gigantic dam. You are training to climb Everest with me. You've got this. Now I need you to get up and walk over to this side of the room." He saw a plastic pail he hadn't seen

on the video feed he'd watched at Guardian Headquarters.

"What if they find you?"

"We are dead, Dani, so you need to do exactly as I
say. Come on now, babe. Get up and walk over here
towards my voice." He could just make out her
movements in the dark. He heard her shuffling to
stand and then the small pads of her bare feet. The
door was still opened only a crack. "Careful now.
Find the wall and use your hands to guide you. Move
to my voice. I want you right up next to the door
before I open it farther. If I open the door too wide,
it will be seen in the video feed." He heard her
getting closer before he felt her against the door.
"Okay, move away from the door about a foot so I
can swing it in. I'm going to ask you to be as tiny and
thin as you can be, so the door doesn't go into the
feed. The infrared will pick it up. That's how they
see you in the dark. It is going to be a tight fit
through the space, but you can do it." he pushed the
door open slightly and then braced it with his foot
and pulled the door handle back towards himself,
keeping pressure on it so it wouldn't swing open if
either of them hit it. He extended his hand to her.
"Take my hand, babe."

*D*anielle reached for the sound of his voice, not really sure if this was real or a dream. She reached out and found him. His gloved hand gripped hers. The feeling of his warm, strong hand supporting her fixed her in reality. Justin really *was* here. Beyond anything she dared to hope, he had come for her. She gripped his hand and squeezed her eyes shut, stifling a sob.

"Okay, come this way."

He tugged on her hand, and she followed. The door was barely open. She squeezed her shoulder through, but the angle of her body against the door blocked any forward progress.

"Wait. If I flip around, I'll be able to squeeze through easier. She let go of his hand and pulled away before she turned and plastered her back against the wall. "Hold the door tight." She waited until he acknowledged her before she used the door as a brace, and squeezed the right half of her upper torso out.

"You're doing great, babe."

She could feel the tension in his arm as he held the door against his foot, not allowing it to move. she pushed through with a gasp of pain. She clutched her right arm to her breast and held the door with her left. She felt the door scrape against her hip, but she was able to move towards Justin, spin her body towards the door and bring the left side through.

She stumbled out past him. The area outside the cell was too dark to know where she was. She groped back and found him.

"Give me a second." A sudden blinding light pierced the darkness. She blinked rapidly trying to get her eyes to adjust. Justin pulled her against him, and she wrapped her arms around him, but whatever he was wearing jabbed her harshly in several places. She pulled back with a hiss of pain. There was a small LED light attached to the shoulder of his black utility vest.

"What..."

"Later. We need to get the hell out of here." Justin grabbed her hand and led her to the base of a ladder. He put his finger to his lips and pointed up. She nodded. He held her hand as he turned off the light on his vest. She heard him pull it off the Velcro and then a small zip. He tugged her hand gently. She stumbled but found the first rung on the ladder. She felt rather than knew they were at the top after about ten upward steps. Justin squeezed her hand, and she returned the pressure. He went still, and she mimicked him although the grooves in the ladder were digging into her bare feet and she longed to shift her weight to alleviate the sharp, biting sensation.

He squeezed her hand again. She heard the complaining of springs and a door open. A very faint illumination filtered down. She could see the outlines of a trap door. Justin sat on the floor as she came up between his legs. He jerked suddenly and put his hand on her shoulder stopping her from lifting out.

Red dots danced on Justin's chest, just above her head. She gasped.

"Motherfucker! Damn it, Justin, we nearly killed your stupid ass. What the fuck are you doing in here? You were supposed to get the fuck out and let us do our job!"

She felt Justin relax. He stood up and extended his hand down to her. "There are no alarms anywhere in this compound." He spoke as she lifted out of the cellar.

She tucked behind him, stupefied by the sight in front of her. Three men. Three M4's with suppressors. The big guy in the middle had two. No. There were three handguns and a bandelier of hand grenades. She shuffled a little farther behind Justin. The types of weapons they carried made them military...or paramilitary.

"What the fuck do you mean there are no alarms?" The big one walked closer, and that is when Danielle saw the resemblance. This had to be one of Justin's brothers. One of the ones he told her worked for a security company. What kind of security company armed their people with military grade weapons?

Justin shook his head. "No alarms, Jacob. Not one. Something isn't adding up."

The man Justin called "Jacob" spun and spoke to one of the men beside him. "Chief, get comms up."

A voice came down the hall. "Structure secure, Skipper."

"Roger that. Standby."

"Comms are up."

A man held out what appeared to be a satellite phone to Jacob, who brought it to his mouth and spoke in clipped words, "Alpha One, we have the primary."

"Affirm. Magus?" The voice at the other end was clear in the still of the room.

"He's secure. Now." Jacob flipped the phone back to the man who had given it to him.

"Fuck you very much, Jacob. I was secure before your ass showed up." Justin shut the door and reached for Dani's hand.

She cocked her head and stared at Justin. She'd never heard him use such vulgar language.

"Yeah, the laser sights trained on your heart told me that, you stupid shit. We could have killed you." Jacob fired the words back at Justin.

"Not likely. You and I both know to identify a target before shooting." Justin headed toward the door and pulled her with him. She whipped her head between the men and hurried to keep her feet as Justin strode ahead. "I thought you didn't like guns?" She didn't know why that of all things came out of her mouth, but it did.

"I fucking hate guns, but I know how to use them.

I was trained by the best." Justin walked into the hallway with her hand firmly grasped in his.

"Where are we?" She glanced at the furnishings. They had a Moroccan feel to them.

"Libya."

"Wait...what?" She half ran to keep up with him. Another massive man stepped out of a hallway. He wore what the rest of the men wore but had an M249 lightweight machine gun—the version her father's company made. She recognized the modified stock. She gasped, and half jumped out of her skin when the man's clone stepped up beside him. Danielle danced to a stop, her feet sliding on the hardwood floors. She jerked at Justin's hand as he headed toward the door. "What is going on? Why are you dressed like this, and that's one of your brothers, right? Do you realize these men are carrying military grade weapons?"

He turned and looked past her to the three men standing in the hallway with them because the man she believed was Justin's brother, the man he referred to as Jacob, had followed them out of the kitchen.

"Chief has the point; Doc is on our six. We need to move." Jacob strode past them and opened the main door a crack. Dani heard a low whistle, and

Jacob opened the door further. He exited the house using tactics she'd seen swat teams use on television documentaries. He rolled out the door, his weapon leveled at his shoulder, and then sank down, low scanning the exterior of the building. "Justin, you and Danielle on my six. Double D, you've got our back. Now move."

Justin stepped out and crouched low, following his brother. His hand clasped hers, and she followed his lead until they reached the gravel. She tried to keep up, but the rocks dug into her feet. Justin paused and looked back. "Shit." He pivoted and dipped down draping her over his shoulder. "Hang on. I'll let you down when we get over the rocks."

Danielle grabbed onto his shoulder and the back of his vest. They moved twenty feet before he dipped forward and placed her on her feet. Jacob halted and held his hand up in the air. Like a rock, Justin dropped to the ground and pulled her with him. Jacob held his ear as if he was listening and then swiveled behind him. He pointed at someone and motioned. Danielle moved her head. She watched the two men trailing them separate and disappear into the darkness. Jacob's whisper traveled the small distance to them. "Incoming. Large caravan. We need to find cover."

"There are several outbuildings on the other side of the vehicles. If we can get to them, we can use them as cover to make a break for the stairs and go over the wall."

"How do you plan to get her down that wall? We'll have to find another way out of the compound."

"I'll get myself down that wall as long as you have a rope long enough." Danielle hissed back. Justin squeezed her hand.

"She can rappel, and she's damn good at it."

Jacob nodded and gave a low whistle. "To the outbuildings by the trucks. Now."

Dani rose off the grass and ran after Justin. A shooting pain lanced the ball of her foot. She stumbled but ran on. Something had cut her, but whatever it was wasn't embedded in her foot. The gravel started again, but Danielle waved off Justin and hobbled through the sharp rocks. By the time they got to the back of one of the buildings, she could feel blood oozing from the bottom of both feet.

Justin pulled her down beside him and made her sit. He stripped the gloves from his hands and carefully fitted them over the toes of her feet. After working each toe into one finger, he pulled the rest of the glove down almost to her heel. He opened his pocket and pulled out a sheet of tape strips. He used them to tape the gloves to the heel of her foot. "It's not perfect, but it will be some help."

"Headlights," Jacob spoke softly to them. "It won't take long for them to realize the guards are down."

"Where's the rope?"

Jacob motioned with his hands again, and a tall man with an eye patch materialized. He kneeled down, and Jacob opened his pack, extracting a rope about fifty-feet long.

"Get up there, get the anchor secured, and get the fuck out of here. I need to be able to concentrate on the shit storm that is going to hit in less than three minutes."

"Give me a gun, I'm trained."

"I know you are. I was briefed, but..." Jacob grabbed Justin. "Take care of your woman, get her the fuck out of here. Take one of the vehicles and get gone. Do you understand me?"

Justin hesitated for a moment.

Danielle's gaze shifted between the two brothers, both warriors, both chiseled out of the experiences of their pasts—different experiences resulting in different scars—but they'd both been through a refining fire. There was a strength in Justin she'd always known was there, but now it was specific and focused.

"Go, get out of here." Jacob spun on his heel and sprinted to a forward position, falling to his knee while he pulled out loaded magazines from his ammo pouch.

Justin grabbed Danielle's hand. The gloves on her feet felt awkward, but the padding helped. She followed him up the stairs and stifled a scream. A man slumped against the wall. Half his head had been blown off.

"Come on." Justin stepped over him, but she jumped, and followed him along the walkway on the top of the wall. "Here." He pointed to an abutment that they could use as an anchor. She held the length of rope as he tied off and tested the knot.

*J*ustin turned from tying the anchor rope just as a swipe of headlights broached the confines of the compound. He took the heavy rope from Danielle and dropped it over the wall. They were shielded from direct vision of the road.

"I need a knife." Danielle held out her hand. He didn't have the time to question her intent, so he handed her his switchblade after he popped it open.

She started splitting her skirt down the front. "I can't climb down in a pencil skirt."

A burst of automatic gunfire flattened them to the ground and served to drive home the danger his brother and Alpha team had willingly put themselves in—for him—and he was supposed to leave them to it? *Bullshit.*

"Get yourself ready to rappel down. I'll be right back." Justin crouched low below the wall and ran back to the man who lay dead at the top of the stairs. He pulled a Russian assault rifle from under the body and grabbed the blood-soaked ammo pouch from the man's belt. He hated weapons, *hated them*, but he'd be damned if he wouldn't help his brother.

Justin locked and loaded the weapon and switched the selector to fire...he hoped. He couldn't read Russian very well. Slipping up over the wall he surveyed the area. He could see Jacob and his men. The enemy was advancing from the flank. That put the twins in between two forces. Justin took aim and let out a breath before he pulled the trigger. His target gave a cry and went down. He terminated three more men before they found his position and started firing at him. Justin ducked below the wall.

Danielle was there directly behind him. Her fingers were busy freeing a fresh magazine from the ammo pouch he'd laid down beside him. "This is an AN-94. Move the selector one more time towards you. It will do two-round rapid fire bursts. You can scatter them quicker."

Justin nodded, flipped the selector and popped

back up over the wall. He managed to clear his clip with the short bursts. He also saw Jacob's team moving forward. They fought as one. It was incredible to see.

A bullet thunked into the wall next to him and he dropped down and hit the extractor button to clear the magazine. Expended brass rolled around him, disturbed by his movement. Danielle handed him a fresh magazine. "Jacob's team is advancing. If I can keep their attention, they'll have a better chance."

Danielle nodded. "Then keep their attention. I don't want to leave them here any more than you do."

His eyes flared at the comment. The woman continued to amaze him. He lifted and identified his target before he fired.

"Justin!" Danielle's scream swung him around. A man in a khaki uniform had her on her knees, her hair fisted in his hands, and a gun pressed to her head.

"Drop the weapon, or she dies." Her captor jammed the barrel hard into the side of Danielle's head.

He could see blood trickle down the side of her face where the skin had already torn, and Justin raised his hands and slowly bent down. The barrel of the gun he held leveled at the man's chest. He'd pull the trigger, but if the bastard jerked, a bullet would kill Danielle.

Justin kept his eyes on the man, his finger on the trigger. He knew without a doubt that as soon as the weapon left his hand, Danielle was dead and so was he.

Justin could see someone approaching from behind. The dark uniform and boots crept up, telling Justin whoever it was didn't want the man holding Danielle to know he was approaching. Justin glanced up and spoke to keep the bastard's attention on him and not on whatever savior happened to be stalking the fucker.

"She's valuable. She's the one you're keeping as blackmail. Kill her and you have no leverage." Justin kept lowering his gun, slowly.

"She's going to die on video—"

Justin watched as the person behind the man reared up, shoved a fist through the crook of his arm and broke the hold he had on Danielle. In one smooth move, the aggressor brought a knife across the man's throat, damn near severing his head. Justin was up and had his weapon pointed at the man with the knife before the dead body dropped to the ground. Danielle scurried on her hands and knees to the wall behind Justin.

"Joseph?" Justin set down his weapon. "What the fuck?"

His brother wiped his knife on his black battle dress uniform and sheathed it. "I didn't get an invite to the party, so I decided to crash it. Not nice to keep us from the fun."

"Us?"

An explosion rocked the front of the compound. Justin twisted in time to see what appeared to be a rocket slam into the rear end of the vehicle convoy parked outside the compound.

Joseph snorted in disgust. "Jared just couldn't keep his mitts off my M72. Get her the fuck out of here. I've got Jacob's back now."

Justin turned and offered his hand to Danielle. Blood still trickled from the gash the bastard had put in her temple.

"You own a light, anti-armor weapon?" Danielle's voice wavered.

A smirk crossed Joseph's face. "She's a keeper. Now go!" He barked the command before he headed down the stairs.

"Come on." They ran back to the rope. Justin pulled an extra set of gloves out of his vest and gave them to her. "Get down. I'll keep watch. When you're on land, I'll drop the weapon to you."

"Got it." She pulled on the gloves and wrapped her split skirt around the thigh she was winding the rope around. Without a second glance, she stood on the wall and let herself drop. Justin thanked God they'd done the rappel off the building under construction. She continued down, slow and steady. He kept her in sight while making sure nobody else was on the wall. The weapon fire behind him was hot and heavy. One more explosion ripped through the night air. Dani reached the bottom and uncoiled. He unloaded the weapon, dropped the magazine first and then the rifle, knowing if he dropped it loaded, it could fire when it struck the ground. He wrapped the rope around him and dropped. Heat from the rope sliding through his hands tore at the skin on his palms, but he dropped as quickly as he could without losing control. When he reached the ground, the skin on the palms of his hand was gone. It was a small price to pay. Danielle held the gun and focused her aim on the top of the wall.

Justin grabbed the weapon from her and nodded toward the deadfall tree. "Leap from the log to the rock in the middle to the ground on the other side. You'll need a running start. Use the log as a catapult and let your momentum carry you through the jump when you hit the rock."

Danielle nodded and backed up to the wall. She studied the jump for several moments. A loud exchange of gunfire triggered her flight, and she took off, the gloves on her feet slapping the ground as she ran. He held his breath as she used the log to launch. Her skirt flew up and away from her legs as she stretched to reach the rock and sprang to the ground. She hit the bank and rolled forward through the dirt. Justin swung the rifle strap across his chest and situated the gun on his back so it wouldn't impede his run. He drew a deep breath and bolted. The log shifted as he punched up. He landed on the rock and literally threw himself forward. He landed half in and half out of the water. He scrambled forward to his feet.

"Are you alright?" Danielle was beside him within seconds.

"Wet, but fine. This way." He grabbed her hand and led her to through bushes and trees towards where they'd left the Jeeps.

Behind them, the sounds of gunfire became sporadic. Justin moved through the underbrush carefully, trying to pick the flattest route. Even though Danielle wasn't complaining, her feet had to be sliced to shreds. A metal on metal noise from near where the Jeeps were parked reached them. He lifted a hand and dropped down, feeling her lower herself beside him. He turned, handed her the gun and whispered, "Stay here," before he moved forward through the brush, soundlessly making his way forward.

In the moonlight, he could see a figure on the far side of the vehicles. Justin crouched waiting. A shuffle of underbrush behind him and a small hand on his shoulder startled the fuck out of him.

"You don't listen." He pulled her into him and pushed the brush back down allowing her to see.

"That's a woman," Danielle whispered to him. Justin whipped his head toward the vehicles. Fuck, a woman. He reached out and grabbed the stock of the Russian rifle. "Wait." Danielle hissed and pointed to Justin's left, toward the compound. A male figure pushed through the brush.

"Well, that took fucking long enough. What the hell am I doing by the Jeeps? I thought I was going to see some action." Jade's pissed off voice rang clear and true through the night.

"They aren't back yet?" Jared ripped off the question.

"Do you think I'd still fucking be here if they

were back? Lord above, did you fire your brains out of that damn rocket launcher?"

Justin chuckled at the snark in Jade's voice, then stood up in the brush and helped Danielle to stand.

"Jacob said he sent them over the wall, but Justin was laying down suppression fire so Alpha team could advance. Fuck, I need to go back. Someone could have..."

"We're here," Justin said as he stepped through the last two feet of brambles and branches, pulling the larger ones away from Danielle as she followed.

"Shit, dude. You've got some explaining to do. What the fuck happened in that compound?" Jared reached for him and pulled him into a hug.

Justin instinctively slapped his back only to be reminded of the abused flesh on his palms. He was tackle hugged by Jade. "Damn it, Justin, can't you follow orders?"

"Ah...no. Can you?"

He pulled away from his sister and watched as her mouth opened and then closed several times. "Well, no, but I'm the one who breaks all the rules. Not you."

"I beg to differ," Danielle spoke from beside him.

"Oh, you got stories to tell about this bad boy?" Jade popped on the LED light on her tac vest and drew in a harsh hissed breath. "Damn it, you two are tore the fuck up. Dani, what the hell is on your feet?"

"Umm...gloves, tape and a lot of blood." She stood with her ankles bowed, all weight transferred to the outsides of her feet.

Fuck, Justin had no idea her feet were so bad. She hadn't complained, not once. He reached down and picked her up, cradling her next to his chest. "Why didn't you say something?" He moved toward the vehicles with Jade sprinting in front of him to open the back passenger door.

"Like what? Please stop saving my life so I can cry about my boo-boos?" Dani scooted back into the seat he placed her on and pulled what was left of her tattered skirt over her lap.

"I could have carried you on my back." Justin reached down to take off the tape on her feet.

"What the hell, Justin? What the fuck happened to your hands?" Jade pointed a flashlight at his palms. The blood and stripped skin rivaled the damage Dani had done to her feet.

"He rapid rappelled off a forty-foot wall without gloves. He gave his second pair to me." Danielle lifted her hands, the gloves were still on.

"Well, damn. You're tougher than I gave you credit for, pretty boy." Jade slapped the flashlight onto the floorboard. "I'm going to get some water and the first aid kit to clean those wounds."

Justin caught Jared's eye. "Why are you two here? And Joseph?"

"It's a long story."

Both of them spun at the sound of brush crunching. Justin grabbed the Russian rifle at the same time Jared lifted his M4. Jade was beside them in an instant, her own weapon raised and ready.

"Don't shoot, it's the cavalry."

"The cavalry had horses, Drake. I don't have no fucking horse. I guess they have tanks and such now-a-days, and I sure as hell don't have no tank." Dixon spouted off from somewhere behind Jacob and Joseph as they emerged from the foliage.

"They were dragoon regiments before they were designated as cavalry and they didn't have horses then." Drake fired back.

"Dude, you didn't say, 'Don't shoot, it's the dragoons,' did you? No. You didn't." The twins went to the other vehicle and started loading their packs into the back.

"Can the chit-chat. Let's get out of here. We have a plane to catch." Jacob's order sent his men into action. Hands on hips, he directed a steady look at

Joseph. "I take it you, Jared, and Jade are flying home with us?"

"That's the plan." Joseph leaned against the front end of the Jeep. He nodded towards Justin. "That boy has balls. He did well."

Justin blinked in astonishment at his older brother. It wasn't often Joseph talked and even less often that he gave anyone a compliment. He dipped his head in acknowledgment.

"I concur. He has stones the size of coconuts. Let's move this to the airfield. Doc can take a look at your injuries when we get airborne." Jacob slid into the driver's seat. Justin ended up holding Dani in his lap on the passenger side. Jared, Jade and Chief crowded into the back seat. Dixon, Drake, Doc, and Joseph bounced after them in the other vehicle. Once again, Jacob used his night vision goggles to navigate the almost-there road.

Danielle snuggled against him, her face tucked against his neck. She held onto his vest as they jolted down the road. "When we get to the plane, I have *a lot* of questions."

Justin hummed an agreement to her exhausted whisper and held her, relishing the feeling of having her in his arms again.

CHAPTER 26

*D*ani didn't fight the exhaustion that pulled at her. She let it consume her and trusted in the man holding her to keep her safe. Jolting awake minutes or hours later, strong arms comforted her, and her lover's voice at her ear calmed her racing heart.

"It's okay, we're pulling up to the aircraft. I'll carry you on board."

The vehicle emptied rapidly. Justin opened his door and carefully maneuvered them out. She would have objected, but exhaustion and whatever rush of adrenaline sustained her during the escape from the compound had drained away. Besides, her feet *hurt*. She held onto his neck as he climbed the ramp leading into the back of the military-style aircraft.

The inside was the size of a small warehouse, and when the Jeeps were pulled in after them, she understood why.

"Here you go." Justin sat her down in a seat made of nylon straps. He kneeled at her feet and cupped her chin, keeping eye contact with her. "As soon as Doc looks at your injuries and we get some water and food into you, I'll explain everything. But first, we'll be taking off. Let me tell you from experience, you need to be strapped in."

She could see a hesitancy in him as he moved around her. It was foreign and unexpected. Dani caught his wrist as he used his fingertips to pull the harness over her shoulder. "Hey." He kept his head down for a moment before he lifted his eyes to hers. "What happened doesn't change anything. I'm not sure what is going on...why this happened to me, but none of this changes how I feel about you." She saw the moment her words registered. The light in his soul that had dimmed, flared, and he smiled that slow, sexy smile that had trapped so many women in the past. She lifted his hand and twisted his wrist bringing his raw palm up. She kissed a spot on his thumb that wasn't injured and whispered, "I love you."

He leaned in, so their foreheads were pressed

together. He lifted his damaged hands and ran his fingertips down the sides of her face. His touch elicited a full body shudder. He drew a shaking breath. She could sense the emotion that ran through him. He whispered just loud enough that she could hear him, "You saw the real me, and you smiled. No one has ever done that. You looked past the wealth and the status, and you found me." He moved a few inches away, he glanced right and left making sure they were alone. "No one knows me. I've kept everyone away. My family has no idea who I really am. I'm an illusion to them. But, you…" his voice thickened and he swallowed once, "…you *saw* me. How can I not be completely lost in my love for you?" A tear slipped from his eye, blazing a slow path through the dirt and blood on his face.

Dani's heart swelled so big she felt like it was going to burst through her body. This sleek, debonair man who wore ten-thousand-dollar suits, and managed a multi-national company had laid his soul bare for her to see. She reached out and traced the tear with her finger. "Even if God were to take my eyes this minute, I would always see the man you are inside of the illusion." She leaned forward and pressed her lips against his.

The emotion that flowed through them was a

physical reaction of two unique persons combining to find in each other the perfect fit. Love consumed them, bound them together and made them both stronger together than they'd been alone.

"Yo, I kinda hate to break this up, but if you don't buckle up, your ass is going to be plastered against the back ramp." Jacob walked past as he spoke and slapped Justin on the shoulder.

Justin dropped his head and shook it.

"You've got an interesting family dynamic going on here." Danielle put her other arm through the harness and tried to figure out the buckling system.

"Here, let me." Justin used his fingers to bring the clasps together. "My brothers are...unique."

"More unique than Jade?" Danielle asked as he sat down beside her.

"Ahh...well, unique in a completely opposite way. Jade's just batshit crazy."

"Hey! I heard that!" Jade punched forward in her harness three seats down. Her hair flew forward at the movement. "I'm not crazy! Guardian has me tested! Once a year!"

Danielle blinked at Justin's sister.

The cabin was still for several seconds until laughter spilled into the hold of the aircraft. The engines roared, and the plane lurched forward sending her sideways into Justin who had just buckled his own harness. Dani tilted her head, laying it on Justin's shoulder. Her arm linked with his as the plane picked up speed. Goodness, she'd never flown in a transport plane before. The lurching and jarring as the aircraft raced down the runway was fifty times that of a passenger plane. She gritted her teeth and literally squealed as the aircraft shot up. Like, straight up! Not a moderate climb.

"It will level out in a minute," Justin yelled over the engine noise.

Dani grabbed his arm. "What is this? A rocket?" She yelled the question back to him. He grinned and winked. What kind of answer was that?

The aircraft banked suddenly and within a minute, leveled off. The red light that had been casting a glow over the cargo space blinked out, and a pale-yellow light appeared. As one person, everyone unbuckled their harnesses and started moving. Dani didn't. There was no way she was taking the harness off. One rocket ride was enough for her, thank you very much.

A blonde man with an eyepatch came across the bay. He carried a canvas backpack. "Hey, I'm Doctor Adam Cassidy. May I look at your injuries?" He knelt at her feet but didn't move to touch her.

She glanced at Justin who winked at her. Danielle turned her attention back to the doctor. "I'm sure it's just a bunch of small cuts."

"I understand, but we don't know what cut you or if any of the lacerations need stitching. The foot takes all the weight of the body, and you don't want a wound to keep breaking open. Plus, you could've gotten dirt or foreign bodies embedded that could cause infection. When was your last tetanus shot?"

"Ummm...maybe high school?" Dani pulled her bottom lip between her teeth when the doctor gently lifted her foot and sat the heel on his thigh.

"Then, I'm going to recommend you let me give you that immunization, just to be safe. May I?" He nodded toward the gloved foot perched on his leg. She nodded and watched as he peeled the tape from around the wrist portion of the glove. He carefully cut the glove off the top of her foot. The material stuck to the sole of her foot. He pulled a small basin out of the backpack and opened a sealed bottle of water, pouring some into it before lowering her foot to soak. He repeated the process on the second foot and also placed it in the water. "We'll let that work to loosen the material for a couple minutes. You have quite a few scrapes and scratches." He motioned toward her arms and legs.

"The branches were brutal." She sighed. The mere mention of the injuries seemed to remind her body that she hurt.

"I don't want to be forward." He glanced up at Justin and motioned for him to squat down beside him. "I can see what appears to be a nasty rope burn on your thigh."

Justin blinked and moved the largest piece of her skirt that still clung to the waistband. "Damn it."

Danielle blinked at the comment. It wasn't like Justin to swear. She knew the rope had chaffed her skin, but she wasn't going to cry about it. She looked down and held the skirt to the top of her thighs, providing some semblance of privacy as she pulled the material away from her sore thigh.

"This is nothing compared to his hands." Dani pushed the filthy wool back over her legs. With her feet in water and her clothes in tatters, she was starting to get cold.

"I've asked Jade to set up an area over there for you to wash. You'll have to remain seated while you do it, so your feet don't get wet again. I want you to get as clean as possible. Then we'll attack those scrapes with some antibacterial cream."

The doctor turned towards Justin. "Let me see them." His tone was nowhere near as kind as when he talked to Danielle. Justin flipped his hands over, and the doctor shook his head.

"Alright. Sit your ass down." He pointed to the netted seat next to Dani. More sterile water was poured into another basin. He set it on Justin's lap and nodded at the plastic tray. Justin dunked his hands down and winced.

"Since we have a minute, would you please tell me what happened?" She rolled her head toward Justin.

He drew a deep breath and locked his stare with hers. "I couldn't reach you." He shrugged. "It wasn't like you, and I got worried. When Max told me that you'd missed two meetings without calling in, I freaked. I tried to get your father, but my call went to voicemail. By that time, I was at the airport, and I'd already called my brother."

Danielle examined his three brothers across the bay who were huddled in conversation. "Which one?"

Justin followed her glance. "None of them." She raised her eyebrows and turned back to him. "My brother Jason is the CEO of Guardian International. Jacob," he pointed to the man on the right wearing the arsenal of weaponry, "is in charge of international operations. Jared, the one in the middle, is the CEO of Domestic Operations and Joseph, the one on the left, well, I'm not sure what he does anymore, but I think he used to work with Jacob. Jade is now one of the people in charge of the Personal Security contingent Guardian has under Domestic Operations. My sister Jewell is in charge of the cybersecurity element. Her fiancé works for Guardian as well. Jasmine is the only one who no longer works for the company."

Dani dropped her eyes and watched the doctor as he tended to her feet. There were several deep lacerations.

He looked up. "Don't worry, it gets easier."

"The cuts?" Danielle was confused as to how it would get easier, because what he was doing stung.

He laughed and lifted her foot, examining the arch. "No, figuring out who is who and what they do."

"What do *you* do?" Dani asked on reflex.

"Well, I'm the Chief Medical Officer at a complex Guardian runs in South Dakota."

Danielle swung her attention to Justin. "Where your mom lives?"

"Yes." Justin didn't lift his eyes from what the doctor was doing to her feet.

"So, she's Guardian?" Dani glanced back down at the doctor.

The doctor looked up briefly with a smile. "No, she's married to Frank Marshall. He owns the ranch where the complex is located. Frank is my wife's father. Jacob," the doctor, nodded at the walking arsenal, "Is married to my wife's sister."

"Frank's daughters?" She glanced at Justin. "So, your brother is married to your mom's husband's daughter? He's married to his step-sister?"

Justin's brow furrowed. "Technically, but Jacob and Tori were married before Frank and Mom married. So, it isn't the way it sounds."

Danielle snorted. "It *sounds* complicated." She leaned against him and plodded through the information dump. She blinked and slid up, so she could turn and look at Justin. "You said Jasmine was the only sibling not working for Guardian."

He nodded.

She pointed a finger at him."That means *yo*u work for Guardian."

"I do."

"And how exactly does that work? You work more hours at JK Holdings than any other person on your staff. When do you find time to work for Guardian?"

Justin moved in his seat, sloshing the water in the basin.

The doctor looked up at him and lifted an eyebrow. "I'd love to know the same thing."

Justin shot the doctor a look that could kill and cleared his throat.

Dani glanced around and noticed all of the people in the cargo hold were standing nearby in a loose semi-circle. He shrugged. "Remember how I told you I got into some trouble and went to jail while I was in college?"

Dani didn't get the chance to acknowledge his words before Jade let loose with a peel of laughter. "Holy Shit! Perfect Justin has a criminal record!"

"No, I don't, brat." Justin drew a breath and slumped into his chair. "Gabriel cleared my record. I was caught breaking and entering a building downtown. I'd managed to deactivate the alarm systems, but some nosey old woman walking her rat of a dog saw me entering. She called the cops. They arrested me for trespassing because they couldn't prove I'd deactivated the alarm. Gabriel showed up and took me back to the dorm. He gave me an ultimatum. I chose to go to work with him. I couldn't face the alternative."

"Juvenile detention?" Dani asked.

"Juvie? No." He appealed to his family. "He was going to tell *Mom*." Several of his brothers visibly winced. "Anyway, Gabriel found the best locksmiths and alarm systems engineers for me apprentice under. I worked learning my trade while I was on summer vacation, and when I had downtime. In return, he got me access to the finest chefs, sommeliers, and restaurateurs in the business. I worked my ass off to be the best at both careers."

"So, the restaurants are a smoke screen?" The brother she thought was Jared asked.

"No, that is my passion. I love it. What I do for Guardian happens once, maybe twice a year, sometimes more, but it isn't frequent. Working for Jason gives me another type of release, I guess. It is a rush. Pure and simple. I live for the rush."

He finally glanced at Dani. She smiled at him and winked, needing him to know that she was more than okay with his need for adrenaline. "That's why Guardian sent you to help rescue me? To break into the compound?" The doctor was wrapping her feet in a dry gauze bandage.

"Yes, except there were no alarms." Justin looked up at Jacob, who cast a glance at the dark, brooding brother, the one who'd stopped that madman from killing both her and Justin. Joseph...maybe?

Tall, dark and broody nodded and glanced around the semi-circle before he looked directly at Justin. "Jason couldn't send you without a verifiable need. Each of us, with the exception of Double D over there, have been where you were. Stopping you from coming on this operation wasn't an option. You needed to be here for your woman."

"How did you three get here?" Justin motioned to him, Jared and Jade.

"Low-level drop." Joseph shrugged as if it were nothing.

"Hell, yes! It was awesome!" Jade let out a whoop of joy.

"Never fucking happening again!" Jared spat the words out and was immediately pelted with catcalls and laughter.

"Okay, the next question is why *are* you here?" Justin looked and sounded perplexed.

"Because you're family, dickhead. No matter how far you push us away. You're family," Jared said and then looked from Justin to Joseph. Joseph raised a single eyebrow and stared at his brother, not flinching or giving an inch. Jared finally glanced back to Justin. Dani assumed there were all sorts of words being exchanged that weren't spoken aloud, but shifted her attention from the testosterone laden battle of wills in front of her when the doctor patted her leg and moved to tend Justin's hands. "But why Libya? I mean I was in a cab, then the man who'd been following me—"

"Excuse me?" Justin cut her off.

"Remember that older gentleman from the lodge? The one I thought I'd seen in Perth? He was the one driving the cab. After I woke up, I figured I was taken for ransom because of what he said. But for what? God...how is my dad?"

Jacob scratched his jaw and glanced at Jared. Dani saw the subtle shake of the man's head. Jacob dropped his hand and laid it on his automatic. Almost as if he was reassuring himself it was still there. "Your dad was working with another security company trying to figure out how to get you back. When Justin got us involved, we pulled the 'national security' card and sent the other players packing. If I had to guess, he is still at Guardian waiting for word we are on approach before he hightails it to the flight line. I might add that we were all impressed with his integrity. Jewell ran a microscope up his company's ass. He runs a tight ship. Something we all appreciate."

Dani nodded, but when no more information

was forthcoming she asked, "Why was I drugged and taken to Libya?"

"You were being held by a terrorist organization. We aren't sure of the connections or how they knew your father had a new weapon. They wanted him to surrender the armament his people developed. If it fell into the wrong hands, it could be devastating on several levels," Justin answered, without looking at his brothers for permission.

"Which weapon?" Dani racked her brain trying to think of which R&D project that a terrorist group would want enough to kidnap her. Not that she knew all the projects.

Justin shrugged. "Does it matter?" Dani heard the inflection change in Justin's voice. It was minuscule, but it was there. He'd been forced to violate his beliefs today. The man hated weapons, and yet he picked up that assault rifle and protected his brother's team and her.

Jade held out her hand. "Danielle, if you'll follow me I'll take you to where you can clean up. We've scrounged up some clothes. They won't fit. These assholes are massive, but at least they brought extras."

Danielle glanced at Justin again. He gave her a small smile and nodded for her to follow Jade. She lifted up and grasped Jade's hand. She had to. The needles shooting through the bottom of her feet made her gasp. Justin lurched toward her, almost knocking the doctor on his ass.

Jared stepped forward and swept her off her feet. "Let me carry you. Justin can give you a ride back when his hands are bandaged and taped."

She glanced at Justin. She could see his desire to be the one to help her, but he needed his own injuries tended. Danielle blushed at being held by one of his brothers but thanked him because, alone, she wouldn't have made it across the metal plating to the corner Jade had sectioned off.

"Here. Take this. It will ease the pain." Doc shook out two tablets. "By the time you get back, you'll be feeling better."

Danielle popped the pills and took a drink from the bottle of water someone thrust in front of her. Jared carried her across the metal plating. It was rigid and had holes in it. She grimaced at the thought of walking across it. He gently set her down on a hard, black, plastic box. "Thank you...for every-thing." She smiled up at him.

"There is nothing I wouldn't do for him, or for you. It is what family does."

Dani blinked and shook her head. "I wouldn't know. It is just my dad and me."

"Well, get used to too many people in your business. They mean well, but...you know...brothers," Jade snarked as she approached with three liter size bottles of water and an armful of material.

"I'll take that as my cue to leave." Jared stood and turned. He smiled at Jade. "We are the best brothers in the world."

"Yeah, yeah. Get yourself out of here so she can get cleaned up." Jade winked at Danielle as she closed off the blanketed portion of the corner. "Okay my new BFF, time to get you out of those rags and cleaned up. I hope you're not bashful."

Dani glanced at the blanket and back toward Jade. "I lost bashful when I had to pee in a bucket in a terrorist jail cell."

"Oh hell, woman, you and I are going to get along just fine." Jade threw down the clothes on another plastic box and set down the water bottles. Dani started taking off the shredded material she still wore. She knew without a doubt she'd get along with all of Justin's family, because they loved Justin. No matter how crazy or unique they were, she'd love them in return.

CHAPTER 27

*J*ustin flexed his hands. After cleaning his raw skin, Doc had applied some ointment, lined his palms with non-stick pads before adding several layers of gauze to cushion the area and taping it all in place.

He glanced over at the corner of the cargo bay.

Jacob sat down next to him."She'll be fine. Let Jade help her."

Justin nodded and glanced at his brother before his eyes glued back on the blanket wall. "Did you know there wasn't an alarm system?"

"Officially? I wouldn't have allowed you to come if there hadn't been documentation of an alarm system." Jacob leaned forward placing his elbows on his knees. "Unofficially? Falsifying the report was foolish and fucking irresponsible on both our parts, but..." he dropped his head between his shoulders and laughed, "...Jason and I would be damned if we would stop you from coming."

"Why? I thought you guys lived and died 'by the book'." He needed to know.

"Because Tori and I met when I sprung her from a warlord's prison cell. She'd been tortured for months. She was nearly dead, but that woman ended up saving my life, literally and figuratively. Joseph saved Ember from a cartel assassin. I can't go into specifics, but the man walked through the darkness of hell on a daily basis. Ember brought Joseph back to the light for us. Faith was damn near blown up and nearly killed in two separate events, but she rescued Jason from his own demons. Hell, Christian was nearly incinerated. Jared damn near went insane at the hospital after he'd pulled his man from that fire. The common factor in all of those events? We didn't rescue them. The people we love saved us. Danielle is your salvation. Every last one of us can see it as clearly as crayon written on the wall. It would have killed you to stay in that damn theater."

Justin nodded as he remembered the feeling of worthlessness and self-contempt that had washed over him when the plans were laid out for the rescue mission and he was excluded. God, he never wanted to feel so inadequate ever again.

"So, you're a good thief?" Jacob nudged him with his elbow bringing a smile to Justin's face.

"Information extraction specialist, and yes, I'm one of the best." Hell, in his mind he *was* the best, but why give his brother any fodder?

Jacob cocked his head, and a wicked smile spread across his face. "You can pick locks?"

Justin snorted with disdain at the comment. "Amateur hour."

"Awesome! Tori has this jewelry box of her mother's that has been locked since her mom died. The people we've taken it to say that there would be damage to the box if they tried to open it. It is the only thing of her mom's she has, and damaging it isn't an option. Could you? I mean, it would mean the world to her if you'd try."

Justin nodded. "I can do that."

"You realize you'd actually have to come to our home. You know, see the boys, too. They miss you as much as Tori and I do." Jacob stared at him sending a spear of guilt straight through Justin's heart. He could see the absolute sincerity in Jacob's expression.

"I'll be there. I'll try to do better." He'd try. Maybe

with Danielle's help, he could learn to let his family get closer.

"Why do you block us out of your life?" Fuck. Jacob was like a dog with a rare piece of prime steak that he wasn't going to let go.

Justin shrugged and focused on the blanket in the corner of the room. "My therapist said it was to prevent myself from being hurt. I don't know if I buy that. I think at first that may have been the case. Then it became a way to hide who I've become. For so long there was nothing in my life but work. I had absolutely no time for family. Hell, I didn't have time for myself. I worked for Gabriel and for my company. When I'd achieved a bit of success at both my jobs, I moved into extreme sports. I'm an adrenaline junkie. I always have been. After that, I moved through life looking for the next big thrill. Family became a distant third to work and play." Justin leaned forward and examined his shoes. "Being lost doesn't have a common face. It doesn't look the same on one person as it does another. I was lost. Until I took a chance on Danielle."

"She's the one," Jacob stated.

"Yes. She is." Justin threw a glance at the blanket. "She was my coworker and that somehow morphed into being my friend. Hell, she's my only friend."

"Hey!" Jacob objected.

Justin smiled. He and Jacob used to be close. He acknowledged that, but time and maturity had frayed that connection. Justin needed to work on repairing it. He didn't know how, or if he could, but he knew he wanted to try. "You know what I mean." Jacob nodded, and Justin continued, "We fell into an easy routine. She's always been there for me, even though it wasn't her job. We decided to explore the connection, but before we could go on a date, I saw her rappel off Gordon Dam in Tasmania." Justin smiled and closed his eyes recalling the memory of her descent. "I knew at that moment, she was the woman for me."

"Why, because she's insane?"

Jacob sent the barb with a laugh, but Justin shook his head and in complete seriousness responded, "No, because when I hit the bottom of that rappel, she saw *my* insanity and embraced it. She saw me. The real me. Not the image the family has of me. Not the image I portray in the business world. She witnessed what and who I am, and she accepted it." Justin leaned back and shrugged.

Jacob leaned back with him. "We all need that one person. I'm glad you found her. I'm happy for you."

The blanket pushed back, and Justin hopped to

his feet as if he'd been spring loaded. Several rushed steps later and he was kneeling at her side. "Hey, you look great in that black uniform."

Danielle chuckled and picked at the shoulder of the black t-shirt she wore. "Oh, this old thing? I just threw it together."

Jade chuckled as she picked up Danielle's old clothes and the empty water bottles. "I'll go tell Doc there weren't any deep scratches. I'm sure Justin will take care of anything else you need."

Dani reached out and grabbed Jade's hand. "Thank you. For everything."

His sister paused, swallowed hard and nodded. She spun on her heel and exited quickly. "She likes you. She doesn't like many people." Justin pushed her hair behind her ear as he examined her, making sure Jade was right and that there were no deep lacerations that he could see.

"HEY." Danielle put her hand under his chin and drew his eyes up to hers. A soft smile spread a happy glow around her. "I'm sorry you had to use the rifle today."

Justin sat back on his heels, stunned at her perception. "I'd do it again. To save you and them," he motioned back toward the cargo hold of the plane, "I'd do it again."

She reached out and ran a finger over his jaw. "I know you would, and I don't know if I could love you any more than I do right now. But remember, I see you. Using that rifle today cost you. I know the price you paid, even if they don't."

Justin dropped his head and leaned into her, his head rested on her lap. He closed his eyes and felt her fingers run through his hair. The emotions her words unlocked rolled through him. "Thank you."

Deep down, he needed someone to acknowledge the fact he'd broken every moral compass point he'd set for himself. That Danielle was the one to know and recognize it proved again how much this woman meant to him. His heart dropped off a cliff and landed into her hands. *She* was the key to his happiness. Not the business, not the work for Guardian, and not the extreme thrills, because there was no better thrill than being with her in a single moment in time.

CHAPTER 28

*D*anielle wasn't quite sure what she expected when they landed, but it wasn't the smooth gliding touchdown. "Wow, that was way better than the takeoff."

Jacob laughed as he unbuckled his belt. "Well, when you're not in hostile airspace, you can afford to have smooth landings and takeoffs."

Dani cocked her head at him and narrowed her eyes. "You know what? I'll leave those experiences to you. I'm pretty much done with all of this."

Justin laughed as he stood and stretched. "I would hope so."

"Keep saying that. I swore off it years ago, and I still get roped into doing shit like low-level drops into hot landing zones." Jared threw his comment into the conversation as he walked by.

"You loved it. Admit it." Jade stood and reached to the ceiling stretching. "Good grief, Jacob, get decent seats in these damn planes, would you?" She rubbed the small of her back and groaned, arching into the pressure of her hands.

"Yeah, I'll get right on that." Jacob rolled his eyes and made a hand gesture sending his team into a flurry of activity.

Danielle longed to stand and stretch, but her feet weren't going to allow it. Joseph walked to the back ramp and opened a large box. He flipped a lever seconds before the back ramp started to drop. As the ramp opened, he jumped off the aircraft and walked away. Danielle glanced from him to Justin who watched his brother leave. "He's not very social, is he?"

"He's come a long way, actually."

Justin's words were nearly extinguished by her father's shout. "Danielle?"

She leaned forward, still strapped in her jump seat. "Here!"

She grasped at the clip, but Justin's fingers beat her to it. She shouldered off the harness as her father slid to a stop in front of her. He enveloped her in a crushing hug.

"Oh, my God. I thought I lost you."

"I'm okay. I'm here." Danielle coveted the display of emotion. She absorbed her father's embrace and whispered words.

"I had no idea how to get you back." He pulled away and cupped her face in his hands. "My God, what would I have done if I lost you?" He pulled her into another hug.

"You couldn't have lost me, dad. We didn't say it." Her tears streamed down her cheeks, but her comment made her father laugh.

"I'll never be ready to say it." He sat back and swiped at his own tears. "Are you hurt?" He ran his eyes over her, landing on the huge black socks that covered her feet. The fact that they were bandaged under the socks were obvious.

"Cuts and bruises. My feet are tender." Danielle mentally rolled her eyes at the understatement. "Justin and his family." She waved at the men who were working to release the straps from equipment. "Jacob's team. They got me out."

"And it was all my fault." Her father's voice cracked.

The crestfallen expression that overtook his face

planted a worry deep inside her. "Really? Did you hire that man to kidnap me? Did you tell them to fly me to Libya? Because if you did, Dad, we need to work on the hotel accommodations."

He looked up at her bewildered. "You aren't responsible for what happened any more than I am. I'm assuming the man you suspected was the leak?"

He shook his head. "I don't know. I turned everything I had, and everything you'd dug up, over to Guardian. I haven't been to the office or taken a call since they brought me here to D.C." He drew a deep breath and scrubbed his face with his hands. "I suppose I should tend to those matters."

"I think you need to rest first." Dani put that comment out there. He looked as if he hadn't slept in days, and probably hadn't.

He smiled. "I'll rest when I get you home."

Dani knew her eyes popped open to the size of silver dollars. "Umm..."

"I'll be taking her home, sir." Justin's tone left no room for argument.

"Really?" He slid his gaze from Justin to Danielle. "Just how serious is this?"

"As serious as it gets," Justin responded for her.

Danielle smiled up at the man she loved. "I love

him. He loves me." She swung her eyes to her dad. "I agree. This is as serious as it gets."

Her father stared at her for several long seconds before he spoke, "Cherish every moment you have together. Don't let this slip through your fingers." He stood, the ramrod straight posture he'd usually carried returned as he glanced around the aircraft. He spoke so everyone could hear him, "Thank you for what you did. For what you risked to bring my daughter home. I am forever in your debt. If any of you need anything, for any reason, ask, and it's yours." Danielle watched him as he went around the hold of the aircraft and shook each person's hand. He made his way back to Justin and held out his hand. "She's my daughter."

Justin took his hand and shook it. "Yes, sir." They stared at each other for several long moments before her father nodded his head and dropped Justin's hand.

"Dinner. Tuesday night." He nodded toward Justin. "You can bring him." He pivoted on his heel and walked out of the aircraft passing a behemoth of a man in an expensive tailor-made suit and a person she recognized, Jewell.

"Justin." The man extended his hand and then pulled Justin into a bear hug that would have broken every bone in Danielle's body. She gazed, wide-eyed, at Jewell who sat down beside her.

"That's Jason." Jewell tossed the words out as if they explained everything. Danielle pulled at the bits of conversation where Jason was mentioned. She whispered, "CEO?"

"Yup." Jewell acknowledged.

Jason finally let Justin go after several murmured comments between them. He twisted and faced her. "Danielle, I presume?"

Dani shook her head. "No."

The look of shock on his face was worth the effort it took to keep the smile off her face. Justin's and Jewell's laughter caught everyone's attention. Jason took off his glasses and pinched his nose while he shook his head. When Jewell managed to quell her laughter, she repeated Danielle's comments to the other's who'd gathered. Jason dropped his head back and said in a clear voice, "Dear God, did you have to put another wiseass in our midst?"

The laughter that had started to subside peaked again. Justin bent down and lifted Danielle out of the jump seat. It felt fabulous to be off the nylon strapping.

"Where do you think you're going?" Jason's gravelly voice asked as Justin turned.

"Home."

"Not so quick. Everyone is going back to Guardian first. Danielle needs to sign some nondisclosure agreements, I need to talk with Chief, Dixon, and Drake after we all debrief. Doc, that new Ortho specialist will be at the offices in four hours. I want you in on the interview. Let's wrap it up here and get going." It was as if the man cracked a metaphorical whip. The casual packing became an intense explosion of activity.

Jewell and Jade walked out with Justin and Danielle as he carried her down the ramp. "So, you aren't getting back to New York tonight." Jewell reached into her pocket. "This is a key to the apartment Zane keeps. He has some friends that make use of it from time to time. It is small, but it's clean. Should have a fully stocked refrigerator, too. I'll text you the address when you get done with the debrief. The little old lady that lives next door is sweet. When you leave, knock on her door and give her a bag full of groceries out of the fridge, would you? She loves the creamer, so make sure you put at least one of them in there. That's the payment for staying at the apartment."

"Being nice to an old lady?" Justin asked as he lowered Danielle into the car. He caught her eye and made a face before he lifted away and looked at Jewell. "I don't understand."

"She is a sweetheart, and she lives on a fixed income. We go over about once a week and make sure she has enough. When people stay there, we ask them to check on her and give her a bag full of groceries."

"We'd be happy to check on her. What's her name?" Danielle asked when Justin got into the driver's seat. Jade and Jewell got into the back seat, and they pulled away. Danielle noticed three other large black vehicles waiting.

"Mrs. Henshaw," Jade responded. When everyone glanced at her, she frowned. "What? She's a cool old lady. Nic and I stop in a couple times a month. Her family doesn't visit." She shrugged her shoulder as if it was no big deal. Dani saw the smile that spread across Jewell's face. She reached over and placed her hand on Justin's thigh. He glanced over at her and winked. Yes, she was going to love this family.

CHAPTER 29

*T*he debrief took about an hour longer than Justin's patience lasted. Now, more than ever, he appreciated his five-minute phone calls to debrief his operations with Jason. He could tell Danielle was over it too. She'd dropped her head on his shoulder and closed her eyes. She wasn't asleep, but she had to be exhausted, although they'd both slept on the flight home. Well...rested, because sleeping in a transport plane took special skills—skills his brothers had gained, and he hadn't.

Every move he'd completed prior to Jacob's team meeting up with them inside the foreign compound was documented. His statement was taken and then Danielle's was also dictated. When he mentioned what Joseph had done, Jason removed his glasses and pinched the bridge of his nose again. He drew a deep breath and glanced over at Zane who sat beside Jewell. The man shrugged his shoulders. Justin glanced at the rest of the room. There was obviously something he was missing, but because he'd placed so much distance between his family and himself, missing the sub context was par for the course when he was with them.

"So, the individual working at Phoenix was the liaison to the terrorist group?" Justin wanted to make sure Danielle was safe, so he would make them repeat themselves as many times as it took for him to get all the answers.

Jewell nodded and clicked her keyboard. "Definitely. We have digital forensics that confirmed he was the one. The day before Danielle was taken, he'd burrowed into the intranet at Phoenix and accessed the email of Danielle's father. He knew Paul Greenfield suspected him and that is what we believe compelled them to act."

Justin leaned forward so he could look directly at Jason. "All the loose ends are tied up? We don't have any reason to worry about Danielle's safety?"

Jason nodded, and leaned back in his chair before he spoke. "I've ensured it. Assets are being employed." He glared across the table, almost daring

Justin to ask the next question. He knew better. He had an idea of some of the 'assets' Guardian had access to and he didn't even want to bump up against them. He'd violated his own moral compass one too many times. He didn't want to know what was going to happen.

"What about the man who abducted me?" Danielle asked quietly from his side. He put his arm around her and tried to give her comfort.

"He is no longer a concern," Jared answered. "A matter of tracking the cab back to the real cabbie, finding out who he'd loaned it to, and then tracking the bastard down. He is being held as a domestic terrorist. I will always have tabs on him. You have nothing to fear."

Danielle smiled at Jared as she relaxed against Justin's side. The rest of the meeting dragged on before Danielle signed the nondisclosure forms. Having her do so was a formality because she held a security clearance. Justin wasn't aware it had been required for her to maintain one to work with her father as a DoD contractor, but it made sense once he found out. She insisted on hobbling through the halls and down to the garage. He held most of her weight as she leaned against him, but he knew that sitting or being carried was uncomfortable and she needed to stretch. When they reached the garage, however, he let his inner caveman emerge and swept her up. He hit the door unlock button on the key fob and found the car Jason's secretary had told them to use when the lights blinked.

"I didn't think traffic could get worse than New York City, but what we just drove through was worse. How does anyone get to appointments? Is there no such thing as public transit around here? Do they all drive their own cars?" Danielle turned toward him when she asked.

Justin chuckled at her griping as he pulled into the parking slot assigned to the apartment number they'd been given. "No more need to worry about traffic."

"Oh, God...I want a shower." Danielle turned a wide-eyed gaze at him. "Shampoo, soap and hot water. That sounds better than chocolate covered strawberries and champagne."

"It does. Let me carry you up?" Justin asked as he shut off the car.

"Let me walk for a while? I need to stretch more than I need to stay off my feet." Danielle opened her car door, but Justin made it around in time to help her out. He hit the fob locking the door as they started inside the building. She wore a pair of Jade's

running shoes his sister kept in the gym at Guardian
. They were two sizes too big and the perfect size for
Danielle to stuff her bandaged feet into.

They walked slowly before they turned down a
small hallway and found the apartment. Danielle
leaned against the wall while he fished the key out of
his pocket.

"Thanks, Mrs. H!" Justin snapped a look over his
shoulder. Someone resembling a linebacker had
walked out of the other apartment. The man held a
stack of cookies. He popped one into his mouth and
winked at Justin.

"Thank you, Cooper. You know you don't need to
bring me groceries. I get by." A tiny old woman
spoke from the doorway.

"Now how are you going to make me my favorite
cookies if I don't bring you the ingredients?" The
man leaned down and kissed her cheek. "I'm going
to be out of town for a while. You make sure you call
Zane or Jewell if you need anything."

The walking wall of muscle ambled down the
hallway eating another cookie. That's when the
woman noticed them. "Oh, hello." She wavered at the
door as if she was unsure she should be talking with
them.

"Hi, Mrs. Henshaw. Justin and I will just be here

overnight. He's Jewell's brother." Danielle smiled at the elderly woman breaking through the anxious look the woman gave them.

"Oh, how wonderful. Would you like some cookies? I swear that Cooper can eat like no other, but I managed to keep a tray. I like to have them available should anyone call."

Justin unlocked the door and thanked all things holy that Danielle politely declined the invitation. Mrs. Henshaw wandered back into her apartment. Justin waited to hear the locks engage before he followed Danielle into their home for the night.

The apartment was tiny, but it didn't matter. Justin threw the deadbolt, and tossed the keys onto the breakfast bar that obviously served as the only dining area. He turned and pulled Danielle into his arms. He'd waited far too long for this and from the way she melted into him, she agreed. "There is so much I want to say, but I don't have the words." His lips lowered onto hers, taking her, claiming what was his. Because she *was* his.

She pulled back enough to whisper, "I hear everything you're trying to tell me. I love you. We almost lost that. We almost lost us."

Justin pulled her closer and tucked her into him. The truth of her words laid bare the fear that he'd fought from the moment she hadn't answered his call.

Danielle moved her head back so she could see him. "I could have died. *You* could have died. A nose to nose look at my own mortality made me face a few facts. I'm not going to hide behind what other people think is appropriate. I love you. I want to know when you go on missions for Guardian. I know I can't go, but I can help you train, to study, to prepare. I want to climb Everest and suit jump down the slopes. I want to live life, with you. Justin, will you marry me?"

In the totality of all the words that could have been shared between them, her question had never been a consideration. A surge of emotion collided inside him, shattering him into a million pieces only to be absorbed by the love that radiated from the woman he held. A smile spread across his face. He couldn't have held it in. "Only if you buy me an engagement ring."

Danielle threw back her head and laughed. "Done. Do you want a diamond?"

"I'll leave that up to you." Justin grabbed her pert ass and lifted her up. She grabbed him by his shoulders and clamped her legs around his waist. "Yes, I'll marry you." He kissed her, teasing her lips open with his tongue. He captured her sigh and consumed it, reveling in the woman he held. He broke the kiss long enough to take the five steps into the bedroom. He let her down, gently. "I want to ravish you, to make you scream my name." He took her mouth again, his hands traveling down her waist and back up again before he pulled away. "We both have to shower."

Danielle leaned into him. "Together."

Justin bowed back and took a peek into the small bathroom. "Close quarters."

"I don't care. I don't want to be apart from you."

"Then you won't be." He'd cater to any desire she had. She was his princess. The One. He'd do anything for her, forever. Justin helped her out of her clothes, kissing each scratch and bruise as it was exposed. He had her sit down so he could unwrap her feet. He held up one, kissed each toe and the ankle before he paid the same tribute to the other.

"Maybe we could shower after?" Danielle reached for him.

He lifted off his heels and met her at the edge of the bed, still on his knees. "Let me take care of you. I promise the wait will be worth it."

Her hands ran through the hair at the back of his

neck. She pulled him in. "Every moment with you is worth it."

He kissed her, letting his fingers trail over her body. Reintroducing himself to the curve of her breast, the plane of her flat stomach and the swell just before her sex. Her legs spread for his hand. Her body was ready for him. His fingers glistened with her excitement. He fought his cock's desire to go straight for that delicious prize. Instead, he broke the kiss and stood up, disrobing quickly. Their eyes locked for a moment before Danielle let hers drop. She leaned forward and traced one of the longer scratches on his ribs. He'd used his body to shield hers from the worst of the entwined, snarled branches they moved through.

He took her hand, moving it from tracing the damage that had been done. He let her use his strength to stand and backed them into the bathroom while holding her, until his shoulder hit the doorjamb. He glanced at the shower and flicked on the water. Danielle caught his hand and peeled the white medical tape off his battered palms, lifting the gauze and pad. The rope burns weren't deep, but the skin was tender. She kissed each hand, mimicking the way he'd worshiped her feet.

He gently maneuvered them into the shower.

The close confines only added to the intimacy of the moment. He leaned her back into the water, wetting her long hair before he shampooed and rinsed it. The sandalwood scent wasn't the normal light floral she used, and he resented not having that for her. He soaped a cloth and worked his way down her body, washing and caressing every curve. He carefully lifted each foot and tended to the tender bottoms before he turned her around and washed up her long legs, over that gorgeous ass, and past the sexy dimples to her waist, shoulders and neck. His hands burned from the soap, but it wasn't enough to make him stop. He wanted nothing more than to commit every precious inch of this woman into indelible memory. With her body soft and pliant, he shifted her and ducked under the water, washing quickly. When he dipped his head back to get his hair wet, her hands found their way to his chest where she drew circles around his nipples before flicking them with her thumb. His body convulsed with pleasure, and his cock stood high and hard. Her hands wandered downward as he lathered his hair. When she palmed his shaft and stroked, he groaned at the gentle tease, a small taste of what he wanted with her.

He reached behind him and flicked off the water.

They stood toe to toe, her soft breasts brushing against his chest, while her hand lazily stroked his cock. Not enough pressure or fast enough to do anything more than torment him. The echo of drops from the showerhead and their heavy breathing drifted around them, tying them to the moment. Justin lowered to her and dropped a soft, lingering kiss. He felt her shiver. Throwing his arm out and back, he reached for and grabbed a towel and wrapped her in it before he helped her out. He dried quickly and followed her into the bedroom. She'd pulled down the blankets and dropped her towel. As he emerged, she leaned over the bed and crawled on all fours to the middle where she turned and looked at him over her shoulder. "The doctor said to stay off my feet." She lifted them off the bed in a flurry of kicks. "How shall we make love?"

Justin let out a burst of laughter and kneed onto the bed behind her. His hands gripped her hips, and his cock jumped for joy at the vision in front of him. "I have plenty of ideas." He tapped her hip, and she lay down, moving to her back. Justin waited until her legs flipped past him before he moved up her body. He stayed like that, on hands and knees, over her, watching her. The woman was beautiful and amazing...and his. "I love you."

He dropped to his elbows, hungry...no starving for the succulent treat beneath him. He tasted her lips, feasted on her tongue, devoured the feel of her skin against his fingers and mouth. Her bouquet became an irresistible song to his senses, combining to be the most intoxicating thing he'd ever encountered. A perfect blend of spice and sweetness with undertones of strength and joy, combined with the undeniable sex appeal that presented her as an alluring feast.

Her hands clenched his hair, pulling him back up to her. "Please, for God's sake, please Justin. Make love to me." Her breasts rose and fell with her panted gasps.

He lowered and drew close to her sex, his cock weeping at the wait he'd demanded of it. "Always, my love. Always."

He entered her, his cock gliding into her heat, eased by the desire that flowed from her. Her legs circled his hips, and he withdrew only to slide back home. Where he belonged. He tortured himself with long, languid strokes, taking his pleasure and watching her climb towards her own. He lifted his leg, shifting his position and thrust again. Danielle's head rolled from side to side. A soft moan and clenched fingers against his skin drove him on, his body took over. He couldn't stop, not now. Danielle shouted his name and begged him to go faster, deeper and harder. Her plea destroyed any attempt at control, and his body took over. Her legs squeezed hard around him. Her hips flexed, slamming herself against him as he drove into her. She shouted his name as she came and, within seconds, her name echoed around them as well. He thrust again and again, emptying himself inside her before he collapsed over her. Their bodies slid together, slick with sweat. Justin managed to roll and carry them both to their sides, still joined together. They lay like that for several minutes—just touching and relaxing in each other and simply being together.

"Thank you...for coming for me." Danielle's sleepy whisper brushed against his throat.

"I'll always come for you." Justin kissed her forehead and listened to her breathing. Slow and steady. Alive and well. Home. Justin closed his eyes and drifted away.

CHAPTER 30

*D*anielle glanced around the venue, and what a venue it was. The soft white fairy lights twinkled against the starlit sky. A warm, soft breeze made her skirt dance around her knees. The white sand to her right separated the soft lapping tide from the manufactured dance floor. She glanced around one last time to make sure the table arrangements were perfect. The wedding party would be here any minute. She and Justin had worked hard to make sure the reception would be perfect for Jewell and Zane. The couple had been married on a majestic old schooner with the entire family on board. The wedding photographer wanted several fun pictures of Jewell and Zane, so that gave Justin and Danielle enough time to get back to

Joseph's...well, mansion...and check on the reception, since they were in charge.

She felt Justin come up behind her and smiled as he pulled her into his chest. "Joseph's estate is beautiful." Justin made a noise that sounded like an agreement as he kissed her neck. "The torches add just the right ambiance and separation." She lifted her hand and held him to her neck. A shiver of desire danced over her.

"How much time do we have?" His words rumbled from his chest to her back. The sexy growl sent another pulse of desire through her. The man just needed to breathe for her to want him. Like this? He was irresistible.

"Maybe ten minutes. Is the food ready?" She glanced over at the buffet. Justin had flown two chefs to Aruba to prepare the feast. They tried to cater to both Zane and Jewell's tastes. The buffet selections embodied Zane's healthy lifestyle. The dessert tables? All Jewell. A chocolate and caramel fountain, and a long table with two hundred pieces of handmade candy. Jewell and Zane forewent the cake and asked for cupcakes. They were the center-pieces of each table, decorated to look like flowers. The effect was stunning.

Justin groaned and stood up straight. "Yes. We

have about five minutes before they bring it out." He grabbed her hand and guided her toward a palm tree that had been adorned with white fairy lights. She could see the whitewater of the gentle waves as they landed on the shore beyond. Justin turned, so his back was to the beach and dropped to one knee. He held a small light blue box in his hands. "I know this is already a done deal, and you beat me to the punch, but I was planning to do this before you asked me, so here it goes. My beautiful princess, even though I've already agreed to marry you, will you do me the honor of wearing my ring?"

Danielle gulped for air because Justin's words and actions were every little girl's dream. He stared up at her, a smile spread across his handsome face. He was her Prince Charming. He'd slain her dragons and brought her home safely. He conquered empires and was fearless in the face of adversity. He was perfect, and he was hers. She nodded, blinking back her tears. It didn't work. She wiped at one that fell down her cheek. "Yes, of course, I'll marry you."

He slipped the ring out of the box and placed it on her finger before he stood, and when he did, Danielle threw herself at him. They held each other, rocking back and forth, dancing to music only they could hear.

"Congratulations."

Danielle jumped back and swung around. Tall, dark and unsociable, better known as Justin's brother, Joseph, stood at the far corner of the dance floor, just inside the shadows.

"Thank you." Danielle smiled and wiped away another tear.

"You didn't stay on the ship?" Justin accepted the handshake and hug when his brother made it across to them.

"No, Blake had reached his limit. He takes after his mom when he's tired. Cranky. I brought him home. My staff here spoil him rotten, so I'm sure he's having a blast inside."

Justin nodded and glanced at Joseph. "Does Ember know you call her cranky?"

Joseph's eyebrows shot up. "Do I look suicidal to you?"

From the embrace of her fiancé's arms, she watched the brothers, happy to know that Justin was here and trying to become a part of the family that he'd shunned for far too long. They had both talked with his therapist, alone and together. Justin knew he had issues to address about his father's death. But he, like so many others who had experienced such a trauma, was a work in progress. She'd stand with him every step of the way.

Danielle wouldn't have it any other way. She glanced down at the beautiful ring on her finger and then at the family that had started to stream in. Laughter, love, and happiness permeated the warm, sweet atmosphere. She glanced up at Justin as he turned his gaze towards her. She held his eyes and knew that her forever was with this man.

*D*rake hung back and leaned against one of the palm trees festooned with little white lights. Chief ambled over with his drink of choice, some fancy cognac that he'd learned to love while he was undercover as David Xavier. He cupped the snifter lovingly in his hand. Drake shook his head and chuckled. "You treat that shit like it was spun from gold."

"I believe it was. You have no idea how expensive it is. I get one bottle every three months from Gabriel. Having it here is an unexpected treat." Chief swirled the amber liquid under his nose before he took a sip.

"Damn, don't have an orgasm." Drake took a drink of his bourbon. Plain ole Maker's Mark. He didn't need the pomp and circumstance. But then again, he'd never figured Chief as needing it either. People change. He glanced around the reception. Damn, how people change.

"Where's Dixon?" Chief swept the crowd looking for Drake's twin.

"Jason wanted to talk with him. Alone." Drake shrugged off the sense of unease the statement brought with it.

Chief cut him a quick glance asking a very clear, but silent question. Drake shook his head. "I have no idea."

Chief took a larger sip of his drink. His eyes gazed across the pool at his wife. He and Taty had married in front of a judge almost six months ago. They didn't tell anyone about it. Just went out and did it. It was typical of them. They were both intensely private.

"We are leaving from here and heading to Russia," Chief said as his eyes followed his woman. "Jewell believes she may have a lead in finding Taty's sister."

"And if it turns out to be nothing?" Drake wasn't stupid, in fact, he was a certified genius. Chief was checking out of the complex for however long it took to track down the lead on his sister-in-law.

Dixon was meeting with Jason. Alone. *Fuck. Him. Standing.*

"Then we say we did our best, and we are able to live with ourselves." Chief turned, giving him his full attention.

Reality slapped Drake in the face with a motherfucker of a left hook. He knew. Dixon was being pulled for an assignment. What, he could only guess. He slugged the remainder of his bourbon. Hell, he'd have to guess because nobody was telling him a damn thing and that pissed him off. He set his glass down on the tray of a waiter who was passing by and crossed his arms over his chest. His mind clicked off the moves that were happening and what counter moves he could employ before Chief was able to take a drink of his cognac.

"I won't let her go alone. We need someone at the Complex in charge of everything. The Shadows need you there to complete their portion. I don't know what mission Jason has for Dixon, but I can only assume it requires his skill set."

"The same exact fucking skillset I have." Drake gritted the response through his clenched teeth.

"No. There is a difference." Chief turned and looked at him. The deadly serious glint in the man's eyes told him he knew. Fuck, if Chief knew, Guardian knew.

Drake stared down his friend. "He doesn't deserve this."

"And yet, you and I both know that what happened haunts him. Let him try to find his solace. He should be allowed to have his peace. No matter how close you are, he is his own man. Jason will give him the option, but this path is for Dixon to walk —alone."

Drake hung his head and clenched his eyes closed. It had happened so fucking long ago. Since then they'd lived to protect others. They'd sacrificed to make amends, but Drake knew how much the past weighed on his brother. He knew Chief was right, but that didn't mean he liked it.

"Your paths will diverge. You will both grow while you are apart. Jason will give him the option, but this is his decision, and if his pain is great enough, this path will be for Dixon to walk alone. A man must make his own journey to his destiny."

Drake hated every word out of Chief's mouth. Every word. He glanced up, knowing with some sixth sense when his twin stepped into the area. His brother met his eyes, and the pain and the resolve were easy to see. Drake shook his head in a silent denial of what he knew without being told. Dixon had accepted the assignment Jason had offered him. All because of misplaced guilt and years of regret. There was nothing Dixon could have done, but they'd had this argument too many times to count. Drake held his brother's eyes as long as he could before he turned and walked off the manufactured floor onto the beach. He gazed out over the water and was immediately surrounded by people. Yet... he felt hollow and alone...and it was just the beginning.

To read the next in the Kings of Guardian Series, Drake's story, click here!

The End

Guardian Defenders Series

Gabriel

Maliki

John

Jeremiah

Guardian Security Shadow World

Anubis (Guardian Shadow World Book 1)

Asp (Guardian Shadow World Book 2)

Lycos (Guardian Shadow World Book 3)

Thanatos (Guardian Shadow World Book 4)

Tempest (Guardian Shadow World Book 5)

Smoke (Guardian Shadow World Book 6)

Reaper (Guardian Shadow World Book 7)

Hope City

Hope City - Brock

HOPE CITY - Brody- Book 3

Hope City - Ryker - Book 5

Hope City - Killian - Book 8

STAND ALONE NOVELS

SEAL Forever - Silver SEALs

A Heart's Desire - Stand Alone

Hot SEAL, Single Malt (SEALs in Paradise)

Hot SEAL, Savannah Nights (SEALs in Paradise)

USA Today and Amazon Bestselling Author, Kris Michaels is the alter ego of a happily married wife and mother. She writes romance, usually with characters from military and law enforcement backgrounds.

Made in United States
Orlando, FL
13 November 2021

0392728R00197